« Shotgun Wedding »

« Shotgun Wedding »

based on the television stories

SHOTGUN WEDDING

and

STEALTH

Neil Corry

First published in Great Britain in 1996 by
Virgin Books
an imprint of Virgin Publishing Ltd
332 Ladbroke Grove
London W10 5AH

BUGS the television series is produced by
Carnival Films Ltd and broadcast in the UK by BBC1

ISBN 0 753 50030 2

Typeset by Galleon Typesetting, Ipswich
Printed and bound in Great Britain by
BPC Paperbacks Ltd, Aylesbury

For Ma and Alien

With thanks to:

David Bailey, Gareth Roberts, Stephen Maginn,
Peter Darvill-Evans, Paul Cornell
and, most especially, to David Smith

« One »

« Remind me to smile »

Anna Fabrizi stepped off the train. The journey could have been better. Stuck for over thirty minutes in that damned tunnel with only some half-mumbled message about signal problems for an excuse. No press conference – just meet the press in the station's concourse, Gina said. Great way to publicise your ideals.

But she was here now. Were they ready for her?

The train station was so strange, so unlike the grandeur of the *Stazione Centrale* or the dirt of the *Termini*. The low, massive arch of the roof was supported by a lattice of blue metal. An overgrown child's climbing frame. Huge windows let in all available light. The brightness of the light, the grey-coloured trains and the white concrete floor made the station appear colder than it really was. Simple and functional. Perhaps that's where its beauty lay. She couldn't see it. For her, the station had no grace at all.

An announcer apologised for the delay over the public address system. She couldn't hear it properly over the roar of the train's engines. Corelli stepped off the train hesitantly, and rubbed his eyes. He had slept on the train when she had wanted to go through that afternoon's itinerary for the conference. And he still hadn't written his speech. No matter how many times she had reminded him, he had dismissed her worries, arguing that there was plenty of time to write the thing.

She fought off the notion that he didn't care any more. That was wrong and unfair. Alberto had worked just as hard as she had building up the Liberty Party. He simply refused to let the election campaign ruin his nerves or his sleep. Basically, his life was his own and his political ambitions would not ruin his health as he claimed it had ruined hers. And hadn't they gone through the conference's itinerary enough times already? She only wanted to ensure things would run smoothly. That was all. Life was too short for mistakes.

Corelli put his arm around her. Anna stepped gently away. His face looked hurt. She knew he wasn't upset at all. How many times did they have to go over it? It was all a pretence. He would just laugh if she complained. She milked their 'relationship' for all it was worth as much as he did.

Corelli wasn't a fool. He knew what he was doing. Mr Public Image.

Still, only another week to go.

The station concourse. Announcements of imminent departures. People staring up at the departures board. The sounds of footsteps and conversations. People in suits and thick heavy coats. Over-dressed backpackers sitting on the cold floor. But not much sign of the press. A few, sure. But was it enough? Anna hoped so.

Cameras flashed as soon as they walked onto the station's concourse. This was more like it. The attention. Feeling special. Anna looked up at a crowd that had gathered on a walkway on the next level of the station. None of them reacted to her appearance. Bizarrely, she felt a little disappointed. She and Alberto were the ones the cameras were waiting for, after all. They were obviously not famous enough in this country. Anyway, she was a politician – and who had heard of screaming politician fans?

'Miss Fabrizi?'

A man dressed in a black woollen coat with a bright red scarf wrapped around his neck stepped through the journalists and camera men that had gathered around them. Corelli snaked his arm gently around her again.

Don't just smile and pretend we're in love, Alberto. The vultures might adore it but I sure as hell do not.

Anna's smile for the cameras didn't falter. OK. Alberto would win – for one final time. The image had to be maintained with the elections back home only a week away. She didn't mind the feelings of anxiety, the stress or the lack of sleep. It was all she lived for. Some might have considered it an abominable way to spend your life but she enjoyed every second of it.

Anna looked at the man in black. He reached his hand out. She shook it.

'SSD – Wence.'

'Hello, how was your trip?' would have been nicer. Even 'Welcome to our green and pleasant land' at a push. Why were – and she knew she was generalising – men so rude?

'I'm in charge of security during your visit.'

How very nice for you. I'm sure your mother's very proud.

Anna recalled the name. One of Wence's troops had been trying to get hold of her and Corelli for the last week to sort out the security arrangements for the conference. With all the media attention in the run up to the election, contacting either herself or Alberto was almost impossible. The rounds of interviews on radio and TV and for the newspapers. God, how she loved it all!

Anna supposed then that she should feel flattered that the commanding officer of the SSD had deigned to meet them, but he struck her as a pompous old fart who would do his best to interfere with her plans over the next few days. And nobody stood in Anna Fabrizi's way – ever.

For a second, she was blinded by a camera flash and

3

the world turned green. Wonderful. Get your face on TV. Get written about in the newspapers. Get noticed. Get remembered. It all helped. Got you voted for. In theory.

She saw Wence being pushed out of the way of an eager camera man and two reporters. He called out, 'There are a number of matters I must discuss with you.'

'The press first, Mr Wence.'

'But, Miss Fabrizi.'

Stop hovering, Wence. If you're in charge of security, go make something secure.

Cameras and tape recorders pushed their way in front of her. Boom mikes were held precariously by lanky twenty-somethings.

A pale-faced reporter in a scruffy trenchcoat stood in front of her. Didn't his mother tell him to eat his greens? And red hair. Fascinating. It was so unusual to see that. Why did they call it red when it was really orange? And it truly did look like wire.

The reporter pushed his tape machine further towards her face. 'Miss Fabrizi. The Liberty Party is only two years old. Why are the Italian voters taking you so seriously?'

Because we're a damn fine party, with honesty and integrity as our watchwords, et cetera. The speech was well rehearsed and well worn through repetition in a dozen different countries. Oh, for some new questions!

But it was Alberto who answered. His deep, gentle voice was so soothing. It was a pleasure to listen to him. The bustle around them quietened a moment. He had a voice that made you listen. Alberto spoke at his own level, his words clearly audible but you wanted to pay him complete attention. He was mesmeric.

'Because we represent a new honesty in Italian politics, and a rejection of the old ways,' he said.

The swine! He had stolen that from her speech that afternoon. Anna refused to let her composure change in front of the cameras. Alberto smiled at her. Two

4

years ago his charm would have won her over completely. His cheeky grin didn't quite have the same effect on her any more.

'We are against corruption,' said Anna. 'We want to clean up politics in our country once and for all. That's why we're here for a conference on open government.'

That wasn't the whole truth but it was all they were getting for the moment.

The journalist raised an eyebrow. 'Isn't your stance against corruption just window dressing? A cynical attempt to win votes?'

Anna wished she could wipe the smirk off his face. But she was used to this and could easily deal with it. 'My enemies don't think it's just "window dressing"; I've had death threats.' This wasn't news. The vultures had heard all this before. They'd want some new meat to feed on. She hoped they were prepared for disappointment.

'But that won't stop me speaking out,' she continued. 'Fighting corruption is the only reason I'm in politics. With me, it's a total passion.'

Another smirking journalist: 'What about your other passion?'

That raised a few half smiles from the crowd of journalists and a few small laughs. They were all at it! Smirking away. Perhaps it was some kind of professional affliction she had never noticed before.

Anna could have written the script for the reporters. She knew they were all playing a part in a small game. All the press she had met recently had the same script: a half-attempt at a serious political question, more or less the same one, and then the other: 'When are you and Alberto going to name the big day?'

Alberto was smiling at the journalist. She was very pretty but looked too severe. Too intense. Her blonde hair was stretched back over her head and tied into a ponytail. Her bright blue eyes stared eagerly at them.

Don't play up to them, Alberto. It'll just make it harder after the election.

Alberto turned to Anna and for a moment she saw a sadness in his eyes. A second later it was gone. That was an old story. Best left forgotten.

It was best if she feigned ignorance.

'The big day? It's next week – the general election.' More smirks. She hoped the condition wasn't contagious. So, there was still plenty of political mileage to be had in their 'relationship'.

'The more we deny there is anything between us,' she added, 'the more you print the opposite.'

There. Neither a confirmation nor a rejection of their media-manufactured affair. They seemed happy with that. It would give them something to write about. Soon, after only another week, that would stop.

Corelli tapped his watch. Time to leave.

Anna increased her pace and stepped onto an escalator that led up to the exit. Questions rolled around her, like a verbal Mexican wave. She turned to see Wence immediately behind her, walking slowly and looking up at the concourse's balcony for, she presumed, anything suspicious.

Corelli turned to face the journalists. 'Thank you. That's all for now.'

Children leaned over the high balcony wall, looking down at the station's concourse. They were excited by the cameras and were trying to get a better view. Bored businessmen hung around on their way to work for a few moments, grateful for the distraction in their mundane lives. Mackenzie stood amongst them. No one paid him any attention. That was good.

He could have been anyone. He blended into the commuter crowd in his conservative suit and shirt and tie. Very little to differentiate him from any part of the rush hour crowd. His hair, already thinning, was cut so short that what remained looked like a fine layer of grey dust on his scalp.

He stared at the escalator. The mini media circus had run its course. And after all the trouble of arranging things at the now-cancelled press conference, too.

There they were. The beautiful couple. Their faces on the covers of so many magazines. Fabrizi and Corelli. Soon to be split up rather permanently. There was Wence, the idiot in charge of the Special Services Department. SSD. Now that was a joke. A department supposed to be so secret that nobody knew about it. Except everybody and his mother did. But Wence did have some good people working for him. Still, it was doubtful they would pose any threat to him.

Oh, dear. What was Wence looking for? Snipers? They would be lucky to get a clear shot with this many people around. A bomb? Again, too many people. Of course, some clients didn't trouble themselves about innocent victims, as long as it meant the target was well out of the way.

The new client bothered. Odd that, considering his connections.

Mackenzie glanced at the ornate clock in the centre of the concourse.

Time to make the call.

He flipped open his mobile and pressed the redial button. He was answered instantly.

'She's arrived,' he said simply. 'Do it now, Starkey.'

A reflected face in the window of the fire exit door stared back at him. Nothing much to look at. Neither handsome nor ugly. Being unnoticeable was definitely an advantage in his profession. So easy to lose oneself in a crowd. Balding on top with jet black hair. Tan could do with a little work. Maybe after the job? Safari somewhere, perhaps. Africa. South America. Somewhere his limits could be tested.

He caught himself day dreaming and gathered his thoughts.

Time to kill.

The good bit.

The best bit.

The money Mackenzie's boss paid – and he paid

well – could never be enough. The down always out-weighed the high.

The money isn't important, he reminded himself.

The life was important. Only the life.

Time to end it.

A chill flew down his spine. The ending of a life. That was all that mattered. This is what it was to be alive: to take the life of another.

He slid his dummy swipe card through the reader by the door. Get you in anywhere. Praise heaven for standardisation of production. The door buzzed and swung open.

Tenth floor, lift lobby. Salmon carpet. Off-white wall-paper. Three lifts. Corridors ran either side of where he stood. Small paintings and lamps lined the plain walls. A sign: ROSEDALE SUITE. Where she would be staying.

Starkey turned left and left again down the corridors leading to the suite.

No one about. No cameras he could see. As it should be.

And when was Mackenzie ever wrong?

The security officer looked at the monitors spread before him. People picked their noses in a lift. Adjusted their clothing as they walked down a hotel corridor thinking no one was around. Checked their lipstick in the mirror behind the bar. Grabbed a quick kiss from a lover in reception. Wence had certainly gone to town on this job. Clusters of optical fibres dotted all over the hotel meant that there was not an inch of it the team couldn't call up at any time. It was not as if the new toys weren't any fun but it did become monotonous very quickly. When people saw a security camera their behaviour would change immediately. But if you let people think they were not being watched, all manner of foibles started to appear.

Why was this delegation getting the royal treat-ment? And why did he have to stay at HQ? At least at the hotel they –

8

Who was that?

Someone left one of the fire exit stairwells. Unusual. Some kid messing about? No. Too tall. Someone lost? Doubtful.

An alarm went off. Its insistent ringing designed to wake up anyone who might have fallen asleep at the job.

He looked over at a computer screen. It read: ILLEGAL SWIPE-CARD USE. Damn. It had tricked the lock.

Whoever had broken in had made a mistake. They might get past the hotel's security but without a registration ident on the card, they were going nowhere.

The security officer picked up a phone linked to the console of monitors.

'Security here. You have an intruder. Rosedale Suite.'

There were so many places to hide the bomb.

Mackenzie said it was unlikely his target would be spending much time at the hotel. Best bet was therefore the bed.

Four leather sofas sat in a square. Two were black and the others white. Both sat in metal frames. Too many lampshades. Expensive, soft carpet. Hideous wardrobe. Great view of the city, though. The room held a mixture of styles: simple and functional, ornate and pointless. Rich – but crass – tastes.

Starkey was so happy with the bomb. So deliriously joyous with the bomb. He would have to be careful with it, so very careful. Such a little thing in its tiny glass container. And so simple. Simple was best. Simple was all that was needed. Simple is perfect. Less to go wrong.

He checked the connections one last time. Admire the workmanship. A couple of wires, a miniature radio receiver and, taped to it, one half pound of high explosive. It was art. Perfectly crafted, singular and beautiful. The artist's skill was clearly evident. Dedication, the eye for detail, the enthusiasm for the work. Hide it then walk out of the room. Wait for the arrival.

Starkey rolled under the bed. He held back a sneeze from the smell of pine and dust from the carpet where the cleaner had forgotten to vacuum.

A sound. The buzz of the fire door. There should be no one there. Something had gone wrong. Hotel security? No. More than that. Remember what Mackenzie said. They were being treated like royalty. That meant whoever was coming would be government operatives.

Footsteps coming closer. Two sets, cautious.

Everything changed now.

Starkey pocketed the bomb. A waste of good material. There would be another chance. If Mackenzie allowed. Mackenzie didn't like failure. Saw it as a terminal disease.

Now the two agents were in the room. One set of footsteps. One of them had stayed close to the door. The other footsteps stopped. Starkey could not see them. He would have to guess their positions.

Starkey rolled out from under the bed and his world turned upside-down for a second. The two men were not good. Left themselves wide open.

Two shots. Fast.

No time for mistakes. No time to let them live. One below the shoulder – could have been better. The other right in the heart.

Seven out of ten.

There was a dull *crump* as the bullets exploded in their bodies. Blood burst out of their chests. A small eruption of tiny pieces of tissue and bone splattered onto the carpet. Music to his ears. It was a good sound to hear and still be alive afterwards. Unlike those two. A bit messy but the bullets had never let him down.

But being spotted was careless. Mackenzie would not be pleased.

There was plenty of time to examine what went wrong later.

Now to get out before any more dummies show up.

* * *

Taylor watched as two operatives zipped up a dead colleague in a body-bag and slung it with only a little care onto a trolley-bed.

Snatchers. That's what the lads down at HQ called them. He moved aside as the trolley was wheeled down the hotel corridor. OK, they had a job to do but how on earth did they get into such a career?

Mum, when I grow up I want to put dead people in black bags and then take them away.

The snatchers gave him the creeps. Their white sterile coveralls looked like something from a science fiction film, not a government department.

Where the hell was Wence? He had made the call to his boss over half an hour ago, and hung around making sure nothing in the room was disturbed.

The hotel staff were terrified. The hotel's manager, a thin, grey-haired man in his fifties, had needed considerable calming. They had shunted the little man away from the suite as quickly as possible, trying to reassure him that everything would return to normal as soon as possible.

But he had to wait. Taylor's eyes turned to watch the sniffers – another nick-name for the forensics team – and then wished he hadn't. They were working carefully through the human debris left by his now dead colleagues. His stomach turned as he saw one sniffer pick up bits of skin and bone from the carpet and place them in small transparent bags.

And Mum, when I grow up I want to be a secret agent and clear up after the dead bodies.

His attention was distracted by the sound of footsteps marching down the corridor towards him. Wence, as ever puffing out his chest and holding in that ever-increasing stomach. Full of his own importance. Black suit, black hair swept back in a vain attempt at covering a balding crown. Wence frowned as the second dead man was wheeled out by two of the workers. Like he cared about the deaths. Every day was Christmas for Wence. Taylor's boss had the most expensive, shiniest and biggest set of toys and it was called SSD.

'Escaped, sir,' Taylor explained. 'Not a sign anywhere.'

Wence strode past. Taylor stepped in line behind him.

Go on. Walk right on by. Look as if this doesn't mean a thing to you.

'For some foreign politicians,' Wence said, 'being against corruption is like writing your own death sentence.'

'Sir?'

Wence sighed. 'This was to be Anna Fabrizi's room.'

« Two »
« Puppets »

Heaven.

Ros was in heaven.

All her birthdays and every Christmas she could remember had been rolled into one.

There were lights everywhere. Every colour imaginable. Kaleidoscopic patterns on the walls that folded into themselves; pastoral scenes projected in the middle of the warehouse that looked so real you felt you could step into them. Technology she had only dreamed of seeing. And, like a child, she just wanted to play.

The walls of Swift's warehouse were stacked with one piece of equipment after another. Beams of light shot out from rods in the ceiling. Consoles with huge flat VDUs displayed computer-animated holograms. A few technicians milled about. They checked pieces of equipment or input information on their computers and analysed the results. Apart from the low murmur of the technicians' conversations and the hum of the machinery, the lights in the workshop looked like a silent firework display. The computational power required had to be staggering.

Ros turned to see a laser-created logo that spun slowly in mid-air. It took her a moment to see it clearly with all the other light shows happening around them. A stylised torch with the word LIBERTA underneath.

Now that was familiar. Where had she seen it before? It was disappointing that the display was only two-dimensional. The equipment Swift had here looked capable of so much more.

Swift led Ros, Ed and Beckett up to his office. Ros turned as they reached the top of the stairs. The view from the balcony was certainly bizarre. Strange, coloured patterns flickered in time with the changes in the light shows. A constant hum of equipment and air-conditioning droned in her head. A comforting, familiar sound.

Maybe she could play later. Now they were here to work.

The team walked into Swift's office. By her side, a drawing of the LIBERTA logo she had just seen. Pulling it from the display board on the wall, she showed it to Ed. He didn't seem impressed. She had hoped he might be able to tell her what it was.

Ros tried to catch Swift's attention. He flitted about his office, checking nothing in particular on his cluttered desk, on his PC, or on the notice board.

Beckett stood at the far end, looking over the office, taking in every detail. Ed leaned by the doorway, keeping out of the way. She and Beckett were the computer experts. Vehicles of any shape and size were his territory. Here, she was on familiar ground.

Ros finally caught Swift's eye. He stopped and looked at the piece of paper in her hand. 'I think I recognise this,' said Ros. 'One of your designs?'

Swift took it from her and placed it on his desk. 'Yes. It's the logo for that new Italian political party.'

That was it. Something on the news that morning. 'I've seen them on TV.'

'They're over here for a conference,' said Swift.

For a second Ros held his gaze but he turned away. His body language was easy to read. Unsettled. Nervous. But that wasn't unusual. Somebody or something was putting him on edge.

Step number one was to get a list of suspects.

'So, Mr Swift,' Ros said, 'who do you design your lasers and holograms for?'

'Political parties are the exception. Generally, I do them for rock concerts, product launches, sports events . . .' He trailed off.

Ros walked over to his desk and started looking through a portfolio. Designs for the packaging of food products that she didn't recognise. Plenty of brand names, though. Ultimately, however, it did not seem very exciting. It wasn't SACROS or the Icarus program was it? Was Swift being paranoid?

Beckett spoke up. 'And you suspect industrial espionage?'

Great tone of voice, Beckett.

He obviously thought that the guy was a brick short of a house.

Swift seemed to ignore the sarcasm in Beckett's voice. 'I want you to check over the whole place.'

Sure he did. But what did he expect them to find? And he had not given Beckett a direct answer. Any additional information would be gratefully received.

Swift and Beckett walked out of the office and joined Ed on the balcony. He seemed hypnotised by the LIBERTA logo that spun in mid-air. Ros checked Swift's office once more. There was an awful lot of money invested in the place. If someone wanted Swift out of business, could there be that many companies capable of squeezing Swift out of the market?

'Forgive me,' said Beckett, 'I didn't realise the laser business was so . . . cut throat.'

Ros stifled a laugh. Beckett was forever doing this. Judging someone quickly, labelling them forever. She wasn't surprised by Beckett's reaction. Was this nothing more than the theft of intellectual property?

Ros caught a whiff of Swift's cologne. Sweet, almost sickly.

'I know it sounds like complete paranoia,' said Swift, 'but I'm sure someone's bugging me.'

That was more like it. Something they could trace,

15

get a hold of, give a good shake and then – *ta-dah!* – reveal the bad guy.

'Don't apologise, my friend,' said Ed. 'It's paranoia that keeps us in business.'

Ros noticed Swift's puzzled expression and he caught her looking. His face became expressionless again. He wasn't giving anything away.

Ed walked down the stairs that led to the workshop floor. The others followed. 'But you said *bugging*, Mr Swift. If someone wanted to steal your designs, why bother to listen to your conversations?'

Swift looked surprised. He didn't know what to say. Suddenly, Ros realised that the story of industrial espionage was a total lie. Swift had asked them there for a completely different reason.

Beckett clarified things for their potential client. 'What Ed means is that a rival company is more likely to steal drawings, or break in and take photographs, or get into your computer.'

So who wanted to know Swift's movements? And why? What was Mr Swift involved in?

'Have there been any break-ins?' Ros asked. 'Any problems with your computers?'

She wasn't really surprised when Swift shook his head. And judging by their faces, neither was Ed nor Beckett. But Swift must know something was wrong or why call them in the first place?

'That doesn't mean there aren't any bugs,' said Swift sharply, 'or some other kind of surveillance.'

'Well, no,' conceded Beckett.

Swift turned to Ros. 'That's what I'm hiring you to check for.'

Ros and Beckett looked at each other. Beckett raised an eyebrow in a silent question. Ros nodded slightly. Swift had got her riled. She wouldn't let it go now until her curiosity was satisfied.

'Don't worry,' said Beckett, 'if anyone gets so much as a crossed line, we'll find them.'

That was almost guaranteed. But Swift was not

16

telling them anything near the whole truth. What was he hiding?

Stevens refocused his telescope. His van was parked outside Swift's warehouse. He was getting a headache from the multi-coloured projections. Through the light shows he could just make out the tall, dark-haired figure of Swift talking to three people. They were coming closer to the exit. Good. Get a closer look.

A voice came through on the radio, making him jump. 'Red Zero. Red Zero. Report your status on William Swift.'

Great timing, HQ.

Stevens sighed and rubbed his temples. He cleared the chocolate bar and chewing gum wrappers on the dashboard to make some room for the telescope. Every time he used the van, it looked like a bomb had hit it. Why couldn't people clear up after themselves?

He picked up his radio from the passenger seat.

Got to get rid of those crisps, too.

Couldn't HQ have waited?

So far, they had found nothing.

Beckett recalibrated his bug detector to another set of frequencies. It bleeped happily to itself as he scanned the entrance.

He looked out of the large windows set in green plastic frames. A receptionist answered the phone. She ignored them as Ed scanned the desk. There were pictures hung on the wall that changed as you stepped close to them – country scenes that broke into a thousand pieces then coalesced into completely different pictures. Very distracting.

Beckett knew they were on a wild goose chase, but it was best to go through the motions to make Swift happy. The workshop was clean. The offices were clean. Not a bug to be found. They had been called out for nothing.

Ed came up to him and pointed out of the glass doors. 'Hey, Beckett. Check out that van.'

Not ten yards away sat a grey, square van, its front almost flat. A delivery truck. Dozens must pass through the trading estate every day. But there was no sign on the van's side. No indication of who owned it. So what? That didn't necessarily mean anything. So what had Ed seen? Anyone looking in from there would have a good view right through Swift's workshop. Sunlight bounced off the windscreen. Was there someone behind the driving wheel?

'Now, I'm no expert,' continued Ed, 'but I'd say that van's had some designer ageing applied.'

Of course. 'The number plate's too old for that model.'

'A little too anonymous, wouldn't you say?'

Finally, the morning was becoming a little more interesting. Perhaps Swift wasn't needlessly paranoid after all. Time to find out some answers.

'I'll go check it out,' decided Beckett.

He walked slowly out of the door, keeping his gaze away from the van. Beckett could just make out a shadow behind the driving wheel. Could be someone having a break. Waiting for a colleague. Or it could be something more suspicious.

Beckett walked around the van on the passenger side. The driver, a man. Red hair, pale face. Beckett couldn't see anything more. He wasn't close enough. Ed wouldn't have noticed anything strange if the plates had been genuine. They were a good few years out of date for the type of van. That smacked of an amateur's involvement – or someone lousy at their job. Some private eye checking up on Swift's whereabouts? Was this just some domestic affair? Swift was married to half a dozen different women up and down the country and they were catching up with him?

Well, it would explain Swift's all-too-apparent anxiety.

Beckett stepped behind the van. Crouching down, he stuck a magnetic bug on the van's undercarriage. He stood up and walked around to the driver's side of the van. Go for the bold approach, he decided.

'You got the time please, mate?'

The driver didn't even turn to look at him. He revved the engine, slammed into gear and raced off. But Beckett had seen everything he needed to. A telescope. A laptop. A radio. Surveillance equipment. Top of the range.

And government issue. He recognised it.

This was not a small outfit.

This was not a domestic.

This was trouble. Big trouble.

Beckett raced over to his jeep parked a few yards away. He fumbled for his key. As soon as the door was opened, he leaped into the driver's seat and switched on his tracking device on the dashboard. A small screen flickered into life. A computerised map of the area appeared. The signal was good and strong. A pulsating red circle indicated the van's position, already a few streets away. With the tracker he couldn't lose Swift's mysterious watcher.

He fished his radio from his jacket and turned the key in the engine simultaneously.

'The watcher's taken off,' he said. 'He looks like a pro to me.'

'I think Mr Swift knows something he's not telling us.'

Ed fumbled with the radio, trying to cut off Beckett's message. Swift presumed he wasn't supposed to hear that. Well, it was too late. Beckett was one hundred per cent correct, of course, but there was no way he would admit that to Ros and Ed.

'So. She was right,' he said.

Ros snapped around to face Swift. She certainly was attractive. Her dark eyes bored into whoever she looked at. He had to turn away from her gaze. Turn his attention to some other part of her. Looking at her and not looking at her. He focused on her coat. Off-white, simply cut. Elegant. Her black, lightly curling hair resting on her shoulders. He wondered if Ed or Beckett was her lover.

'Who was right, Mr Swift?' she asked.

Swift hesitated before replying. 'Er, a friend who suggested I should get you in.'

The blond Australian raised his eyes to the ceiling. Ros just sighed. They didn't believe a word he had said since they had walked into his warehouse. Telling the truth was out of the question, though. They could be working for anybody. And what the hell was 'Gizmos'? Sounded like a high-street game store.

The phone call that morning asking him to call in Beckett and his team hadn't exactly been brimming over with information. All in all, there was not much information with which Swift dared trust them.

Still, the team had checked the place over and given the green light. No taps on the phones. No interference with the computers. No hidden cameras. No bugs anywhere. It gave him only a little reassurance. Who was the man with the van?

The three of them walked into Swift's presentation hall. Racks of seats were arranged on all sides of the hall with a stage in the middle. Ros's heels clicked on the polished wooden floor.

Ed's voice echoed in the empty hall. 'The question is, Mr Swift, why are you under surveillance?'

'Somebody wants to put me out of business,' said Swift. It was the only line he could come up with.

Ros shook her head. She didn't believe it. He couldn't say that it wasn't obvious. He had never been a good liar.

Ed turned to Swift as Ros carried on to the exit. 'Is this really just about lasers?'

Ed could keep pushing but he would get nowhere. 'That's all I know about.'

Ros stopped. 'Well, bugs are what we know about and there aren't any here.' She stared at Swift, her eyes showing her anger and impatience. 'So, whatever secrets you have – feel free to discuss them.'

She sounded tired of the rigmarole. Swift couldn't help but agree. He had used them. They had done

20

their job. That was all he wanted.

I must be as transparent as glass.

'Look, thank you for all you've done –' he began, but Ed and Ros turned and started walking briskly out of the building.

'Let me know what your colleague turns up,' Swift called after them.

Ed shouted back, 'Of course.'

'And if you want anything else,' added Ros without turning, 'you know where to find us.'

Beckett took his time following the van. The streets were almost devoid of traffic and he didn't want the driver to realise he was being tailed.

He looked out of the windscreen. The roads were wet from the early morning rain. Grey clouds threatened rain again at any moment.

He had travelled only a few miles when the signal on the tracker stopped. He pulled around a corner and there was the van, parked in front of a large, modern building. A security barrier returned slowly to its rest position. Two security guards. Armed. Beckett looked through his binoculars. Small but powerful pistols.

Beckett parked the jeep around the corner from the building. Stepping out, he could see no sign of the van's driver. Obviously inside. He paused for a moment. He had to assess the risk of following the driver in. Swift's place was clean but he was under surveillance. Probably a government job. Some security outfit. Well, if he met up with anyone he could bluff his way out. He had dealt with plenty of civil servants in his time. Chewed them up and spat them out. He should be OK. And he had to find out what was going on. Swift was up to his neck in something. His reservations with the truth only made Beckett more determined to find out what.

Cameras ringed the building at irregular intervals. They were perched on tall poles, slowly turning back and forth. He had to find one that was isolated from the others and had to be by an entrance.

He looked at the building's grounds for suitable cover. A few trees. A few bushes surrounded the building. All bare. God, it was quiet. No vehicles had passed down the road in the last few minutes. There were other similar buildings along the road but hardly anybody about. It looked as if he was in some new business estate where hardly anyone had moved in. So few people around meant that there was less chance of his being observed but it also made it easier to be spotted by the security guards at the gate.

Beckett stepped into some bushes, wishing it was summer so he would have better cover.

It suddenly didn't matter. He was in luck.

Above a side entrance, a lone camera travelled steadily left and right. Checking to his left, Beckett saw the security guards chatting. He would have to make a run for the door and hope he wouldn't be seen. Not that that was very likely.

First thing: fix the camera.

From a pocket, he produced a thin box about the size of a personal CD player. Ros's RT73. Government issue. He never liked to ask where Ros managed to find half her stuff. He was just grateful she had it.

Beckett flipped up the box's cover. A small red light flickered on to show that the unit was powered up. Beckett pulled up the aerial and pointed it at the camera. The RT73 had two sliding controls. What had Ros said? The left was for the horizontal, the right for the vertical. He slowly and gently pushed the left control upwards, keeping an eye on the camera all the time. The camera scanned left – but did it reach as far left as it had a moment ago? He waited a moment and then adjusted the horizontal control. This time, the camera came only half as far around again.

Beckett took a quick look left. He couldn't see the guards. Where were they? He checked left and right. They weren't around. He darted for the door. He had to be quick. The RT73's interference with the camera's motor would not last long.

The door had an electronic lock. He pulled out his wallet and found his swipe-card that would trick any such lock. He slid it through and the door buzzed open.

He was in at the bottom of an emergency fire escape. He looked up. Fourteen, fifteen floors. Windows facing outside ran up the side of the building. The walls were gleaming white. There was the smell of fresh paint. No cameras inside.

No one around.

Beckett ran up to the first floor. The sound of his heavy footfalls echoed in the stairwell.

He checked outside. No sign of any security.

A door led out onto the rest of the floor. Locked. No door handle. Nothing to break, trick or pick. Just a solid wooden door.

It was the same with the second floor. The third. The fourth.

The fifth had a card reader.

He tricked the lock. Hydraulics hissed and from behind the door came a dull clang from what Beckett guessed was a heavy duty lock. They really meant security here. There was no time for worrying about that now. The door slowly slid open.

Beckett stepped through the doorway. Dark. The familiar hum of computers. Eight arranged in three rows on three long workstations. Blue light shone from the terminals. There were no other lights on.

So who was using the computers?

Beckett's eyes adjusted to the lack of daylight. Suddenly, out of the shadows, five figures stepped out.

Five clicks of safety catches.

He struggled to overcome his instinct just to turn and run. One wrong move and he'd be dead.

Men in black. Faces like stone. Cold eyes. Unsmiling. Their pistols were pointed directly at Beckett's head. He hardly dared to breathe.

'Do you think you can go anywhere with an RT73, Beckett?'

The voice was familiar. Almost a whine. Self-confidence bordering on arrogance. Where had he heard it before? He couldn't think properly with the guns pointing at him.

A man sat before a computer. Even in the half-light he could tell who it was.

Dark haired. Balding. Double chin. A self-satisfied smirk on his face.

He might have guessed.

'My office,' snapped Wence. 'Now!'

« Three »
« Conversation »

Lying to them. Bad move.

Ed wasn't happy as they stepped outside Swift's warehouse. He wasn't the only one who felt they'd been taken for a ride.

A cold wind whipped round them both. The clouds had thinned out after the morning's rain. Ros unlocked her car door and slumped in the driver's seat, her arms over the steering wheel. She made no attempt to start the engine. 'I didn't believe a single word Swift told us, did you?'

Ed climbed into the passenger seat. Ros looked how he felt. Fed up and angry. Swift could have been on the level with them. There was no need to mess them about. He had to know a little of their past history. After all, the team had been recommended by some mystery character. Well, it was up to the client to tell them all the facts. They weren't some run-of-the-mill security firm but that was exactly how Swift had treated them. Swift could have hired anybody to check over the building.

A man had his pride. A little trust from the client would have gone a long way.

They would have to get to the bottom of this.

'He ought to be in politics, not lasers,' said Ed.

Ros smiled and bent to fish out a scanner from her

25

handbag. She flicked a switch to turn it on. The radio whistled and crackled as she adjusted the frequency. A voice came through, barely audible through the hiss of interference. Swift.

Ed shook his head. She hadn't. She couldn't have. Surely it was against the rules? Unethical for one thing. Immoral for another. Plus it made it a little difficult to tell her what he had done.

'Bugging the client, Ros. Isn't that against our – um – code of practice?'

Ros turned. Her eyes held that resolute stare that always made him worried. She wasn't going to let Swift get away with lying to her.

'He started it.'

Well, that was fair enough. And if you thought someone was lying, with Ros's boxes of tricks you could find out for certain.

Next was the tricky bit. Hey. Great minds think alike and all that. Ros would be flattered that she could be beaten at her own game. The scanner continued to crackle. Swift's voice faded away.

Sounded like electronic interference. With the amount of equipment in Swift's warehouse that wasn't a surprise. Ros continued to fine-tune her radio with little success.

'Tune to 34.9 megahertz.'

'Why?'

'You'll get a better reception.'

There was no need for Ros's stony glare. A smile quickly followed the glare. Ed breathed a sigh of relief. You didn't want to get on Ros's bad side.

'I stuck one on his desk,' he added.

Ros re-tuned the scanner. The crackling faded almost completely but there was nothing to hear. Ros stared out of the windscreen, seeing nothing but listening to everything coming through on the radio.

Typing. Probably Swift at his PC. Papers shuffled. Footsteps. Heels clicked on the floor. They came closer to Swift and then left the office. A phone rang loudly. It must be close to the bug. A mobile. Ed could tell by the ring.

The beep of the phone being activated.

Swift's voice: 'Hello?'

A chair scraped on the floor. More footsteps. Swift was moving away from the bug on the desk.

'Anna, darling,' said Swift. 'How was the journey?'

He was speaking too low and too far from the bug.

Ros smiled and re-tuned her scanner again. 'Lucky my bug's on the phone itself.'

Ed smiled back. He had to concede defeat to the high priestess of surveillance.

Swift's conversation became crystal clear. A woman's voice.

'All the press wanted to know was when Alberto and I are getting married! If only they knew the truth.'

Very precise English. A southern European accent. Spanish? Italian? Kind of sexy.

'Listen, Anna. Something happened this morning. There was a man outside the workshop keeping a watch. One of the experts chased him off.'

'It's possible he was on our side.'

'What?'

Ros raised her eyebrows. Swift sounded as surprised as they were. What was going on here?

'I had to tell security about us,' said the woman. 'Look, I'll explain when we meet.'

Swift sounded disorientated. 'Er, yeah, sure. Can you get away this morning?'

'Of course I can.' Confidence. Determination. 'As long as I'm back for my keynote speech at three.'

'Have they given you a bodyguard?'

A gentle laugh. Friendly. Reassuring. 'Yes, but don't worry. I can easily give him the slip.'

Someone who thinks she is important. What was Swift's relationship with her?

'So where shall we meet?'

'Do you remember that big courtyard?'

'Royal College Green. Where I proposed.'

Ed should have guessed. Lovers. But why all the secrecy? It didn't make sense. Perhaps Swift really was scared of his own shadow. No, that couldn't be right. It wasn't Swift who was being protected. It was this Anna, whoever she was. Swift had used the team to check over his place for her safety.

He was distracted from his thoughts by laughter. 'Yes!' exclaimed Anna.

'We can sit on the very same bench!'

'I'll see you there in an hour. Bye, darling.'

'Ciao.'

Italian. Thought so. Two clicks. The phones were switched off. Ros unplugged the scanner.

Ed leaned against the dashboard, and stared out at the car park. 'Well, whoever she is, she's the reason for his paranoia. Let's go and put a face to the name.'

Ros nodded her agreement and started the car. 'What about Beckett?'

Beckett could look after himself. 'By the time he's finished playing tag, we'll have all the answers for him, won't we?'

It didn't matter where Starkey set up the Celltrack. The car park was as good a place as any. Wet grey blocks of concrete. Puddles of oily water. A good view of the city. People going about their little lives.

So easy to snuff out.

The call between the two love-birds finished. Starkey closed the line down. The Celltrack – a combination of mobile phone and laptop – let him, through satellites, monitor any conversation anywhere in the world. Top of the range technology, naturally. He always tried to obtain government issue. The security services never went for anything less than the best. Pity the same couldn't be said about their operatives. Mackenzie had warned about them, but what was there to worry about? If you were good, you worked freelance. More money. More action. More to get the adrenalin pumping. If you weren't top-notch, you worked for the government. Kept yourself safe with a mortgage, wife, kids. Things that tied you down and sucked the life out of you.

Starkey picked up his mobile and pressed a number. The call was answered almost immediately. He drew out a portable cassette player from his black leather jacket pocket.

The tape annoyed Mackenzie. That was tough. The boss should be used to it by now. Security was everything. It could be anyone on the end of the line. You didn't trust anyone. Ever. Life was too short for trust.

An electronic voice: 'Confirm your identity'. He could hear sighing on the other end of the line. 'Confirm your identity', the tape repeated.

'This is Mackenzie. You've been out of contact, Starkey. What happened at the hotel?'

Starkey's face flushed red with anger. Mackenzie would already know what had happened. He was trying to wind him up. He had to ignore the jibe. Stay calm.

'Tell your boss to have my money ready. Fabrizi will die – very soon.'

By the book.

Beckett didn't know which book but felt sure it wasn't SSD's operations manual. Probably some cheap spy thriller.

Two of Wence's grunts shuffled him into a lift and took him to the top floor. Standing either side, they stared at him all the way like he was something they wouldn't like to find on the bottom of their shoes. Their breathing was shallow. Faces set hard. Eyes boring into Beckett as if daring him to make a move. Their attitude wasn't even laughable – never mind threatening – just tedious. Beckett knew the ropes. The apes in the lift should know that. But he had trespassed onto their territory so now it was their rules. They could do anything to him. He no longer worked for the government. Another reminder of his descent into civilian life.

Feeling it was better to be safe than sorry, Beckett resisted the urge to knock their stupid heads together and stared up at the LED display showing each floor they passed.

He turned and waved at the security camera in the corner of the lift.

'Nice day for it.'

A click of a pistol. Beckett froze. For a second he was scared. They could so easily kill him. Quickly. Easily. A bullet in the back. From here, even one of Wence's in-bred half-wits wouldn't miss. All the same, Wence wouldn't shit where he ate, would he? Beckett would have been taken out of the building; not killed in the lift on the way to Wence's office. His fellow passengers were simply trying to frighten him.

Sorry, lads. It takes a bit more than what you've got.

It was still a relief to be bundled into Wence's office. He was left alone. The lock in the door turned behind him.

A desk in the far corner. Windows on three sides of the room. Good view of the city. Open blinds in all the windows. Dark grey carpet. A leather chair behind the desk and two light grey chairs in front. No papers left lying around. A camera in the corner of the room followed him as he walked about the office. A portrait of Wence's family sat on the desk. The wife, he presumed. And two teenage girls who took after dear daddy rather than their mother. Pity. A phone sat next to the framed picture. Beckett picked up the phone's receiver. Dead. Either Wence had cut the line or you needed a special code to get an outside line. He took his radio out of his jacket and turned it on. Static. It was worth a try. SSD was obviously screened, like the Hive had been, to stop unauthorised messages being sent and received. There was no way he could send word to Ed and Ros.

Beckett sat down in the chair in front of Wence's desk after almost choosing to sit in Wence's leather chair. Diplomacy wasn't his strong point and neither was respect for authority, but both would be useful here. Beckett waited quietly.

As far as he knew, SSD were supposed to be the good guys in the government's security operations. That meant he was only here to be frightened off. They weren't going to do anything. If they had planned to, they would have done it already.

But from what exactly was he being frightened off? Swift had clearly involved himself with something political, otherwise SSD wouldn't be interested. SSD were in charge. Other government security departments wouldn't be involved. Big time, no-nonsense stuff. And SSD were supposed to be the best of the lot. Though there were plenty of rumours that suggested the opposite.

There were too many questions flying around his head, and Beckett knew Wence wouldn't answer any of them. If he still worked for the Hive, then maybe. As it was, he had nothing to go on other than Swift was up to his neck in something big and probably very nasty. But that didn't make sense. Swift didn't have a clue about surveillance. Unless his business was a front?

His train of thought was derailed as Wence unlocked his office door and stepped inside. Beckett watched him closely. Wence held his gaze as he stepped around the desk and sat down in his leather chair.

'Right, Beckett,' he began. 'I hope you're going to be co-operative, because, if not, there are a certain number of sanctions SSD can impose.'

Beckett leaned back in the chair and rubbed his eyes. 'Spare me the lecture, Wence. I know this department is so secret that nobody admits it exists, and you could bury me in wet concrete and tell my friends I'd died in a car crash, and no one but no one would ever be any the wiser. But you're not going to, are you?'

Wence stared at him for a full half-minute before replying.

'No.'

Something in the way Wence stared made Beckett

31

shiver. Wence could have issued a formal warning. Beckett could have been held on suspicion of helping Swift in whatever the hell Swift was up to. Neither had happened.

Wence had been talking to someone.

Someone who knows me. Someone who's watching me, knows what I'm doing. Wence has been told to let me go. By whom? What for? It's a game. So who was rolling the dice? Who was making up the rules? Who was playing with his life?

Anger burned inside him. It was pointless to think about it now. He just wanted to get away from SSD, Wence and all the others like him. No, it wouldn't be fair to take his anger out on Wence. He was following someone's orders. But Beckett had stopped following orders. No one told him what to do anymore.

'I'm leaving.' Beckett stood up.

Wence leaped up out of his seat. 'A word of advice. Keep away from William Swift.'

'William Swift has employed us to do a job, Wence.' Beckett spat the words out. 'I'm not giving it up on your say so.'

'He's mixing in dangerous company. Take my advice: keep your nose out or you will end up buried in concrete.'

Beckett only half heard the warning. He was already out the door.

The conference room was large enough to hold the two hundred or so attendees. Why did the colour scheme have to be such a drab mushroom brown? You walked into the room and thought 'boredom' immediately. Probably so the speakers held your undivided attention; there was little else in the room to distract. A podium stood in the middle of a raised platform at the back of the room. Three large metal urns were set up on a table to one side. Hotel staff were busy opening an endless line of bottled water.

A few late delegates collected name badges from the

admissions desk at the side of the conference room. There were faces Anna knew, faces she had seen in magazines. But she didn't want any distractions. She had waited three weeks for her meeting with William.

Ah, there was Alberto.

He was supposed to be in the bar talking to their fellow delegates. And it was very unlike Alberto to pass up the chance of reacquainting himself with the delegate from Napoli.

Anna looked over Corelli's shoulder. At least he was finally writing his speech. Well, that's what it looked like.

'Alberto?'

Alberto spun round. He looked as if he had been caught out, like a naughty schoolboy. His left hand went over the paper to hide his writing. She wondered what he had written.

'I need a favour, Alberto. I need to go out.'

He didn't look up at her. 'Take Mr Wence's body-guard. I'm not going anywhere.'

His voice was severe. Not unusual. Without journalists and cameras around his charm was set firmly in the 'off' position.

'I'm meeting a friend.'

Corelli nodded his understanding and smiled. 'And you don't want a chaperone?'

Good. He got it. Why did she always have to tip-toe round him? Never mind. She would keep smiling. 'Exactly.'

Alberto pulled back his seat and got up to leave. He couldn't leave yet. There were things to make clear to him. He had to be told. But it was so hard. The way he looked at her every time William was mentioned. His sad eyes. Hurting him could not be helped. Not now.

Anna took the seat next to Alberto and took his hand. He placed his writing pad to one side.

'Alberto, I don't like all this secrecy. Pretending people who are close to me don't exist. Pretending our relationship is something it's not.'

33

He leaned forward and put his other hand on top of hers and squeezed gently.

'Everyone is so in love with the idea of us being a couple, why spoil their illusion?'

Really. The man was too much sometimes. 'We're meant to stand for honesty, Alberto, not deception.'

He stared hard into her eyes. 'Other parties would pay millions for the public affection we have. The more they love us, the more chance we will have of winning.'

Anna felt her resolve crumbling. He never listened to her about William. He ignored it as if it was something that would, one day, go away of its own accord. Like a bad cold.

'After the election, we'll come clean, yes?' she asked.

Alberto sat back in his chair, withdrawing his hands. 'After the election, it won't matter one way or the other. Now give me a minute, then take the fire exit.'

Anna stood. 'I know the way, Alberto. Thank you.'

She had blown it. Every time she was about to tell him her plans she would suddenly get cold feet and put it off for another day. But she knew she was running out of time. Perhaps Alberto would find out from the newspapers after all. No, she couldn't do that to him. The Liberty Party was about honesty and she was holding back the truth with her most trusted colleague.

She checked her watch. If she didn't leave now she would be late meeting William.

Telling Alberto would have to wait another day.

Slow down.

Beckett gradually lifted his foot from the accelerator until he was within the speed limit. More or less. He had cut up one driver after another, trying to take his aggression out on his driving. He wanted to hit something and hard. If he wasn't careful, it would be another car. Not clever. Damn stupid, in fact.

The back of his neck ached with tension and frustration. Something was going on. Wence had been told to back off. That much was certain. Otherwise, Wence would have brought every single rule and regulation he could have thought of, and a few more besides, down on him. Gizmos could have been disbanded. There was no doubt that Wence had the political clout to do it. Ed and Ros could have been implicated in whatever it was Swift was up to. Ended up in prison, maybe.

No. Somebody was watching him. Hell, maybe even watching out for him. The thought wasn't a comfort.

The carphone rang. He stabbed a button without picking up the receiver.

'Beckett here.'

It was Ed.

'Hey, Beckett. Good to know you're still with us. Where've you been?'

'I'll tell you later. What are you and Ros up to?'

'We've found out a little bit more about Mr Paranoia.'

'Watch yourself, Ed. Swift could be into something bigger than lasers.'

Beckett was being patronised and he knew it. Still, Ed needed things spelling out very clearly every now and again. Where angels feared to tread, Ed had many a time barged in without considering the consequences. Beckett felt a little envious of his colleague.

And maybe that was his problem. He thought too much about everything.

'Ros and I kinda get that feeling too,' said Ed. 'Don't worry, we'll watch our backs. We're going to check out a meeting he's got. Ros suggested a rendezvous back at the office. Sound OK?'

'Sounds fine.'

It was time to stop worrying and get on with the job.

The bodyguard – a short, stocky thug with a crew-cut – stood by the entrance to the conference room.

This was too easy.

The bodyguard looked up at Corelli questioningly. He looked more like a bouncer than a security operative. What did it matter? Well, he wasn't paid to do anything more than watch their backs.

What mattered now was that the bodyguard wouldn't be covering Anna's back.

'I need to go to the Embassy,' he said. 'You'd better come with me.'

Wearing her long black coat, Anna stepped around him. Why did she have to make it obvious that she was about to leave?

The bodyguard asked, 'And Miss Fabrizi?'

'Don't worry about Miss Fabrizi,' Corelli smiled and winked at Anna. She smiled back.

So trusting. So honest.

So sickeningly, dangerously honest.

He held Anna close, wrapping his arms around her, savouring the smell of her perfume. 'She'll be staying in her room. OK?'

Anna kissed him on the cheek and walked out of the conference area into the hotel lobby.

The bodyguard didn't move. Was he uncertain whether to carry out the request? Suddenly Corelli hardly dared to breathe.

Everything hinged on the bodyguard's actions. The future. Corelli's friends' futures. A whole country's future.

Corelli stared at the bodyguard. He raised an eyebrow in a silent question.

The bodyguard didn't move.

And that was confirmation enough. The hired gorilla wasn't going to do anything. He had played his part perfectly. But would he truly understand the ramifications of the duping he'd fallen for? He would probably find out in the evening papers. Corelli smiled at the bodyguard who turned away.

Corelli pulled out his mobile phone. Ten digits in quick succession.

'Hello? Is that Mackenzie?'

« Four »
« Sister surprise »

The two women walked confidently down the alleyway.

Jackie looked at her partner. Her exact double. In the pale foundation make-up, Ruth looked even more ill than usual. Silly girl. Up all hours, popping anything she could get her hands on. Jackie knew she should keep an eye on Ruth but the girl seemed to live a thirty-hour day and there was no way of keeping up with her over any stretch of time. Like last night. Downing vodkas as if there was no tomorrow. And judging by the way she drank, you could never say with any certainty that Ruth would have a tomorrow. If only Jackie wasn't so scared of Ruth's boyfriend – but how much of that was her concern?

Whatever else besides alcohol Ruth was on last night, there was no way of telling. The heavy make-up hid any trace of the effects of drink and drugs. They looked like six-foot china dolls. The make-up would appear strange under the studio lights. She had told them that, but they treated all models like bimbos who knew nothing about their job. More fool them. Their faces would simply white out and all they would see on film would be two pairs of bright red lips dancing about in mid-air.

And the wigs were bizarre. Straight black hair with a blonde streak running down the centre, tied into a long ponytail. Jackie was glad of the sunglasses. Thin strips of black plastic stretched around their faces and over their ears. It didn't matter how naff they looked. If she saw anyone she knew, they would never recognise her.

Her little black dress was tied at the waist with a thick black belt. PVC jack-boots with block heels completed the ensemble. They looked ridiculous. Sort of thing found in seedy bars.

The black dress made the desperately thin Ruth appear more under-nourished than she already was. She was a walking eating disorder. A six-foot tall skeleton, nourished only by drugs. She acted as if it was all part of the job.

Ruth stumbled in the high, thick heels. Jackie held out an arm to steady her.

'Are you OK?'

Ruth laughed and steadied herself. 'Silly bugger, aren't I?'

'Come on. We're there now.'

'Thank God for that. I'm freezing.'

From behind them came a woman's voice. 'Excuse me.'

Jackie turned. Two women. Almost as tall as they were. One blonde, hair cut short and elf-like. She had a small nose that turned up ever so slightly. The other was dark-haired, cut short in the same style. She had bright, large brown eyes set in a slightly rounder face. She looked slightly older than the pretty blonde. It was obvious they were sisters.

Two arms whipped out and Jackie's head smacked into Ruth's.

Muggers? *Women muggers?* What was the world coming to? But neither she nor Ruth had anything worth stealing.

Ruth fell to the floor and didn't get back up.

Oh, brilliant.

Pumped full of God-knows-what, able to dance for every single second in a twelve hour period but, when her augmented physical abilities were really needed, utterly useless.

Jackie turned to the two women, rubbing her head. 'I

don't know what you want. We've got no money on us. Just the clothes we're standing in.'

A fist smacked into Jackie's face.

'Exactly,' said the dark-haired woman.

Jackie fell to the ground and didn't get back up.

It was all his.

O'Neill wandered slowly and deliberately around the studio. He had to keep an eye on everything, especially the car. It was quite beautiful.

Lights in the studio gantry glared down. Everywhere and everything apart from the jet black car glowed white. Technicians were setting lights up in different parts of the studio. The director had said they'd only need two cameras for the video shoot. Bloody poof. Mincing around the place, clipboard in one hand, his feeble-looking assistant trailing behind him. If O'Neill had his way, they would be looking for the git who got the photos at last week's trial, not be messing around with a damage limitation exercise.

The shiny black car sat on the round tilted dais in the centre of the studio. It looked as if it was waiting for something. Like a camouflaged animal about to pounce on unsuspecting prey. Black frame. Thick black tyres. Tinted windows. A century of development in the motor car industry had led to this: the Trancer. Tronix had worked directly on it for years now. It was his last, and best hope. O'Neill had put everything he could into the project – and a few things he shouldn't. But now wasn't the time to worry about that.

Setting up a multi-media press release wasn't that bad an idea of Cray's. And Cray had got things moving quickly with the studio. Good little worker. Just a pity that the editor at *Autofuture* hadn't had the decency to spike the pictures taken at the test track. And *Autofuture*'s editor hadn't even said that he was going to print them. Not the act of a gentleman, was it?

You couldn't trust anyone these days.

* * *

The door was dull and grey. An illuminated white sign with black lettering read STUDIO STAFF ONLY. Sarita checked that the strange wig was straight and then rapped again on the door with a black-gloved hand.

Why were they taking so long to answer? They should be expecting the models. She checked the time. Almost late. Keep checking for anyone who could ruin the plan.

No one about. Good. Heaven knew how long they would have to get the car once inside the studio. Sarita hoped that the models wouldn't be found until they were well away from there. Bit bad tying them up and gagging them. Davina was always the more physical one and the whack she gave the second girl. *Ouch*. But they would get over it.

They didn't have much choice but to knock them out. You had to be callous in this business, that's what Bob said. You didn't let anything stand in your way. That sounded like it could be Uncle Dave's motto. In a way, it would be good to see the old bastard again.

And even better to see the look on his face when all his dreams go up in smoke.

That was, of course, if they got away with it.

There was so much that could go wrong. So many things that might catch them out.

Go in. Get out. See Bob. Get the money. Leave the country for a while and start all over again. Perhaps not the best profession in the world, but it paid the rent. It sounded so simple. So why was her heart thumping against her chest?

Why wasn't anyone answering the door? Perhaps they had the wrong day? Impossible. The models had turned up. And this fiddling wig. A bit of a makeshift job. A damn good disguise, though. All the tools for the car were in the vanity case. What a lovely shade of pink.

Sarita checked on Davina who stared at the door as if she was willing the thing to open. Davina tapped her feet and, under her breath, muttered, 'Come on!'

What was that? The sound of heavy-duty bolts. The door swung outwards. The two women took a step back.

A man appeared. Young. Late twenties, early thirties. A few years older than them. Attractive but not distinctive. Medium build. Mousy hair. Nice jawline. Not too square. Light brown eyes. Freshly shaved. Good suit. OK tie. Sarita remembered him from Bob's pictures. Paul Cray. She never forgot a name. Cray was the technical director at Tronix Design and Development. Hard worker. Very loyal to Tronix, apparently. Shame about that. Otherwise, Cray was supposed to be rather a nice chap. That was according to all the reports she had heard. So what was a nice man like him doing mixed up with the Spawn of Satan himself – David O'Neill?

'Where have you two been?' said Cray, looking at his watch. 'You're cutting it a bit fine.'

Neither woman replied. He might have known the two models. Might have even hired them himself. You never knew. In this get-up they would easily pass for them. Sarita stepped inside and walked past him. Davina followed.

The door slammed shut.

Sarita took a deep breath.

Now the fun would really begin.

Cray bundled the models off to Kenny, the floor manager. Now he was a spare part in the video shoot. The cameras were all lined up, apparently. What would he know? The studio lights were in place and technicians were checking the sound levels.

It was no fun having nothing to do. And Cray wanted to keep clear of O'Neill. The man had been in a foul mood all week and Cray had had enough of his whining.

O'Neill wanted a close eye kept on the car and had automatically assumed that as Cray had organised the shoot – within a week, was that some kind of world record? – he had to come along. From technical director

41

at Tronix to tea-boy-stroke-runner. Cray laughed. Here, he was out of his depth. It wasn't a feeling he was comfortable with.

And there was O'Neill, lording it over his manor. Common little toad. He had the manner of an escaped convict trying to be on his best behaviour. Not that Cray would tell his boss what he really thought of him. O'Neill's recently acquired acquaintances were terrifying. Soldiers. Some strange military outfit. Not a government's armed forces, that much was certain. A small mercenary unit.

With friends like that, Cray would make sure he kept O'Neill smiling.

If only the pictures hadn't been taken at the test track.

O'Neill spotted Cray and walked across the studio floor.

'The girls have arrived,' said Cray.

O'Neill pretended to ignore him and carried on looking around the studio. Why did O'Neill persist with such an attitude? It didn't win him any friends.

After a moment, O'Neill spoke. 'I hate going public in a rush. And I especially hate being forced into it.'

Oh, change the bloody record. Didn't they all know it? For the past five days O'Neill had spoken of little else.

'It's only for the dealers,' said Cray.

'Reassure me some more, why don't you?'

'Security reckon it was someone at the test track who sold the photos.'

'Whoever it was, I hope he likes hospital food.'

That confirmed a theory. O'Neill was looking for the photographer, after all. And, knowing O'Neill, he would not stop until the photographer had been found.

'And you can inform Security I'm going to make some big changes,' O'Neill continued. He turned to face the car that was his pride and joy. 'Tell the bimbos to keep smiling, don't fall over, and most importantly,' he stressed, pointing a finger at Cray, 'don't touch the car.'

42

With that, he walked off.

Sometimes, you just wanted to hit him. Not that O'Neill was a bad boss. Cray always knew exactly where he stood with him. None of the deviousness of some of his ex-employers. Come to that, O'Neill simply didn't have the intellectual capacity to be devious. It was doubtful he could even spell 'intellectual'.

A tannoy voice. It was Lawrence, the PA. 'Everyone in position, please. All non essential crew will kindly leave the studio.'

Well 'crew' wasn't exactly how Cray saw himself but he assumed the request to leave included him. Perhaps they would let him watch in the gallery. He had always wondered how they made an advert.

Kenny the floor manager relaxed slightly as the lights came down. Even though this would be the first of many takes that morning (why, oh why couldn't they rehearse a little first?), the majority of his work was done. The car was there on the podium. The crew had rigged up the set – such as it was. A dais, four white billowing curtains that ran from top to bottom and two blue screens. The lighting guys had worked wonders in a very short time. Sound were their usual obstreperous selves, but the PA had sorted them out.

The cameras trundled into position. They had been pre-programmed with all the shots. Camera technicians followed them keeping a close eye on signs of malfunction. The technicians were only a failsafe. Looked bored out of their skulls. In Kenny's view, they were a waste of time and money but he had heard stories of berserk cameras, so perhaps not.

The shoot had been quickly organised. Nothing fancy or complicated was going to be filmed. There hadn't been enough time to organise anything better. A couple of good shots of the car, the girls and then to the interviewer and O'Neill. Basic stuff. With luck it would all be over by one o'clock.

'Is everyone ready, Kenny?'

43

Kenny spoke into his headpiece. 'When you are, Lawrence.'

'Okay. Counting down a minute.'

'One minute everyone!'

This was his favourite moment. The few seconds before you started to create something. Everyone working as a team, pulling together. Decades of experience coming into play.

'Thirty seconds.'

It was the tension he liked. It wasn't stress. More like a buzz in the air as people prepared to show off their skills. Got the adrenalin pumping. Made the senses sharp.

'And cue.'

A huge light flashed on behind the car, its silhouette the only thing the camera would pick up. Camera One slowly tracked from left to right.

Over the speakers, a pre-recorded audio sequence blasted out: 'Well, a secret as good as this one is bound to get out sooner or later. You've heard all the rumours, now see it for yourself. The car they're all scrambling to imitate. The car that's going to change what motoring's all about. From Tronix, the continent's leading automotive design and development company. The new Tronix Trancer.'

Music. Loud. Modern stuff. He must be getting old. It wasn't his taste at all. But it was on cue, so that was good. A bank of overhead spotlights slammed on. Perfect timing. Both cameras focused on the centre of the studio where the car sat. The car was indeed very nice. And so were those two girls. Their poses weren't exactly what Lawrence had asked for. Not that it mattered much. One of them looked a little uncomfortable. Hmm. Lawrence was bound to ask for another take. Maybe it was going to be a long day after all.

Then Camera Two pulled away so that both interviewer and Mr O'Neill were in shot.

'There are a lot of people who would love to know what's hidden inside this amazing looking package,' said the interviewer. 'Well, I can tell you that the technology developed by the whizz-kids at Tronix's car division leaves all the competition standing. Here's the head man at Tronix himself – David O'Neill.'

Kenny stared at the monitor by his side. O'Neill looked straight at the camera and smiled. It wasn't a pleasant sight.

'David, this is really a fantasy car, isn't it?'

'The technology inside the Trancer may be fantastic but it's no fantasy, Phil.'

O'Neill grinned at the camera again. Oh, dear. You couldn't have a more wooden delivery if a tree had been asked to step in.

'Is it true you brought the prototype here in an armoured truck?'

'That's absolutely true. Our competitors would pay a king's ransom for a sniff at what's going to put them out of business.'

'Can't you even give us a hint?'

'I will say this, Phil. This car's going to have a built-in level of intelligence that has no parallel in any other model.'

What were those girls doing? Why were they climbing inside the car? They weren't supposed to do that, were they?

Since when had that changed?

The car hadn't been locked. Sarita lifted the door upwards. It lifted easily. Hydraulics hissed into action. Wouldn't be a good idea to make too much noise. But there was little time to be worrying now. They had sussed the exits. Getting out was as easy as pie. O'Neill could try to stop the car but he would not want it damaged. His security team were powerless. No guns and only three of them to stop two very determined young women.

Over the blaring music, Sarita barely heard the interviewer ask O'Neill, 'And the performance?'

'Racing standard all the way, Phil. All in a mass-production vehicle with a lot of Beauty and not a little of the Beast.'

She had to ignore them and concentrate on the job at hand. She put a hand inside the left thigh-boot. Dancing around the car had been a pain. But a girl couldn't be seen at any function without her fully adaptable ratchet screwdriver, could she?

Sarita examined the car's controls. The ignition was standard. That didn't feel right. The steering seemed perfectly, boringly normal. Well, this was the car that Bob wanted, so it was the car he would have.

Sarita extended the thin steel rod from the long plastic cylinder of the screwdriver. With a click she locked the rod into position then slammed it into the plastic of the steering column. It fell away easily.

Standard wiring. There didn't seem to be a screw or a wire out of the ordinary – nothing she or her sister had not seen before. Wasn't this car supposed to be special?

The music stopped suddenly. The studio staff were on to them. Time had run out.

'Hold it, please, everyone. Kenny?'

A tannoy voice. Had to be from the gallery.

'Will you ask the girls what they're playing at?'

O'Neill turned towards the car, looking stupid. The interviewer looked puzzled. Camera men looked bored. The rest of the studio crew looked confused. The floor manager looked irate. And all of them were staring at her and Davina.

The passenger door opened upwards. Davina stepped inside.

'Come on, sister, it's time to make our daring escape.'

Sarita opened her jacket pocket and fetched out a coin-sized piece of metal with a thin copper wire extending from its centre. She pressed it into the ignition switch. The device beeped, registering that it was functioning perfectly. They would be out of there in a few seconds.

If the car had petrol in it.

Sarita gave a sigh of relief as the engine kicked into life. She wanted to kiss her little lock pick. Davina locked her door and put on her seat belt. People were coming closer to the car.

Sarita revved the engine. People backed away. O'Neill's eyes were wide open. He couldn't believe it was happening. His beautiful little car was going for a long drive and would not be making the return trip.

'Hey!' he shouted. As if that would do much good.

Davina laughed. Time to go. Foot down slowly. Don't go too fast. Wouldn't want to hit anyone. More importantly, she didn't want to damage the merchandise. This was going to be a nice little earner. Bob would be pleased.

Two uniformed men came forward, one either side of the moving car. They tried to open the doors. Idiots. The two cameras backed away as the car rolled forward. Monitors on stands were hurriedly pushed out of the car's path. A regular little slalom.

Inside the car they heard O'Neill's voice. Sarita couldn't make out what he was saying. Barking some order, probably.

Sarita gently pressed the accelerator and turned the car to leave the studio.

What was that?

She'd clipped somebody.

'Who was that? Is he hurt?' she asked.

Davina turned to look back. 'A security guard. It's OK. He's getting up.'

And there was the exit. Two huge black doors. The gateway to freedom and a cool couple of hundred thou. Perhaps they should raise the price. After all, there were a lot of people interested in Tronix's new machine.

The open road. No more than a tarmac strip. She had to turn left on to the main road.

Sarita checked the rear mirror and adjusted it for her eyeline. A couple of people were running after them. Was one of them O'Neill?

It was worth the risk if stealing the car really hurt him. Forget the dosh (up to a point). It didn't matter nearly so much as ruining him and his empire.

And Sarita could just imagine the look on his face as they sped off in his precious car. Shocked. Angry. Despondent.

The thought made her a little happier.

But then it was only a car they had taken. O'Neill had taken so much more.

Well, they'd made a good start.

« Five »

« Down in the park »

There seemed to be no one around for miles as Starkey crossed the green. He constantly scanned left to right for anyone who might be following. Nothing to disturb him. A vague hum of traffic in the distance. An occasional plane crossed the sky every few minutes. That was all. As near to silence as you could get in the city.

The college was an excellent site for cover. He could hide almost anywhere and not be seen. Massive. Solid. Built a couple of centuries ago? Didn't matter. Rows of pillars. Windows everywhere. He couldn't see inside because sunlight reflected off the windows.

Did he need to hide? If Fabrizi and Swift saw him, he would just look like another member of the public.

Starkey glanced up at the balcony above the ground floor windows. The short wall ran along the balcony. Would that hide him from prying eyes? Well enough.

Mackenzie would have him killed if he fouled up again. He had become too much of a liability. No one ever let Mackenzie down for long. And there was no running from him. Somehow, he would always catch up with you.

Why was he thinking of letting people down?

Starkey gently lifted the bomb from his pocket and almost allowed himself a smile. It wouldn't be wasted.

49

He would get the job done. He had never let anyone down. Ever. And he wasn't about to start now.

Starkey had to hold the bomb so very carefully. The glass tubing was extremely delicate. The explosive, so solid. Beauty and power.

He kept checking for anyone watching. He couldn't afford to slip up again. He had a reputation to think of. And then there was the money. And the life. The life was all that really mattered.

He pocketed the bomb and rubbed his hands together. Hell, it was cold and the wind was making his eyes water.

Look left and right, left and right. Green everywhere. Not a tree in sight. Nowhere for cover. He had to stay for this one. Not like the hotel where he would have planted the bomb and sent a radio signal to detonate the explosives. He had to watch Fabrizi die.

Wence might have got wind of her plans to leave the hotel and the conference. That wasn't likely. From her phone call with lover boy, it sounded as if she could pull the wool over people's eyes with no problem. But security was everything. You could never be too careful.

And there was the bench. The one where Swift had proposed. Where the two lovers would die. How romantic. The bench sat alone in the middle of the courtyard. It had to be the one. There was no other bench around.

Starkey felt his heart start to pound. Adrenalin surged through his body, the exhilaration swamping his thoughts.

The air seemed so clear. He could see for miles. His senses were so sharp. Expectation burned. The life was coming. That was all that mattered. The life was coming to an end.

All he had to do was keep calm. Just sit on the bench. No need to rush. Ensure that he didn't do anything that a passerby might think of as strange. He didn't want people to remember. No one knew his face. He was too good. He didn't get caught.

The bomb was too small to be noticed under the bench. Perfect. The lovers would never suspect a thing.

The bomb, fitted snugly on the underside of the bench, almost invisible. It sat waiting for Fabrizi.

Waiting for the life.

Ros's car came to a stop. Huge black gates blocked the path. There was no way of driving the car through the grounds of the Royal College Green. This assignment would be better done on foot.

Well, they didn't make buildings like that any more. Ros loved modern architecture with its tall, straight glass and metal monoliths. Elegant in its stark functionalism. She found beauty in a building by its simplicity. Sharp, straight lines or unusual geometric designs she saw every day but the college was from another time. A world before computers, before telephones, before electricity. And it was beautiful in that no other building she had ever seen looked quite like it.

The site was really two tall and long buildings. One the exact twin of the other, running parallel to each other. Black domes topped both, contrasting strongly against the brilliant white structures. Both had sets of huge windows. A cold but bright sun shone on the buildings, reflecting the light back and causing the college to somehow glow. A clock sat below each dome. Black face, golden roman numerals and hands.

It was 11.15.

Swift and Anna (girlfriend? partner? co-conspirator?) would arrive in a little over ten minutes.

Ed tapped Ros's shoulder. His bright blue eyes glinted in the light.

'If someone's tracking Swift, it might be a good idea to have a look around, yeah?'

Ros agreed. 'We need to be quick. I don't want Swift finding out that we're snooping.'

They left the car and walked through the gates. The path divided into two, leading to either college site. A few yards beyond the left path, Ros noticed a raised platform on which sat a bench. Wide concrete steps led up to the courtyard between the college's two sites. The blue plastic bench looked incongruous among the historical splendour of the college. But there was no other bench. This was where Swift would meet Anna. And they would be here any minute. Ros looked for suitable cover.

'Is that the kind of place you'd like to get a proposal?' asked Ed.

'Depends who it's from, Ed. This place is romantic all right. But with all these windows . . . it's like being in the middle of a stage.'

Ros realised suddenly what she had said. The arrangement of the bench in the courtyard would be a perfect opportunity for any assassin.

'Very exposed.'

Anyone sitting on the bench could be targeted from a long way off. Anyone could hide in the college and never be seen. Anna had a bodyguard but she said she was going to shake the guard off so an extra layer of protection had been removed. From what Beckett had said, Swift had a government department on his tail. But did that make him the bad guy?

Ros had to trust her instincts. There was not enough information to do anything else. Damn, it was frustrating. A decision. Swift was worried when he heard he was being spied upon. Anna had a security team watching her back. But her bodyguards weren't here. For some reason, she wanted to give them the slip. Criminal motives?

Ed and Ros turned to face each other. Swift could be in a lot of danger here.

'Good place to kill someone,' she said.

This meeting place was downright assassin friendly. A would-be killer had a thousand places to hide. There was practically no time to give the place the once-over before the lovers met.

Still, they had to try.

Ros ran into the courtyard, passing the bench, and lifted out a pair of bulky binoculars from her bag.

'Come on, Ed. Let's check it out.'

Ros needed a good vantage point between the two college sites. Standing at the back of the green all she could see were a few birds and, in the far distance, a figure of a man walking his dog. Bright sunlight cast strong shadows of the pillars that ran alongside each building.

Nothing moved.

No flicker of a shadow.

Perhaps she was being paranoid. There really might be nothing to worry about. Swift's meeting might be entirely innocent. So why had he lied to them all that morning?

Ros lifted her binoculars to her eyes and pressed a small button on the side, hearing a whine that increased in pitch as they powered up. The whine quickly became inaudible.

Through the binoculars, Ros glanced over at the building. The computer-enhanced image showed her nothing.

'Increase magnification five per cent.'

The image faded but quickly returned, showing a sharp, enlarged image of a set of windows. The resolution was impressive. It had taken her for ever to perfect it. What was more of a surprise was that the voice-operating system still worked.

Still, it was getting her nowhere. She couldn't detect anything out of the ordinary.

'Switch to heat sensor,' she whispered.

Again, the image faded. This time it took a moment to return. The colour of the world viewed through the binoculars changed into different hues of light-blue and green. Ros could see everything and its ambient temperature. If someone was hiding in the shadows, the binoculars should pick them up.

Ros checked over the college. Colours ranging from

53

a pale, whitish-blue to a light green showed the extent of the temperature range around the college. If someone had been around, they would have shown up as a yellow-to-orange figure in a sea of blue. But there was no one. Another dead end. The morning was becoming increasingly frustrating.

What the heck was that? An orange shape rose from the ground. She dropped the binoculars.

Of course. How could she have forgotten? Swift. Running up the stairs to the bench.

11.30. Right on time.

She had to run out of his line of sight before he spotted her.

11.30 am. Time had just run out.

It could be a coincidence. Ed believed in fate. What will be will be and all that. It made him the way he was: a man who took a day at a time, taking whatever was thrown at him with a feeling of 'This was meant to happen'.

And the aerial sticking out over the balcony could be a coincidence.

Like hell. Every ounce of his experience said that the aerial was unlikely to be anything innocent. It just didn't happen.

He had run around the entire college, checked every hiding place he could see and found nothing. If he had stayed where he was and looked upwards, he would have seen the aerial poking out over the balcony.

It could be a radio. But then, it could also be a radio transmitter.

If Ed was a gambling man, he would have bet money on the latter so he had to get a better look.

He kept to the shadows. If he could see the aerial, the owner could probably see him.

Loud footsteps echoed as he ran down the colonnade. That was no good, he had to slow down. The owner of the aerial might hear him running.

Time: 11.33. Anna and Swift could be together by

now. He would have to risk being heard. He was on borrowed time already. His decisions would affect whether Swift lived or died.

'Ros?'

She came through clearly on his head-set.

'Yeah?'

'I think I've got something. On the, er, west wing.'

'Right. I'll go and find Swift and his friend.'

From his hiding place, Ed lifted his binoculars to his face. The aerial was clearly visible. It jutted out from a small black box.

A man's face appeared over the wall. He seemed to be checking over the courtyard between the two college buildings. Hell, he would be looking over Swift's bench.

No coincidence. It *was* a transmitter. And probably for a bomb.

And then Ed saw the man himself. Swift. Sitting patiently on the bench waiting for his fiancée.

What if he shouted out a warning? No good. The assassin would hear it. Swift would simply turn around confused, wondering what was going on. He would have no time to escape before the bomb exploded, scattering Swift far and wide.

So why hadn't the bomb been detonated?

What was stopping the assassin from pressing the button to get rid of Swift?

The mysterious Anna. Had to be. The killer wanted them both dead.

Ed looked up at Swift who glanced at his watch.

11.35. Anna was late.

It gave Ed more time to stop the assassin.

If Swift was lucky, Anna would stand him up.

Starkey's fingers caressed the remote control.

He knew he was being impatient. That was not good. It couldn't be helped. He was always like this. With every single job he had taken, he was the same. The hunting, the stalking, the waiting, the life. And

55

now he was so close. It was almost a shame to end it. Keeping his impatience in check was another part of the ritual. This wasn't a job. It wasn't just taking pride in his work. This was what Starkey was, all he had ever wanted and needed to be.

It wasn't joy. It was everything.

The ending of not one but two lives. What more could he ask for?

Three lives? Four?

He had been there. Gunned down six people at once. It had felt good, really good. But it had been just the one experience. The six lives extinguished all at once. It would have been much better to kill them one after another.

But he did what he was paid to do. He had never before let any employer down. He wouldn't be starting now. The Italian woman would be dead very soon.

Starkey took a quick look over the wall. Still no sign of Fabrizi.

Where was that damned woman? She should have been on that bench by now, laughing with Swift and then – boom, bye-bye.

Starkey looked at his watch. Fabrizi should have been dead by now.

He ducked his head back under the wall, crouching down with his back against it. He put the remote on the floor. He had to wait for the right time, control his anger. The delay would make her death all the more pleasurable. Fabrizi had escaped him once. It would not happen again. Could not.

Footsteps. High heels.

Yes.

Starkey turned and peered over the wall. He had seen her photograph from a dozen press cuttings. A complete personality profile had been supplied by Mackenzie. He knew her so totally. Her politics. Her family. Her school friends. Things Fabrizi herself would have forgotten. And he knew her exact movements for the next two days.

56

But Anna Fabrizi wasn't going anywhere. Not now. Not ever.

Starkey reached for the detonator. Let them have their meeting. Their happiness was his happiness too. Because he was ending their happiness.

Swift spun the woman around in the air. Smiling faces. Kissing. Holding one another tight. Their joy was nothing compared to his. Nothing.

Time to die.

Footsteps.

Behind him.

Starkey turned.

Male. Blond. Handsome. Tall. Fit.

Head-set.

SSD operative?

No. Wence and his men would go through the rigmarole of giving him a chance to surrender.

This guy was running at him full on.

No weapon.

Starkey barely had time to put up a defence.

'You're going nowhere, mate.'

Australian?

The intruder tried to lift him from his crouching position.

No. This guy was not going to beat him.

His jacket was being pulled. He allowed himself to be lifted up.

Starkey butted the man on the chin. He reeled back, unsteady on his feet.

Damn him for being so tall.

The Australian was off-balance.

Now. Kill Fabrizi now.

Starkey dived for the remote on the floor. He should never have let it out of his hands.

Stupidstupidstupid.

The Australian was up on his feet and managed to kick the remote control before Starkey could grab it. Starkey almost screamed his anger.

He clenched his fists. Blood pumped violently round

57

his body. His muscles were taut and hard.

Starkey grabbed the Australian's legs and pulled. The man fell, catching his head on the balcony. He collapsed to the floor, stunned. Starkey jumped up. He had to hurt him while he was dazed. There was no time for the gun.

A kick to the stomach. His assailant doubled up. A punch to the face. Another kick in the ribs.

This guy was no match for him.

Over the side.

Starkey picked up the Australian and lifted him onto the edge of the balcony. The Australian groaned. He was coming round very quickly.

Get a move on, Starkey!

The man would survive the fall. They weren't up that high. Broken back. Pain for the rest of his life.

That would be good enough.

There were a few stone on him, though. Judging by the man's build, the weight would be muscle. Not enough to stop Starkey. No one and nothing could match him.

A hand pushed Starkey's head backwards. He wouldn't let the Aussie stop him.

A few inches more and he would be able to tip him over the wall.

'William! William! Move! There's a bomb! Move!'

No! That couldn't happen!

A woman's voice. From below. On the ground. Shouting a warning. There was no time for getting rid of this guy.

Where was the remote? There. Just a few feet away. His attacker wouldn't be able to stop him.

No. Swift and Fabrizi had stood up. They looked back at a woman running towards them through the courtyard.

He still had time. Swift and Fabrizi were confused. They didn't know what to do. Perfect.

Starkey let go of his attacker and jumped for the remote. The man leapt on his legs, bringing him down.

58

Starkey twisted, and hit the blond guy's neck with the side of his hand. At a better angle he would have broken it. This time, he just fell back.

It was enough.

Starkey pressed the detonator.

The explosion was beautiful.

Starkey pressed the detonator.

« Six »

« A question of faith »

As Beckett entered Gizmos he heard the answering machine switch itself on.

A message was recording. A man's voice. Educated. Young.

'– Cray of Tronix here. I've been asked to contact you regarding a security check. If you can get back to me today I'd be very grateful. I hear you're pretty good.'

Their reputation was getting around. Good. It meant more work. He hated being idle.

The caller left a number and rang off.

Tronix. A household name no less. Top of the range motors. Sports stuff mostly. Every kid wanted to drive one of their cars, or so the adverts said. Also into advanced automotive R&D. One of the world leaders in it, if he recalled rightly.

Beckett picked up the phone. Might as well call him back there and then.

Cars.

Ed would be pleased.

Ed didn't want to look up.

The assassin had pressed the detonator. Small chunks of debris had been thrown everywhere. Some had fallen on his back as the ground shook beneath him. The explosion echoed through the courtyard. It had been huge. Ed's ears were still buzzing. The killer had wanted to make sure Swift and Anna were very dead.

And now Ros could be dead because he hadn't stopped the bomb going off.

There was no sign of the hit man. He wasn't important right now. He looked over the wall, steeling himself against the possibility of looking down at three corpses.

Where the platform had been was a massive hole.

Oh God, no.

Three bodies lay prostrate on the ground, unmoving. Ros had cleared Swift and Anna from the bench but it seemed they hadn't been able to escape the bomb's blast.

He felt empty.

A head moved and turned.

'Ros!'

Ros looked up at him. She put a hand up to shield her eyes from the sun.

Oh, yes! YesYesYES!

Right now Ros was the most beautiful woman he had ever seen.

'Are you OK, Ed?'

'Me?' Ed shouted from the balcony. 'You're worried about me? I thought you were dead!'

Ros sat up – not without a little difficulty. 'You don't get rid of me that easily.'

Anna and Swift stirred. Ros helped Anna up.

Ed grinned and shouted, 'I'll be down in a second.'

He was the happiest man alive.

Ros felt dazed and battered. That wasn't such a shock. It happened when you were in the vicinity of a few pounds of detonated plastic explosives. She was covered in dust and small chunks of bench debris.

It could have been a lot worse. They had only just made it. A few feet nearer to the bench and Ed would have been taking what was left of her home in a body bag.

61

Anna sat up and immediately glanced over at Swift. They seemed all right.

Ros stood up and winced. She had landed badly. There would be a bruise on her leg. It wasn't anything serious.

Swift looked up at her, completely bewildered. He had grazed his hand but that was about the extent of his injuries. He might need something more than a sweet cup of tea for the shock.

His near-death experience didn't stop Ros being furious with him. It made her temper worse. If he had been honest with them from the start, the assassination attempt would never have happened.

'I think you've got some explaining to do, Mr Swift. For a start: who would want to kill you and your fiancée?'

Running footsteps clumped behind her. Ros knew it would be Ed, but her nerves were shot to pieces so she had to look.

'Thank God you're all right, Ros. For a minute I thought you were a goner.'

'Well, I'm about as all right as I can be.'

Ed helped Swift get to his feet. 'You can walk OK?'

'Yes, I'm fine,' he said. 'Just a bit shocked, that's all.'

'And you must be Anna,' said Ros, helping her to stand.

'That's right. And you are?'

The woman's tone of voice spoke volumes. Here was someone who got what she wanted – always. A proper little madam. Would she stamp her feet if she didn't get her own way? She dare try it and Ros would make sure she regretted it.

'We're the team William hired to sweep his place for bugs.'

'Ah, yes.'

Her tone of voice became conciliatory but the atmosphere changed. Each had found out that everyone was fine and that there was no further need to depend on each other. Without that need, Ros felt a distinct feeling of distrust from the two lovers. Ros took a step back and stood next to Ed. The movement was almost subconscious.

'Look, this was all as much a surprise to you as it was to us.'

'No, it wasn't a surprise. Not at all,' said Anna. 'I've been expecting an assassination attempt for some time.'

Ed raised his arms in exasperation. 'And do you think we had something to do with it? We just saved your lives!'

Anna shook her head. 'I've no real idea what to think. Look. Let's go back to William's warehouse and talk about this.'

'Fair enough,' said Ed. 'And we'd like some answers if that's not too much trouble.'

How badly could things go wrong in one day?

Holed up in the most secret security department's HQ then Ed and Ros almost blasted to nothing by an unknown killer.

Beckett wished they could have met up somewhere a little quieter than Swift's workshop. And they were supposed to be at the Tronix headquarters that afternoon to sort out something about a stolen car.

But first, one case at a time.

The droning of machinery in the background filled his head. Beams of light danced here and there in all sorts of colours. Add the smell of fried onions mixed with candy-floss and the warehouse could be mistaken for a fairground. Trying to think straight was almost impossible.

Ros seemed quite at home, as did Swift. Both Swift and Anna appeared unperturbed by the assassination attempt, although Anna constantly fidgeted and looked at her watch. She had to leave soon for her conference or Wence would notice her absence. Even Wence could not fail to see that the conference's main speaker was missing. But Miss Fabrizi was not leaving before they had some answers.

Every now and then Anna would reach over for Swift's hand and then pull away again. Beckett wished he could interpret body language. He found Anna quite attractive but in a glamorous, film star way. Her dark hair swept back into a ponytail made her features hard. It gave her a determined and earnest look. Perfect for a politician.

Ed kept staring at the two lovers across the table. He never took his eyes away from them. It was *that* look, Beckett thought. Ed had been pushed too close to death – his own and Ros's. The look didn't show fear. It was the effect of the fear the would-be assassin had instilled in him. Vengeance. Ed was out for blood.

And that might not be a good idea if they were going to catch the killer. Well, that was what Beckett wanted to do, if the others would follow.

'So let me get this straight,' he said. 'The Italian public want to believe that you and your partner Alberto Corelli are lovers. You go along with it because it's good for your image and will win you votes? Right?'

'You make us sound so cynical.'

Ros smiled and nodded. Beckett agreed. There really was no other word for it. Perhaps Miss Fabrizi would have preferred dishonest?

Ed pointed at Swift, but looked directly at Anna. 'And now you plan to marry William, yeah?'

Anna looked at Swift when she answered. 'So far we've kept our relationship secret.'

'But after the election,' added Swift, 'the truth will have to come out.'

'After the election is a bit late for us,' said Beckett. 'Wence obviously knew all about you. We were completely in the dark.'

'I didn't know if I could trust you,' said Swift. He looked at Anna, taking her hand. 'I was frightened Anna's enemies had found out about us.'

Anna looked up. 'That's why I wanted William to have this place swept for bugs.'

So Anna had recommended them.

'Listen, Miss Fabrizi,' he said, pointing at Ed and Ros at his side. 'These two just saved your lives. Perhaps you can trust us now?'

For Heaven's sake! Rescuing two people from an assassin should make them the firmest of friends! Christmas cards every year, the occasional drink, being godparents of each other's children, all that sort of thing. The two lovers didn't seem at all grateful. Well, gratitude Beckett could live without. In a world where anyone could monitor a person's movements at the touch of a button, listen in on conversations being held halfway around the world, or intrude into lives without ever being noticed, trust was all he wanted.

Swift nodded almost imperceptibly to Anna. Good. Maybe now they would get somewhere.

Ros asked, 'So who wants to kill you. And why?'

'A number of people,' said Anna, almost too casually, as if she had become used to life as a living target. 'The Liberty Party wants to clean up Italian politics. It's a vote-winner. But those with their hands in the till don't like it.'

So any number of people could be taking pot-shots at her. And all she had for protection was Wence – and maybe the team. If Anna agreed.

'You didn't bring your own security people with you?' Ed asked.

Good point.

'My partner, Alberto, thought we would be safe here. And, of course, Commander Wence's squad was supposed to protect us.'

'Wence couldn't look after a pet goldfish in a bowl.'

Ed laughed, which was reassuring. Perhaps his fury was on the wane already. Beckett didn't want to think Ed could be a liability.

Anna slapped the table. 'I don't want "looking after". I want to catch the people responsible.'

She paused. Either she trusted the team or she didn't. She seemed to weigh something up in her mind. 'Could you help me do that?'

Beckett refrained from smiling. Trust. So hard to win. So easy to give.

'Unless you'd rather follow Wence's advice and stay clear of us?' asked Swift.

Ed's cold blue eyes stared at Swift. Beckett knew his answer.

Ros smiled at Swift and Anna. 'Sorry, staying clear and giving up just isn't our style.'

Ed checked over the computerised security system in the warehouse's reception. A young brunette named Tamsin had, on seeing him, bent over backwards to show him every intricacy of the program. Normally, he would have lapped up the attention. But it was the image of Ros, Swift and Anna he kept seeing. Lying face down in the courtyard after the explosion. Thinking they were dead.

The killer had been too close.

Ed couldn't get it out of his mind. And then there was the other job for Tronix. Cars were as near as damn it to what he lived for yet, try as he might, he couldn't feel excited about it.

But getting inside a place like Tronix was the stuff he had dreamed of since he was a kid. Maybe once he got there, he would feel differently.

Ed had almost been thrown twenty metres to the ground by the assassin. He had almost been beaten. It had been luck – no skill involved at all – when Ros cried out to Swift and Anna and so distracted the assassin.

That was what had angered him the most. He had not been good enough. His pride was well and truly dented.

There was no way he would let himself be beaten again. The team had cooked up a plan to trap the killer. Like the spider said to the fly, 'Come into the parlour.'

'I'm sorry?'

Ed's thoughts were brought back to the here and now. 'Nothing, Tamsin. Just thinking out loud.' He smiled at the young woman and pointed at the computer screen. 'Thanks for showing me around this. Would you mind, er, leaving me for a while? I've got to check everything on this and –'

She looked a little disappointed. 'You don't want any distractions. OK.' She started to move away, towards an office behind the reception desk. 'If you need any help . . .'

Ed waved without looking up from the computer terminal. 'I'll give you a shout. Thanks a million.'

Swift had cameras positioned all around the outside of the warehouse. Very wise considering the amount of equipment inside. There was not one angle of the exterior of the building that could not be called up on the computer. The main exits to the building led directly to the rest of the trading estate. Using the computer, Ed changed his view of the area. More oddly designed warehouses and offices. The roads were lined with lamp-posts. At the rear of Swift's workshop was a building site. The basic infrastructure of new buildings was in place. Colossal cranes. Masses of building materials. Workmen in day-glo overalls and hard-hats drilled and hammered. Nothing unusual.

The locks on all the windows were also monitored by the computer system. According to Swift, every door and window in the place was linked up. No one could get in or out, without his say-so.

The computer alerted him to the fact that the rear exit had just opened. His fingers tapped commands into the keyboard. A picture appeared of a technician in a white coat. A man. He was lighting a cigarette. Tut-tut. Nasty habit.

He changed the picture. Beckett stood alone in the presentation hall. His arms were raised as if looking down the sights of a rifle.

It was time to pay Beckett a visit. Ed had finished with the security system. He needed cheering up and perhaps a trip to Tronix would do that.

* * *

67

If the guys at the Hive could see him now.

They would say he was mad. There was a certain amount of risk with Ros's plan – and also to Anna Fabrizi's life. But Anna said she wanted to catch this guy no matter what it took, so Beckett took her at her word.

The assassin was close on Anna's tail. She could leave the country immediately. Head back home and hide until the elections were over. In short, be safe. Anna said she had never been the type to cower and it would be impossible to hide during the last week before the elections. She had numerous television and public appearances to make and an election to win. Beckett wondered if Anna had a death wish. Her attitude bordered on arrogance.

As Anna was the target, she accepted that, logically, she would have to be the bait. Swift had attempted to convince her that it was not a good idea. Anna had turned to him and said that if it was the best way to catch the killer, she would do it. She wasn't messing about. Beckett admired that no-nonsense attitude in anyone.

Swift's presentation hall was the perfect place to catch the assassin. Large and empty, the killer would be brought onto their territory. It was a small advantage admittedly, but every little helped. And with what Ros was cooking up catching the killer would be made even easier.

Beckett looked across the hall. Swift had pulled out all the racks of plastic seats and had them arranged on all four sides of the raised central platform.

'Hey. Beckett!'

It was Ed miming firing a rifle. 'Just watching you on the security cameras.'

OK, so Beckett might have looked a bit stupid, but there was an important side to his earlier pretence.

'For any marksman worth the name, Ed, Anna will be a simple target.'

'I wish I could be so sure. He used a bomb before.'

'That's the beauty of setting it up here,' countered

Beckett. Ed had no need to be even remotely worried. 'The hall is open enough to attract the assassin but controllable so we can limit his options. His only choice will be to go for a rifle.'

He was becoming excited and he knew it. This was what he had been trained to do, after all. And it beat sitting behind a desk at the Hive any day.

'If he picks up the bait,' said Ed.

Of that, Beckett was certain. With what Ros and he had planned, there was no way the killer would want to miss this opportunity.

'He'll take it. Now, about this evening. You collect Anna. I'll be here, ready for our man.'

'Oh, come on!' protested Ed. 'I'm a lousy chauffeur. You collect Anna. I'll do the ambush stuff.'

Ambush stuff? Very technical. There was no way he would let Ed risk his neck.

'No, Ed. You haven't had the training.'

'Training!'

'Yes, *training*.' Beckett began counting them off. 'One: unarmed combat; two: night pursuit; three: survival; four: small arms –'

'Beckett, I'm doing this. All right?'

There was that cold, hard look again. Ed was not going to accept any job other than preparing for the assassin's arrival.

Beckett sighed. He really should be harder with the pair of them. Sometimes Ed and Ros, particularly Ed, lacked the discipline needed for some of the situations they found themselves in. They had to be co-ordinated. It wasn't a case of him pulling rank on them, nothing of the kind. Each of them brought their own experiences to the team. They dove-tailed brilliantly. It was just that preparing to trap an assassin was his field of expertise.

But reluctantly, Beckett nodded his head. Perhaps Ed had to learn sometime. And there really was no better way to learn than in the field. He just hoped neither of them would regret it.

'Great,' said Ed, flexing his biceps in Beckett's face. 'And don't talk to me about small arms.'

Beckett looked at his watch. Time seemed to be speeding up.

'Right. We best be making a move on Tronix. I'm supposed to be meeting Anna this afternoon at her hotel.'

Ed waved a finger in mock seriousness in Beckett's face. 'Just make sure Wence doesn't spot you. Don't want to ruin all your plans, do you?'

Beckett ignored him. 'Is Ros back yet?'

'Yeah. Ages ago.' Ed pointed in a vague manner across the hall to the entrance to Swift's workshop. 'She's making pretty pictures with Swift.'

There was nothing Ros liked doing more than playing with new toys. Swift's workshop was a dream. In most cases, the equipment comprised the very latest models and they were from companies around the world. Swift did not do things by halves, it seemed.

They were in a sectioned off part of the workshop. She had given him a list of the equipment she needed to use: a computer linked up to one of the laser projectors (with the appropriate software); a desk; three chairs; a series of miniature laser scanners they normally used to create corporate logo holograms; a metal cuboid frame and a coffee – white, none.

Two technicians quickly assembled everything Ros had asked for. She looked around her play room. The floor was covered with black cables of varying thickness, leading from the computer terminal through various junction boxes arranged seemingly haphazardly about the room. A number of cables were coiled around the metal cage. Flickering lights shot out from each inside corner of the cube. In the centre of the cube sat a rather old and scruffy teddy bear on one of the requisitioned seats.

Her fingers blurred as she typed one set of instructions into the terminal after another. Swift sat behind her, closely monitoring everything she did. Ros was almost oblivious to his presence. She was having fun.

Swift gave a quiet laugh and said, 'You've achieved more with this in a couple of hours than I have in years of research!'

He sounded amazed. *Years?* Ros hoped he was lying. The equipment he had here practically ran itself. A little time and a little patience – OK, and not a little skill – were all that were needed. Ros wondered how successful his company was.

'It's actually a bit of a lash-up,' she replied. And it was the truth. 'It might not even work at all.' Which was not true at all. It wasn't that she lacked confidence in her own abilities. But she wasn't about to go around bruising a client's ego. Bad for business.

'Well there's only one way to find out,' said Swift.

True. Ros input a final set of instructions. The computer program started up and the hum from the equipment around the metal cage grew louder.

Come on. Let's show Mr Swift how we're going to save his wife-to-be.

Tiny beams of light danced over the stuffed bear, flickering faster than the blink of an eye. It appeared that the bear was sitting in a dense fog.

The lights suddenly went out.

Ros crossed her fingers. This had to work. If there was any chance of ensuring Anna's safety tonight, this had to work. She held her breath. Swift didn't move or make a sound.

The laser projector attached to the ceiling shot out a fierce beam of light to the floor. Ros covered her eyes. The beam quickly lost its intensity.

And there it was.

Swift gasped. Ros wasn't feeling blasé about her achievement either.

In the middle of the beam was another teddy, the exact double of the original, hovering in mid-air.

Swift walked around the beam of light being careful not to cross it.

71

'I've never been able to create a three-dimensional laser image from an original. That's amazing.'

As quickly as it had appeared, the projection beam cut out. The replica teddy vanished.

'That's a shame,' said Swift. 'Pity you can't hold the image for very long.'

That wasn't a problem, Ros consoled herself. And there was no such word as 'can't'. The hologram's life-span was determined by the processing power of the equipment being used. All she needed was to work on even more powerful machinery. Then she would definitely achieve better results.

'No need to worry, Mr Swift. By this evening, it'll be perfect. We'll have a three-dimensional image that could fool anyone.'

Swift looked thoughtful for a moment. 'Yes, I was meaning to ask you. How can we guarantee the killer will turn up at all?'

'He knew you were meeting Anna at College Green, didn't he?' Swift nodded. 'So there's a leak of information somewhere.'

'But you checked my place and Anna's hotel room. There were no bugs.'

'There are other ways of listening to conversations, Mr Swift. This is where you and Anna come in.'

72

« Seven »
« Machine and soul »

Cray hadn't known what to expect of the team of security professionals he had called in. It had been O'Neill's idea to get outside help. That was typical. But with the amount of money that he had invested in Tronix and the Trancer, Cray wasn't surprised at the man's paranoia. You couldn't be too careful.

The tall blond guy had wanted to be known as 'Ed'. That was different to the people Cray normally worked with. With potential buyers – a dying breed as far as Tronix was concerned – you always used their title: Mr, Miss, Ms, whatever. Not only that, referring to employees by their titles ran through the rest of the company. It probably appeared to be unfriendly. It was just another example of Mr O'Neill's running of an efficient operation. Right down to the way language was used.

Ed kept quiet as he checked over the place. He looked eagerly over designs of cars that hung on the walls. Every now and again he would nod as if confirming something in his mind. Perhaps he knew something about the auto industry?

The other man in the group, Mr Beckett, didn't make a point of being informal. The word from Mr O'Neill was that Mr Beckett had been a government operative in his time. It had been one of the reasons O'Neill

73

wanted the team. Experience counted for so much. But Beckett no longer worked for the government. Did that mean he wasn't good enough for them or the other way round? Beckett's reputation for unorthodoxy had preceded him. Cray worried about that. All Beckett's team were there to do was keep an eye on the test car. Cray did not want any unusual methods being used to keep the car safe. He wanted life to be as simple as possible.

Cray turned his attention to Ros. Intelligent, beautiful, stylish. Her eyes betrayed her thoughts. She didn't look around the auto bay as obviously as Ed did but she wasn't missing anything.

It was time to tell them why they were here and to meet the boss. The trio followed him as he slowly walked around the large bay.

'We don't mass produce cars here. We make prototypes for the manufacturers who do. We've got two very different test models. One we lost this morning. Mr O'Neill, the boss, wants you to make sure the second one doesn't go the same way.'

Ed asked, 'When does the car go into production, Mr Cray?'

At least he was observing Tronix formalities.

'That's two years away.' At the very least, and presuming Tronix didn't go under before then.

'So why take the risk of a press show this early?' asked Mr Beckett.

'Our hand was forced. A rival got some pictures of the body shape. One of our spies told us they were about to pirate the look and call it their own. So we had to pre-empt that.'

They all turned at the sound of footsteps behind them. Mr O'Neill. Looking his good-humoured self as always, wearing a white polo shirt. Not very flattering.

'But it all went wrong,' he said.

There was no need for O'Neill to glare at Cray like that. Was it Cray's fault they had all been duped by two thieves disguised as models? The real models had been found, bound and gagged in an equipment room, banging against the door.

And was it Cray's fault if some people were so persistent that nothing anybody could do would stop two very clever women who were in the right place at the right time?

O'Neill continued. 'That pair of Sharons could have done me a lot of public damage.'

He always talked about women like that. And got away with it. Too intimidating.

'But,' said Ros, 'you still have a lot of secrets worth protecting.'

What did she know? Oh. She was talking about the car. Cray hoped she was. For her sake.

'Oh, that's for certain,' said O'Neill. 'They didn't get away with quite as much as they thought. I'd like to see their faces right now.'

Bob shivered in the echoing workshop and gazed sourly at the two women.

The smell of grease and oil. It churned his stomach. Bob felt a little dizzy. It was freezing cold. He supposed that those working here didn't feel it. The lock-up was a dump, and that was putting it kindly. Didn't give potential employers the best impression in the world. Dented metal lockers. Work-benches with pieces of machinery and paper lying on metal shelves. He had faith in the girls, though. He just wished they would become faster learners and think before they rushed in.

Amateurs.

You gave them a helping hand, pointed them in the right direction and still they messed it up. The girls didn't realise what they were dealing with. They would soon.

Both of them looked over the whole of the car's chassis, desperate to find something they could sell. But they were new at this. Maybe they would improve.

They had succeeded in breaking into O'Neill's place.

An act of which, if ever questioned, Bob would deny all knowledge. That wasn't a bad piece of work. And obtaining the photos without getting caught was pretty well done. Petty criminals or industrial spies? It was too soon to decide.

The women were wearing mechanics' coveralls. The gleaming car, bonnet raised, sat incongruously in the middle of the floor. Sarita was leaning inside the engine compartment. A light hung to the left above her bent head. Sarita had been staring into the engine compartment for the last ten minutes.

'It's a fake,' she said finally.

They got there in the end.

Davina walked from a workbench to her sister's side and peered inside.

'They've put a Trancer bodyshell on an ordinary car,' continued Sarita. 'This won't tell us a single thing about the new engine.'

It was time to put them out of their misery. 'That's not unusual practice. What you've got here is just a showpiece. It's only meant to be photographed. It was never meant to be driven.'

They both looked blank for a moment. Yes, all their time and effort had been wasted and that was a shame. But these lessons had to be learned.

'So where do they keep all the fancy technology?' asked Sarita.

Somebody give him strength. Why did he have to give them all the answers?

'They keep "the fancy technology" almost certainly in a road-test model disguised so you wouldn't look at it twice. That's the one you should have lifted.'

Davina spoke up. 'You still have to pay us, Bob.'

He tried not to sound too amazed by their cheek but failed. 'Why?'

'Because it's not our fault you hired us to steal the wrong car,' she protested.

They still didn't see how the relationship worked. 'Look, I know you're both new to this. Let me clarify

76

something. My employers do not hire people to steal. If you get some commercial information we can use, I'm authorised to buy it from you. That is not illegal. But the responsibility for how you come about that information is entirely yours.'

He was being hypocritical and he knew it. But you had to watch your back.

Like a child, Sarita stamped her foot.

Temper, temper, little lady.

'The money is still on the table. You are more than welcome to try again. If you're interested. And assuming no one else beats you to it.'

The sisters looked at each other. Ah, competition. They hadn't thought of that.

Both seemed resigned to the fact that it was back to square one and Bob turned and walked out of the garage and into the fresh air.

It was a big risk he was taking. If the stolen car was traced and he had been seen making a personal appearance at the girls' lock-up, it would ruin him. He was involved in the stealing of the car as much as they were.

Thankfully, the lovely Sarita and Davina didn't realise that. Their naivety was not only charming but, in practical terms, a godsend.

Ed might as well have been dipped into the burning pits of hell. He was staring at his worst nightmare. The car. It didn't matter that it was surrounded by banks of strange equipment that displayed every piece of information about the car that sat in front of him. That was Ros's department. The car had been what he wanted to know about. And if the lump of metal was the car of the future, he might as well end it all now.

The car was dull. Matt black in colour. Boring shape. Square windows. Hell, even the registration plate was dull.

This couldn't be the car that he, Ed, Captain Speed of the Speed People, was being asked to drive. He had just about managed to cheer himself up after the morning's events. Now looking at the test car, supposedly the best thing since the wheel was invented, his good mood started to fade.

It sat in a gleaming white car bay. And that was just wrong. You walked in and all your attention was focused on the most embarrassing and ugly car in the world. At least two decades out of style. An utter nothing. No sleek design, no smooth contours, no additional extras to make it that little bit special. Nothing. Nada. Nix. It looked like a black box on wheels. And this was what Beckett had tried to get him all excited about? It even felt horrible. Rough paint-work. Enough to make a grown man break down and cry.

He managed to find his voice. 'And ... *this* is the shape of things to come?'

Beckett moved nearer to the monstrosity. 'What's wrong with it?'

Heathen. 'It's not the kind of shape I had in mind.'

'The body's a disguise, Ed.' Ros carried an equipment case into the bay and set it on the floor. Cray was immediately behind her. 'The only way to generate genuine road test data,' she continued, 'is to go out on the road. This version's not supposed to look exciting. All the secret new technology is hidden inside.'

That made sense. Still, there would be no fun for Captain Speed this afternoon.

Paul Cray walked up to the car and opened the door. 'Get in, Ed. I'll show you.'

There was only one seat in the car's front. Ed took it. The dashboard looked very temporary. Wires were uncovered and hung loosely, but connected each instrument in the car. The instruments seemed very modern despite the temporary housings in which they were held. There were no buttons to press, only small screens that, at a guess, were similar in design to touch-screens that Ros had used at Gizmos. It was more like a spaceship than a car.

78

Ed looked up at the rear-view mirror. A small motor whirred into life and the rear-view mirror moved. Ed moved his head slightly and the motors responded. Now that wasn't bad.

Cray laughed. 'The rear-view mirror automatically adjusts to the driver's eye-line.'

Ed moved back and forth and from side to side. The mirror immediately tracked every move he made. This was beginning to be fun.

'How does it do that?'

'Magic,' said Cray.

Ed felt silly for asking. No one at Tronix was about to divulge their secrets, were they?

'You'll notice there's no ignition key in the keypad,' Cray added.

Nope. A little strange. You probably had to press some screen on the dashboard.

'We're going to code it to recognise your thumbprint.'

Cool. For the security-conscious, this car was going to be a dream. Pity the dummy model looked so damn awful.

Beckett and Ros leaned in through the door. Ros said, 'Tomorrow you drive, Ed. I'll monitor from base and Beckett, you stick close in a shadow car.'

'Where will I be going?' asked Ed.

'We've got a schedule for you to follow,' said Cray. 'Just normal motoring and nothing adventurous. The job is to drive the course, attracting no attention.'

'And Ed,' said Ros in a warning tone, 'that also means handing it back in one piece at the end.'

Hey! He had never trashed a car in his life. Scraped a few, dented a few, but never smashed one up. Oh, there was that plane. But that was a long time ago so it didn't count. He knew how to handle a car. Cars were what he lived for. As long as you treated them with respect, how could you go wrong?

Beckett sat on a roller platform underneath the test car. Cray and O'Neill had left him and Ed to go over the car. They'd fit a couple of bugs and that would be that. A few technicians were working on another machine in a neighbouring bay. No one seemed interested in what they were doing.

Night was beginning to fall. Beckett dusted his hands. And another tracker fitted. He couldn't remember the precise details of setting it up. It was as if he had gone through the motions on automatic. Should have been keeping his thoughts on the job. He checked over the wiring. Not a thing wrong with it.

A screwdriver dropped to the floor.

'Damn,' said Ed.

'Are you almost done, Ed?' asked Beckett.

Ed's muffled voice came from above Beckett where Ed was working in the engine compartment. 'Shouldn't be long,' he said. 'Five, ten minutes.'

Beckett checked his watch. Anna Fabrizi would have finished her speech an hour ago. She was probably waiting in the hotel bar for the next part of Ros's plan.

Unless the killer had got to her first.

She needed full-time protection. At the hotel she should get that from Wence and his mob. It was no good thinking about things that might happen. You would be so busy worrying about the consequences of every action that you would never do anything.

He looked over his handiwork in the car. Simple enough. He put down his screwdriver. O'Neill was an odd bloke. His rat-like features and his abrupt way of talking showed no sign that he either trusted or respected anyone. Cray was all right. There was the impression that nothing would be too much trouble for him. And the way he followed Ros around was funny. Ros, of course, acted as if she didn't notice. Was that a pang of jealousy there, Beckett? No. Ros was a good friend and colleague. That was all.

And where was she?

'Ed? Where's Ros?'

'Building security check,' came the muffled reply. 'O'Neill wants advice on how to improve it.'

'Considering the lack of luck he's had lately, that's not a bad idea.'

'Ros said she would check in with us every half hour.'

But the last time either man had seen Ros was in the canteen. He and Ed had been fitting the car with transponders and trackers since then. Beckett put his hands on the floor and rolled out from under the car. 'And how long ago was that?'

Ed looked down at him, then checked his watch.

'Perhaps we should go and find her?'

Only the spotlights moved.

Ros, you shouldn't be here.

It hadn't felt right when she had come across the srange room and it certainly didn't feel right now. Was there really a need to check out the military division? Well, Mr Cray hadn't said anything about not giving it the once-over. And they had to do their job properly.

It was pitiful justification, when all she wanted to do was find out what else Mr O'Neill was up to. So, once again, Ros ignored the small voice of caution in her head and walked through the double doors and down a flight of steps into a totally different part of Tronix.

Six lights roved randomly in different directions. Programmed to behave like that, no doubt. The lights were hung from long metal arms suspended from the ceiling. They could move through three-sixty degrees, and they were set in spherical casings that allowed almost the same freedom of movement. Like arms and hands dancing to an unknown tune, they jerked back and forth or glided gently from side to side. Ros watched the lights play about the room. Good security measure. You couldn't hide here. You didn't know where the lights would shine next.

The annexe put her on edge. It wasn't the fact that the floor and ceiling were all black. The brutal industrial look was just a façade, designed to put you on edge. Nor was it that the air was so very still, bordering on stale. It was obvious that the company's air conditioning didn't extend to the annexe. No. It was the six huge vehicles, covered in metallic-looking tarpaulin that spooked her. You couldn't tell what they were.

There were three vehicles on each side of the huge building. They could be trucks, harmless freight carriers. But then, why cover them up? A light shone at her feet. Tyre tracks. Fresh. Out on manoeuvres, or recently tested? They could be freight carriers, but what did they carry? Tronix was heavily into military R&D. What contracts were they working on?

Ros cleared her mind. This had nothing to do with her. She was checking the security system only. That's what she had to concentrate on. Still, the anxious feeling wouldn't leave.

Thick, black square pillars, four to each bay, supported the ceiling. A string of small circular holes, arranged in a vertical line, ran up each side of the pillars. Curious design.

Ros walked over to the access doors that led outside. It appeared they were operated remotely and, if she was not mistaken, by a radio signal. Perhaps the vehicles could open the doors? The panel on the wall by the exit would be signalled to by a transmitter from the vehicle. And Ros couldn't see any way to trick the lock without knowing the transmitter frequencies. The annexe was about as secure as you could make it without having an army standing guard.

Cameras. Ten in all. Excessive. One above each bay and on either end of the annexe. No one does anything without being seen. It would be good to have a similar set-up in Swift's presentation hall. Especially for what they planned in the evening.

Ros checked her watch. She should have phoned in eleven minutes ago. Better give the boys a ring now or they would be getting worried.

The annexe was more than secure. Whatever Mr O'Neill had down here, he was positively paranoid about it. After only the briefest of meetings with the man – and she knew she shouldn't judge him – the security system told her more than enough about him. Maybe O'Neill was right to be so paranoid. The shell of the new car had been stolen from right under his nose.

Ros spotted a telephone hanging on the wall in one of the two empty bays. Perfect. The light shone on the floor. Ros knelt and dusted her hand on a set of tread marks. Recent. And leading out of the bay.

Ros stepped into the bay and picked up the phone. It was dead.

Then all hell broke loose.

The roving spotlights became frantic. A siren started to scream. It was deafening. She clamped her hands to her ears. There was no way to think, the alarm was so loud. She had to close her eyes and concentrate on keeping calm. The siren's shriek reverberated around the annexe.

Then there was a new sound. A pulsing, electronic *thrum*.

Ros opened her eyes. On each of the four sides of the empty bay, bars of green light ran horizontally from pillar to neighbouring pillar.

The alarm cut out. The sudden silence was a shock.

A cage. She was trapped inside a cage. She turned to the nearest set of bars. Her left hand moved closer. The bars gave off heat. The stale air was suddenly thick with the smell of ozone. Small sparks shot from the bars to her hand. It smarted. No permanent damage.

At any rate, she must have set off at least half a dozen alarms. All she had to do was stay in this evil-looking cage and wait for rescuers.

She hoped they would be friendly.

« Eight »
« The hunter »

The doorbell chimed. Someone was at home. Sarita could hear music in the back of the house. A light was on upstairs.

Sarita brushed a hand through her hair. She tapped the heels of her shoes in nervous anticipation as she stood on the doorstep. Pulling her sombre grey jacket tight, she drew in a deep breath. A light came on through the frosted pane of glass in the door.

She was supposed to be feeling confident about this. Instead she felt bloody stupid.

Come on, Sarita. You can do this. You will do this. You have to do this.

She tried to think of Dad. No good. That just brought her down. She couldn't shake the nerves. Uncle Dave. That made her feel angrier but still scared. There was the money they would make if they pulled this off.

Getting away from all this, away from Dad's legacy. Almost too much of a dream but it made her feel better. It was an insane plan. Oh, she and Davina had laughed together when she had first suggested it. She hadn't expected to be following it through.

Davina had telephoned Tronix, not to speak to anyone nor to listen to anyone but to check their networking system. Completely illegal, and always boring. Tronix's e-mail mainly consisted of dull memos from one department to another. Or inane gossip or childish insults.

Almost useless.

The time taken over Tronix's e-mail wasn't wasted, though trawling through the crud was no fun at all. But what else could they do? The shell of the Trancer wasn't enough to make any serious money or – more importantly – break Tronix Ltd and its damned owner. They couldn't sell the shell. Everyone had seen the photos in the papers. Thanks to them.

So with a hunk of horrifically expensive but totally useless metal, they had to go back to Tronix for more information. Thankfully, no one had found, or even suspected, the tap on Tronix's computer network.

Davina had finally found something interesting. The Trancer was due for a test run which was to be held the following day. Tomorrow afternoon. That meant they had to work quickly.

A stop was scheduled at a road-side cafe. There was their chance. They could break into the car, retrieve a mass of information then sell it to Bob.

Maybe they could even steal the car.

The thought made Sarita's heart skip a beat.

But it all depended on how this meeting went.

The front door finally opened.

The woman had a pale face. Long black hair. Wild, dark eyes lined with thick mascara. She was tall and thin. A bright red-lipped smile. Perfect teeth. Mid-fifties at a guess. Black silk dressing gown.

Now or never.

'Mrs Pearce?'

'That's right.'

Sarita showed her the badge. It looked good. Very official. Completely bogus. Mrs Pearce glanced at it and then back at her visitor.

'My name's Deveraux. Special Services Division.' Her mouth had gone dry.

Come on. Keep this up. You'll be OK.

There was no change in the woman's composure.

She kept smiling. It was a little disconcerting. The smile being held like that.

'And?'

'It's about your tea-shop. I've just been there but I didn't realise you closed at three in winter. I wonder if I could come in?'

Mrs Pearce frowned. The smile vanished. She stepped back from the door.

This was her cue.

Enter Sarita (disguised as a government operative).

She wouldn't corpse. She wouldn't dry. She had practised every line over and over again. Every scenario. She was word perfect. Prepared for anything.

She prayed that her audience would be convinced by her performance.

All the rooms Beckett and Ed checked were empty. There was no sign of Ros anywhere.

Beckett marched down another corridor, checking left and right for any sign of her. There were various ways to return to the test car bay. With luck, Ros would meet up with them before she arrived at the bay. If she got back before them she might start searching for them. They could spend the rest of the day going round in circles.

The gleaming white walls in the long narrow corridor were suddenly replaced by walls painted sky-blue. All the doors they tried to check were now locked. To open them required an electronic key and a swipe card. Ed produced his electronic lock-pick. His eyes glinted. The man was always ready for a little breaking and entering.

'Not the best idea in the world, Ed,' said Beckett. 'Anyway, Ros would've left a door open.'

Ed pocketed his lock-pick and pretended to sulk. 'So where are we in the building?'

Beckett pointed up at a sign. It read: UNAUTHORISED ENTRY STRICTLY PROHIBITED.

'At a guess, and it's a good one, we're in Tronix's military division.'

They carried on walking. Ed checked every single door. All locked. It was pointless but at least he would feel like he was doing something.

Ed asked, 'And what do they make?'

'Toy soldiers. I don't know.'

There was no need for Beckett to sound exasperated but it couldn't be helped. Ros wasn't the sort of person to be out of contact. She was the last person to forget to make a call. It made him nervous. There was something wrong. He could feel it. And working for a client with unspecified military interests didn't help.

'And I bet O'Neill has some dodgy customers,' said Ed.

'It's like the space programme,' Beckett replied. 'The technology filters down. The military buys up the toyshop and when they're finished with it, the rest of us get to play with the toys.'

They turned left at the end of the corridor. A set of stairs led to a set of open double doors. Beckett stopped. That was a weird noise. A strange half-buzz, half-drone. What was going on through there?

The phone was still dead.

Ros sat down on the cold concrete floor and sighed angrily. What did she expect? A sudden miracle? That, wondrously, a supernatural force would come to her aid in this, her hour of need?

Hey, she could get herself out of this. There were two options. One: turn off the cage. Problem: there was absolutely no circuitry that she could see. Two: repair the telephone. After all, there wasn't a phone in the world that she couldn't fix.

Ros stood and lifted the receiver. First, check the wiring. Oh, that was marvellous. The phone had been set up but not connected. And no plug, no socket for it to be plugged into.

Footsteps. And in a hurry. Friend or foe?

Beckett and Ed were running towards her. Good,

with their help she might get out of the bizarre prison some time before breakfast. And they were infinitely better than dealing with Tronix's uniformed security. She had no time for O'Neill's over-dressed gorillas.

She held out her arms as a warning and shouted for Ed and Beckett to stop. Beckett looked amazed by the beams of light that ran around the empty bay.

'Don't get too close!' said Ros. 'Step back both of you. I don't know what it is.'

'What happened?' asked Beckett.

Ros shrugged. 'I was heading for the phone and then *ka-zam*.'

'No warning?' asked Ed.

Ros shook her head.

'Maybe we can switch it off,' Ed ventured.

'I can't see how.' Then she had an idea. 'Just stand back. I want to try something.'

She tied the loose wire around the phone receiver and then threw it at the light beams. The phone exploded in a shower of sparks as soon as it touched the green light. A blob of melted plastic slapped onto the floor and bubbled gently.

Ouch.

More footsteps. The dancing spotlights played over a man's face. Cray. A couple of security men. All running towards the cage.

'Wait! Just wait!' Cray shouted.

Beckett turned to face him. 'What is this thing?'

'It's a plasma cage,' said Cray, as if that explained everything and that everyone had such a thing in the comfort of their own homes. 'We only just put it in.'

Another man entered the annexe. He was a little shorter than Ed but looked almost twice as wide. The man's swagger as he strode towards the cage gave Ros the impression of a tank rolling towards an enemy.

The man was middle-aged. His hair was covered by a leather cap. A thick moustache rested on his thin lips. Lines around his deep set, dark eyes. He didn't acknowledge their presence. He didn't ask questions.

He only stared hard at the three of them. The guy was creepy.

'Why did you install the cage?' asked Ed, not taking his eyes away from the older man. Was that some sort of black uniform he was wearing? Black cotton trousers. Heavy boots. Thick black leather jacket. The man practically disappeared into the background. If it wasn't for the spotlights he would have been invisible. And he was so still. Not a muscle moved in his huge frame. His face was impassive.

'It's for security,' Cray hesitated, 'on another project.'

Cray moved to one of the pillars that made up Ros's cage. He pressed the palm of his hand on the section of the pillar that was level with his chest. A blue light appeared and scanned his palm. As quickly as they had appeared, the beams around the cage shut off.

Ros gratefully stepped out of the bay. She was impressed. Not only was a screen camouflaged in the pillar, the cage was operated by recognising palmprints.

'So what project's that?' asked Ed.

Cray looked sideways towards the man in black. He seemed to think for a moment. 'Sorry, can't tell you about it.'

The man in black was a client – and by the looks of him a pretty formidable client at that. Ros felt there was an air of menace about him that was almost tangible. Either that or it was her own fear.

'Major Cardenas,' said Cray. The man stepped forward. 'These are the operatives hired by Mr O'Neill to advise on project security. Their being here is a mistake.'

Nobody had told Ros there were no-go areas. 'We were given full clearance,' she protested.

Cray turned to her and gave an intense stare. She could see that Cray desperately wanted her to shut up and keep out of the way.

Why was Cray warning them away from this Major Cardenas? What did this Major have on Tronix?

Cray continued. 'The job we're doing for the Major's people is not part of your brief. The Major and his team handle their own security.'

Ros was in no doubt they would. She guessed he had his own private little army to deal with small matters like security. But what else? What was Tronix involved in?

'Please,' insisted Cray, 'go back to the car lab.'

Beckett and Ed exchanged glances. The *what the hell is going on?* look.

'Major, perhaps you'd care to come to the hospitality lounge?' asked Cray, trying to usher Cardenas out of the annexe.

The Major didn't reply. He stared hard at the team. Where was he getting off with that attitude? They all stared back. As far as their brief went, Ros knew they had done nothing wrong. The Major could stick his attitude where the sun didn't shine.

The Major turned and was led away by Cray. Strange behaviour from the Tronix employee. He flustered around the older man, chattering nervously. He had seemed to be the epitome of self-confidence when she first met him. Now nothing remained of that confident young man.

Cardenas ignored the agitated Cray. He walked at an even pace. Self-assured. Powerful. In control of everything he did.

But Cray's body language was practically shouting at her.

'Cray's terrified of the Major. I wonder why?'

The hotel bar buzzed with conversation. Beckett heard a man talking in Italian, translating a colleague's conversation into German and French hardly pausing for breath.

The skyline looked impressive from the top-floor bar. Massive windows framed silhouetted skyscrapers and a deep red sky as the sun sank below the horizon.

Anna had said that Wence was in charge of security

in the hotel. Beckett had half a mind to inform SSD of how easy it was to pass Wence's men. He had listened to a part of a delegate's speech in the conference hall, showing nothing more than a quickly lashed-up name badge. The security staff that he had seen, all armed he noted, looked terminally bored. That was not good enough when covering an assassin's target. Not even remotely professional. They should be alert, looking for anything remotely suspicious and checking it out. They were protecting the probable future leader of another country for crying out loud. Even Ed, with his gung-ho enthusiasm and desire for excitement, managed to keep awake during the most tedious parts of their jobs.

The whole arrangement in the hotel made Beckett nervous.

This was not a good place to be. Too many faces. Too many unknowns.

Ed's description of the assassin had been vague. The assassin was not tall, not short, lightly tanned, dark haired but balding, and had jet-black eyes.

The killer could be in the room with them. The plan would mean nothing if Anna was shot right now.

Beckett sat at the bar and ordered a drink.

This was madness.

There could be a bomb here. A bomb that would rip a hole in the side of the hotel. The hit man could kill them all. Right now. He might not care who he killed just as long as Fabrizi was out of the way.

It certainly made you appreciate life while you had it.

Over a hundred delegates were in the room. Making contacts. Networking. Favours asked for here, friend-ships made there. And so what if they each had a name badge with their photograph attached? A photo and a signature to show you belonged with the delegation. Badges weren't security. They were far too easy to duplicate.

The killer could be there in the bar, waiting for his prey.

Beckett looked at his watch. The call would be coming through to Anna at any minute. There was still no sign of her.

A tap on the shoulder.

Beckett turned and smiled. Anna.

'I'm sorry if you've been waiting long,' she said. Beckett could hear the tiniest trace of her accent.

'I've only just arrived myself. How was the speech?'

'Oh, fine. Fine. Cameras everywhere,' she laughed. 'A huge round of applause at the end. It was great. Pity about Alberto. Lost his speech. Idiot.'

She showed Beckett her mobile phone. 'Shouldn't we go somewhere quieter?'

'No. Here's fine. The background noise will make it more realistic. You're sure you know your lines?'

'Now, now, Mr Beckett. Surely you realise politics is ninety per cent acting?'

The phone rang.

Rage.

Fabrizi had survived. He had been cheated.

Starkey sat in the driver's seat of his car. The Cell-track was at his side. Where was he? A street. Quiet. No traffic. Suburban. Parked cars on either side of the road. How had he got there? He couldn't remember.

Starkey could wait. Fabrizi would make a call. He would have her life. He could wait forever if he had to. But Mackenzie wanted her dead *now*. And he had failed. Twice.

Starkey struggled to remain calm. His heart pounded. His thoughts running over the events at Royal College Green. Defeat. Humiliation. Anger.

It was becoming more difficult to restrain his emotions. Defeat was a new experience. An impossibility. But it had happened.

He had run away. Deserted his post.

Coward.

He couldn't reconcile his thoughts and feelings. He lived to kill but had left her to live.

It was the defeat. Had to be. The confusion caused by his failure. That's why he had left.

He had *lost*.

The life had been snatched away from him. A second more and the life would have been his. Just one second. The life *had* been his. When Fabrizi and her lover had sat on the bench, they were his. He owned them. It was his right to kill her.

He wanted to destroy everything. He had to kill. He wanted to kill everyone. Eradicate. Eliminate. Exterminate.

No. Starkey breathed deeply.

You had to treasure the life, cherish it until he was ready. Life was a miracle. Everyone was so very different. Indiscriminate killing debased life.

The phone rang.

'Hello? Anna Fabrizi here. Oh, it's you, William!'

'I thought you'd like to come over and see a demonstration of the laser logo.'

'The Liberty Party torch? Excellent! What time?'

'How about eight o'clock? In the presentation hall.'

'That's fine. Will there be a crowd?'

'Just us. In that huge empty space. I wanted you to be the first to see it.'

'Marvellous.'

'I'll meet you there.'

'At eight, then. Bye.'

'Bye.'

Faultless.

Beckett wanted to shake Anna by the hand for her bravura performance. Even he, with his experience, would have been fooled. The intonation of each word exactly right. One hundred per cent flawless in her delivery. Anna Fabrizi was the perfect politician, coming across as totally natural but totally fake. No hint of the practice that had been put in learning her lines. William hadn't done so badly, either.

Beckett's confidence in the plan shot up.

'So why did I have to use a mobile?' Anna asked.

'We reckon that's how he knew your movements this morning.'

Anna frowned.

'Talking on a mobile phone is like discussing your private life with a gossip columnist. Anyone with the right equipment can listen in on any conversation held on a mobile.'

Realisation dawned. 'Ah.' She lowered her voice to a whisper. 'So that's how the killer knew I was meeting William this morning?'

'Exactly. All I have to do now is work out how I'm going to get you to the warehouse for eight o'clock.'

'That shouldn't be a problem. I can ask Alberto to cover for me.'

'No. I'm sorry, Anna. You don't mention this to anyone. There can't be the slightest chance of a leak to Wence. If he and his men interfere we might never find the assassin.'

Anna nodded. 'OK. I'll see you later. I should go. My bodyguard will be thinking I've been kidnapped or something.'

'Oh don't worry about that. Wence's men have a hard time standing up straight, never mind thinking.'

The anger left him. His thoughts were clear. The pounding of his heart calmed to a normal, regular beat.

He could see into the future. The one future, the only future, where he held the life in his hands.

Fabrizi stood next to Swift. A picture hung on a wall of a kaleidoscopic pattern that constantly folded in on itself. She looked up at it. Swift stepped away. A clear shot. Starkey savoured the moment. He was a hundred yards away in the presentation hall, rifle in his arms and Fabrizi in his sights.

No sound as the bullet was fired.

Fabrizi fell to the floor, a bloody hole in the side of her head. The bullet exploded, ripping the side of her skull apart. Swift screamed.

Rapture.

Mackenzie had given Starkey the layout of Swift's workshop should he ever need it. Starkey knew when, where and how he was going to take Fabrizi's life as soon as the phone call between the two lovers finished.

Whether he was still employed by Mackenzie after his failures didn't matter. The life would be his.

So Beckett and his so-called team were still interfering.

Wence knew he was seen as a bit of a fool by the other security departments – and his own, if truth were told. But he got things done. Yes, lives were risked and lost. That was the job. You didn't get called up by the government to serve your time in the security services. You volunteered. And he had no time for people like Beckett who didn't make the grade.

Beckett was a little idiot. Sometimes, people didn't know when to take a hint. And it wasn't even a hint. He had told Beckett to steer clear of Swift. Yet there he was, bold as you please, walking through the hotel foyer.

Beckett must have been very pleased when he walked past his men in the conference room. Sat in the bar having a drink with Miss Fabrizi. Hadn't seen the fibre optic cameras though, had he? Wearing that smug little grin on his face.

Wence wished he could wipe that smile from his face. But Beckett could prove useful.

'Mr Wence, sir?'

Wence turned from the bank of monitors. A tall, blond man stood next to him. What was his name? Somers?

'Yes?'

'Do you wish to have Beckett detained?'

Wence sighed and turned from the rack of monitors before him. Taylor sat at the console, changing the controls so that Beckett's face filled the monitors. Not a pleasant sight.

'No. I don't think there's any real need for that. Yet. Just don't let him out of your sight.'

Beckett and Miss Fabrizi were up to something, Wence was certain of it. If it had nothing to do with the morning's events he would be very surprised. And wouldn't Beckett's little team be surprised to learn that the SSD knew of that farce?

But Beckett had obviously won the charming Italian woman's trust. How, didn't matter. Watching him would be good enough for now. If Beckett pulled any stunts, his men would be ready for him.

And give a man enough rope . . .

Failure. Not a word Mackenzie liked to hear. Not a word he heard too often. If you didn't come up to scratch you were out. And out meant dead.

And he didn't like hearing bad news from a third party, worse still from the client himself. Starkey should have been in contact by now.

Mackenzie felt tense. Explaining to a client why a job hadn't been completed was something he rarely did. This was his office. His haven. Spartan. Efficient. A mahogany desk. A leather sofa. His chair. A phone. No pictures. No plants. Nothing to distract. From here he ran his world.

The phone rang.

He paused before answering.

The client sat on the sofa, a cigar in his mouth. A man who seemed to have not a care in the world. Except Mackenzie knew differently. Mackenzie's driver, Spencer, stood as unobtrusively as a large man could in the corner of the office.

Mackenzie picked up the phone. Starkey.

'Confirm your identity. Confirm your identity.'

Mackenzie sighed. Starkey's tape was very aggravating. A child's toy.

'It's Mackenzie. Must you use that stupid tape?'

'Haven't you heard of security?'

Starkey's voice. No accent. No way of telling where

he came from. It was a surprise that Starkey had phoned at all. He knew that failure wasn't permitted. It must be good news or Starkey would have been very stupid not to have already left the country. Not that anyone could get away so easily.

And no apology for his failure was forthcoming. For his *failures*.

'I'll kill Fabrizi tonight at Swift's workshop,' said Starkey.

Not the news Mackenzie would have preferred to hear. Still, Starkey wasn't the type to give up. If Starkey was on your tail, you were as good as dead. Expensive and the best.

Or was he still premier league material? Two missed chances in one day. That must have been a record. Maybe Starkey was passing his prime.

Starkey's bland voice continued: 'I want a car waiting to take me to the airport. By the canal lock on the north side of Swift's place. I'll be there by 8.30.'

No request to continue with the job. Perhaps Starkey assumed the job was his right?

'We'll send a car.' A confirmation that the assassin could carry on with the job.

Mackenzie realised he had never seen Starkey. The man was just a phone number, a disembodied voice on the other end of the line.

'How will my driver recognise you?' From the corner of his eye Mackenzie could see Spencer stand straight.

'There'll be no one else around at that time,' said Starkey. 'Tell your driver to flash his headlights twice. I'll find him.'

'Just get it right this time, Starkey.'

The line went dead. Mackenzie replaced the receiver. He opened a drawer in his desk and lifted out a piece of paper. He had to write Spencer's instructions very precisely. His driver was loyal and aggressive, but not particularly bright. Three characteristics he looked for in certain employees.

He beckoned to his driver and handed over the instructions.

'This man, Starkey,' said the client, extinguishing his cigar in an ashtray by the sofa. 'He's failed twice. Send your car. But, Spencer, don't take him to the airport.'

Spencer said, 'You want him dead, Mr Corelli?'

Corelli winced slightly as he heard his name. Naughty boy, Spencer. The client never liked his name being spoken out loud. You could never be too sure who was listening. But the client should know better than that. The phone lines were scrambled. The offices were constantly checked for bugs. They were secure.

But Corelli shouldn't be in the office. The meeting had been set up at the very last minute. An emergency session. It was a risk. Time was running out for Corelli. If Fabrizi wasn't killed soon, his 'friends' would put his life on the line.

'If he kills Anna this time –' Corelli seemed to weigh something in his mind '– then maybe I'll relent.'

Mackenzie pointed with his thumb over his shoulder. Spencer got the message. Time he left.

The double doors behind Mackenzie clicked shut. 'And if Starkey fails again?' said Mackenzie.

Corelli shook his head vigorously. 'Anna must die before the election. I don't care how this is achieved. Her death will mean the Liberty Party and I come to power on a wave of public sympathy.'

Power. Such a wonderful word.

Mackenzie smiled. 'And then you quietly forget all your anti-corruption policies.'

Corelli looked sharply at him. Mackenzie had done his homework. Corelli's links with certain strands of Italian society were well hidden. But if you knew where and how to look, all sorts of political embarrassments came to light.

'Those policies are Anna's policies,' said Corelli. 'They are not mine. If Anna ever actually got to power, certain friends of mine would be very inconvenienced.'

And wasn't that the truth? Mackenzie was surprised

98

Corelli had let the woman live for as long as she had. But killing her now had the excellent advantage of being so wonderfully media friendly. For the next week, the Italian media – and much of the rest of the European media – would extensively cover the death of such a prominent and well-loved political figure. The other parties wouldn't receive nearly the same amount of coverage.

A real vote winner.

'You're lucky she hasn't uncovered your links with it so far.'

Corelli looked at his latest employee carefully. Mackenzie smiled, as friendly as he could. He was giving himself away. Knowledge was power, but also dangerous. Corelli might not appreciate an employee knowing so much.

'But Anna will find out,' Corelli said. 'That's why I want her dead.'

Ros and Ed had gone back to Gizmos. Swift had called. He wanted them round at his workshop as soon as possible. He was not happy when Ros told him he had no need to worry about being left alone. The killer wasn't after him, just his fiancée.

Ed had checked and double-checked Swift's security system. He had walked around the entire warehouse making sure every connection was functioning. No problem with a single circuit. Then Ros had checked over the computer system's programming. Not a glitch. The only place he could think of as more secure was O'Neill's military division.

If everything went to plan, the computer system would help them locate the killer and contain him so they could find out who was behind the assassination attempts. And behind every great hit man, there had to be a great motive. With Anna's political inclinations, that meant a great many people could be out for her blood.

It must be nice to be so wanted.

'Ouch!'

Ed turned to see Ros sucking her finger.

'Now that's something I never expected to see.'

'What? Me sewing?'

'No. You doing something badly.' He laughed and looked at the top of his jacket from the lapel of which Ros had removed a button. Now she was trying to sew a slightly larger button into the same place. No, it wasn't a button but a microphone the size of a large button. She seemed to be having limited success; the button was barely attached to the jacket. Professional it was not. The underside of the lapel showed the stitching was all over the place. But it only needed to stay on. Did it matter how it stayed on?

Ed sat next to her on the sofa and peered more closely at the strange button.

'That's a bit large for a microphone, Ros. What is it?'

'Guess.'

'Don't tell me. A tracker.'

'No. Both. A mike and a bug.' Ros caught her finger with the needle again and swore. Ed stifled a laugh.

'Damn. I never was any good at sewing.'

'You should've asked me. Man of many talents.'

Ros continued to stitch. He was putting her off.

Ed looked at the new button. It was half an inch wide. How did Ros fit all the circuitry for the tracker, the mike and the power source into something so small? Another one of Ros's little mysteries.

'That's incredible.'

Ros smiled modestly. 'Thank you. It's super-miniaturised with only minimal loss of power and range. Took me weeks to get it right.'

'And this is the only one?'

'So far. It's the prototype. I thought you could give it a field test tomorrow with the test car.'

'Sure. But aren't our normal radios good enough?'

Ros stood up and held out the jacket. 'You'll still carry a radio. This is only a mike – not a receiver. That little miracle, I'll start next week.'

Ros watched Ed carefully slip his arms into the jacket.

She asked, 'You and Beckett are certain it won't be another bomb?'

'We've made sure he's got no choice but to use a gun.'

'Well you better be right.' Her voice suddenly showed how tense she was. 'If it all blows up in your faces, don't think I'm sewing you back together.'

« Nine »

« Exhibition »

Anna had to get rid of her shadow.

He just stood there like a statue, looking incapable of
smiling. And Anna Fabrizi needed some joy in her life.
She wasn't going to get that with Mr Misery in the
corner. OK, so bodyguards weren't hired for their
charm, but please!

Some fun. A drink with friends. Her family. To drink
herself stupid. The world, at that precise moment in
time, could look after itself. Its cares and woes catered
for by somebody else. Tonight, it would not be her
concern. Perhaps a drink with Gina, her secretary and
her closest confidante? Gina, she suddenly realised,
was closer to her than Alberto. And he had been in
a bizarre mood all day. She dismissed it as stress
brought on by the election.

So, a drink in the bar later with Gina? No. Perhaps
not. Poor girl was exhausting herself running around
after her. Let her lie in.

Tomorrow was going to be such a wonderful day.

A warm glow filled her chest. William. Simply
thinking about him made her smile. His proposal on
that bench had been so sweet, so romantic and sincere
that she could not have turned him down even if she
didn't love him.

But the bench was no longer there.

Anna suddenly wondered if she would live past tonight.

Her reflection in the huge window stared back at her. It seemed grey and tired. It might be how she looked but in no way did the image reflect how she felt. Oh! If it was only tomorrow and if only the next six days would hurry up!

'Anna Fabrizi. Italian premier.'

She smiled, pleased with herself. She pressed a button on the wall and the curtains closed. She turned to face the room.

The bodyguard stood motionless in the corner. Gina fussed with some papers. They hadn't heard her whisper.

Italian premier. It sounded right. Sounded like it was going to happen.

That wasn't arrogance. She was a woman who knew where she was, what she was capable of, and where she was headed. And if the European media were anything to go by, she was heading for the top. And with Alberto at her side, they would make a perfect team. An invincible team.

It had been a long day and was getting longer. She was used to it and she loved it. The rounds of interviews, whether for television, radio or the press. People paying her and the Party's cause lots of attention. The media coverage she and Alberto received was part of why she loved being a politician.

A thought struck her at a tangent. She still hadn't told Alberto about tomorrow.

He would be furious with her. Why hadn't he been told of the plans sooner? Et cetera, et cetera. She would tell him over breakfast, with plenty of other hotel guests around so he would be less inclined to make a scene.

That was all tomorrow. She had plenty to think about here and now.

Her hotel room had become an office that afternoon. Gina was rushed off her feet, trying to keep everything running smoothly. Now the room was spotless. Her secretary was priceless.

Gina put her briefcase down by the coffee table in the centre of the room.

'*Bueno notte, Signorina Fabrizi.*'

There was a cheeky glint in the girl's eyes. A smile lit up her face. Anna laughed.

'Thank you, Gina. See you at breakfast.'

Anna looked at her watch as she took it off her wrist. A present from William. She slipped her shoes off and gently rubbed her feet.

'I think it's going to be an early night for you, too,' she said to the bodyguard. He didn't move.

'I'm going to stay in and work.'

Again, he didn't move. Perhaps Beckett was right about Wence's agents. Perhaps they didn't think. She suddenly wanted to shout at him to get out but thought better of it. She didn't want to make the operative suspicious.

Time for Plan B. Stronger tactics.

Anna started to unbutton her orange silk blouse. As she stepped towards the bodyguard, he took a step back.

'But right now I'm taking a shower. So, if you wouldn't mind?'

She stepped lightly over to the door. He still wasn't getting the message. She opened the door and pointed outside.

Finally.

The bodyguard lumbered out.

Anna rolled her eyes and whispered, 'Thank heavens for that.' But she still didn't know how the Gizmos people were going to get her out.

She had been in the country a little over twelve hours, seen William – which was just wonderful, she hadn't realised how much she had missed him – survived not one, but two assassination attempts, delivered a successful speech, held lots of interviews, eaten a great dinner and was about to attempt to catch her potential killer.

Certainly something to write in her diary.

A quiet but insistent tapping came from the window. Anna's stomach clenched. Oh, no. The killer couldn't have found her. She had moved into the room which was registered under Gina's name. That had been Wence's suggestion.

Anna turned slowly.

Tap. Tap.

She tip-toed towards the curtains. Had Beckett's plan been for nothing?

She pressed the button that drew the curtains. They swished open. She sighed in relief. It was Beckett, apparently standing in mid-air just outside the window. She was on the twelfth floor. How on earth . . .?

Beckett smiled. 'Room service?'

She slid the window open and peered out. He was standing in a metal cradle. A window cleaner's lift.

Great way to make an entrance. Now, if only her heart would stop hammering against her chest.

'Going down?' he asked, offering her a hand.

Anna put on her shoes. 'Just let me fetch my coat.'

She darted over to the bed and picked up her black woollen coat. She had to hurry. Wence or one of his men might come in at any moment with another discussion on security arrangements.

Reaching the window, Anna looked down. Not a good move. It was a long, long way to the ground floor. Vertigo was a luxury she couldn't allow herself.

The cradle was only a small step down from the window. Ignoring Beckett's hand, she jumped in. The cradle juddered as Beckett activated the controls. The lift's motors whirred into life.

'Next stop,' said Beckett, 'William's warehouse.'

'They're making their move, sir.'

Taylor put his pair of night-sight binoculars on the back seat and started the car.

'Wait,' snapped Wence, without looking up. 'I want to make sure they don't realise they're being followed.'

Wence held a monitor in his hands. Its colours flickered from black and white to colour, lighting his face. The resolution was not brilliant but was good enough to see that Miss Fabrizi's room was empty.

He hadn't told her about the cameras installed in her room. He couldn't tell her. There was no way she would have conceded to such an invasion of privacy. But he had only her best interests at heart. And now she was stupidly risking her life. Wence hoped they wouldn't have to mop up any mess afterwards.

He hadn't got a clear view of the face that had appeared as she opened the curtains. He hadn't needed to. It could only have been Beckett.

An agent had watched him all afternoon. At every opportunity a camera had been trained on him. Beckett did not go anywhere without the head of the SSD knowing about it.

Wence peered out of the windscreen as the window cleaner's cradle descended. Before it had reached the ground, Beckett opened the door of the cradle and jumped out. Fabrizi followed.

Taylor instinctively sank back into his chair as Beckett looked towards the hotel's small car park. Silly idiot. There was no way Beckett could see them across the car park. Wence had removed all operatives out of the area as soon as it had become obvious that Anna was leaving. Was the woman demented? And she was about to become Italy's prime minister.

Wence picked up a radio from the dashboard. 'Wence to base. Wence to base. Beckett is leaving with Miss Fabrizi. This is an unauthorised departure. Repeat: this is an unauthorised departure. Back-up required.'

Taylor started the car. Wence re-activated the monitor and attached it to a stand in the middle of the dashboard. The picture of Anna's room dissolved to be replaced by a map of the locale. A red dot pulsated on the screen. Beckett's Jeep.

They weren't going to lose the little idiot now.

* * *

The lights in Swift's presentation hall went out. Ros couldn't see a thing. Her eyes slowly adjusted to the darkness. Still nothing. You couldn't see your hands in front of your face.

Time to experiment.

She flicked a switch. Racks of the strongest lights suspended from the auditorium's ceiling flashed on. White light flooded the hall. Her view of the hall was tinged with green from the after-effects of the light. Too bright. Not what she wanted. She flicked them off and the hall fell into complete darkness again.

Another switch. Four spotlights, one in each corner of the hall. A large circle of light illuminated each of the four seating areas. Much better. The lights weren't for her benefit. The killer had to see where he was going.

Ros lifted a pair of binoculars to her eyes and heard the whine of the unit powering up. A blurred image of the hall appeared. It was too dark in the corners of the hall to see anything.

'Night-sight.'

She whispered the instructions. If the killer was in the hall already, she wasn't about to give her position away. The blurred image remained. Oh, for the love of . . . Absolutely perfect timing. Trust the binoculars to fail now!

'Night-sight,' she hissed. 'Manual magnification.'

The image transformed. Ros breathed a sigh of relief. Her view from the top of the hall was represented in various green hues. She scanned the hall. She was the only one there. She hoped it stayed that way. If Ed did his job, the killer wouldn't get into the building.

But you never underestimated your opponent. If the assassin had the equipment to listen in on conversations transmitted via satellite, what other tricks did he have? You always had a back-up plan. And a back-up for the back-up plan.

She gently lifted the mouthpiece of her head-set.

'Ed. It looks very quiet. No sign of anybody.'

* * *

'There's nothing going on out here,' whispered Ed, bringing his radio close to his mouth. 'I hope we haven't got this wrong.'

Nothing moved. Not a car. No one out for a stroll in the cool, clear evening. The rain had stopped. The wind had died down. Apart from the rumble of far-away traffic, it was almost silent.

Street-lamps illuminated the warehouses and offices neighbouring Swift's studio. No one had left a light on in any of the offices. No one was working late. No cars were parked outside any of the buildings. It was as if the area had been evacuated. An unexploded bomb had been discovered or a poisonous chemical had been released into the atmosphere. Totally lifeless.

What if the assassin didn't show? What if he could tell he was being set up? As he had failed before, would he necessarily try again? Would it be the same guy?

Ed snapped his head round when two new lights came into view. Car-lights. Ed could hear the scrunching sound of tyres on the wet road.

He picked up his binoculars. Infra-red. The streets altered, coloured in various hues of grey and red.

Beckett's Jeep. Beckett and Anna unsmiling, staring straight at him. Beckett lifted his hand from the steering wheel for a second, acknowledging he'd been seen.

Ed picked up his radio from the pavement. The radio whistled. Batteries running low? Couldn't be. He had only changed them that afternoon. The whistling suddenly stopped.

'Ros?'

'Yes, Ed?'

'Beckett and Anna have just arrived. Let's hope we're not all wasting our time.'

Swift's cleaning lady was at rest. Peaceful. Her eyes stared at the ceiling.

He had had to kill her.

Quickly. A sharp turn of her head as he came up behind her. A satisfying crick. She never knew. No struggle. No pain. Only death.

Starkey had dragged her into the cupboard with all the mops, buckets, dusters, polish.

And then he'd sat with her.

He needed to hide. The cleaner's cupboard was an ideal place. By six, almost everyone had left the warehouse. Swift was working with one of his assistants on something. The Liberty Party logo he would be showing his fiancée? It didn't matter and Starkey didn't care.

It would be foolish to arrive immediately before Fabrizi appeared. He could have been spotted entering the building. Swift's extensive security system would have registered his entrance whether he walked through the front door or broke in through a window. And that could not be allowed to happen. Nothing would be permitted to stop him now.

So Starkey waited with the dead woman.

She was so thin. Auburn hair. Light grey shadows under her wide brown eyes. Her face was wrinkled. Her jaw was slack. A bead of saliva dangled from the corner of her mouth. Her clothes stank of cigarettes.

Starkey watched her. Torch-light on the back wall of the cupboard. After almost two hours, he had noticed hardly any change in her appearance. Her face paled slightly. Her hands grew cold as he held them. The warmth ebbed out from her so much more slowly than the way the life had ended.

He had never stayed with a life after its end. This was new, exciting and different to the feelings he usually had. He was grateful to be able to savour a life's end.

But the cleaning woman hadn't been a challenge. Not like Fabrizi.

He had finally admitted his failure. But failure to kill her didn't mean defeat. He hadn't lost. He had never lost. He could never lose. Fabrizi would die and her death would be glorious. Better than all the others.

His rifle was immaculate. Polished till it shone. The night-vision sights were clear. Light bounced off the bullets he had picked out of his leather jacket pocket. Golden.

The door clicked open as he unlocked it. Carpeted floor in the corridor hid his footsteps. There was no need to rush. Darkness. No need for light. The floor plan was in his head. He knew exactly where he was at all times. No view to outside. No one could see in. Silence. His breathing became shallow. He was calm. His heartbeat slow.

He focused on the life.

Swift's heart skipped a beat as he sat at the security desk in reception. The computer displayed a picture of Beckett's Jeep coming towards his studio.

Anna.

Smile, Ros had told him. Act as natural as possible. But how could he ignore the fact that Anna's life was at risk?

This was no time to panic. It was too late to think about any danger. Just obey. All he had to do was follow Ros's instructions. It would work out.

Swift felt he was in a play. It didn't seem real, trying to capture an assassin. He felt like a minor character or a stage hand. The assassin was the star, the focus of that evening's activities.

Swift just hoped the killer would know his lines. Do everything that was expected of him. Most importantly, the killer had to be trapped.

Anna swung open the entrance. Beckett hadn't followed her in.

'Beckett's gone to check the rear of the building,' said Anna and then smiled. 'William.'

It was the smile that had grabbed hold of his heart all those months ago and gave it a damned good squeezing. Swift stood up and hugged her.

She pulled away, looking surprised. 'William. Everything's going to be all right.'

He could only manage a half smile. The plan was almost suicidal. He was only going along with it because Anna had wished it.

'Yes, I know,' he lied. 'I can't wait for it to be all over.'

'And tomorrow?'

'I especially can't wait for tomorrow.'

They held each other again. Swift smelled her perfume. The way her body felt next to his made his heart feel as if it would burst at any moment.

'Now,' said Anna in her no-nonsense, demanding tone. 'The control room.'

Swift performed an exaggerated bow, placed his left hand on his chest and held out his right arm, directing her. 'If you would care to follow me to the control room, Miss Fabrizi.'

Anna laughed and kissed the top of his bowed head.

Ros stood in the shadows, unmoving, her binoculars permanently at her eyes. The infra-red image of the hall showed rack upon rack of seats. But nothing else and no one at all.

Suddenly, there was a blaze of light to her right. Startled, Ros almost dropped the binoculars. The control room. Swift was setting up the computer program. Anna sat on a stool and beams of light danced all around her. From where Ros was standing, she would be the only one in the hall to see Anna in the corner of the control room. Ros quickly scanned the hall with her binoculars but the light from the control room whited out the night-sight image.

'Heat sensors,' she hissed.

The image faded, then re-formed. Ros was looking at a blue picture with vague outlines of the racks of seats.

An orange shape. Heat. Over at the other end of the hall, halfway up. Opposite to where she stood. A heat source and near an exit.

Her heart leaped into her mouth.

'Normal picture. Zoom in.'

A face filled the computer-generated image. Balding with dark hair.

The assassin.

'Ed,' she whispered into her head-set. 'There's someone here. By exit three. He's got a rifle.'

'He never passed me.'

'Well he's here now.' It didn't matter how the man had done it. All that mattered was that he was there.

'Right. I'm on my way.'

The rifle pointed up at the control room.

Ros wanted to shout, scream at the assassin, do anything to put him off. But she couldn't. The killer had to be captured or all their work was for nothing.

She hoped that Swift had followed her instructions to the letter or Anna was dead.

Fabrizi.

Smiling, laughing. Swift passed by her and blocked Starkey's shot.

Starkey didn't care. He wanted to sing. The rapture. This was all he needed. Life. That was all. Rare, special, unique life. Billions of people. Every single one of them so different. He wanted them all.

Right now, all he needed was the one life.

And he had Fabrizi's life in his hands.

Strange lights played over her face. He couldn't see the whole of the control room but that wasn't a problem. Starkey had her in his sights.

Her forehead. His premonition hadn't come quite true. Once the bullet hit her, Fabrizi would fall back, then the bullet would explode and destroy her entire face.

It would be beautiful.

Look at me. Look at me. Just glance over here.

Swift again passed by Fabrizi. Starkey could wait. The obstacle would only be there for a few seconds. The life was coming to him. Starkey was her master. She owed her life to him.

She was looking directly at him.

Starkey fired.

He ignored the recoil punch into his shoulder. He had to see the body fall back, see the bullet's explosion. He had to see the life end.

Fabrizi closed her eyes.

No.

That wasn't possible.

« Ten »

« Replicas »

For a second, Beckett was confused. Ros had done her work well.

Two stools and two Annas, both looking equally shocked. One the exact twin of the other. But only one had cried out as glass shattered and a bullet sang through the air embedding itself in the concrete wall before suddenly exploding.

Anna was still alive. The plan had worked. Beckett breathed a sigh of relief.

Swift tapped an instruction into the computer. The Anna by the holed wall faded to grey and then vanished altogether.

The killer had fallen for the hologrammatic doppelgänger.

Swift stepped away from the computer and walked to Anna who stood up. They held each other tight.

'You two OK?' Beckett asked. The shock he had seen a moment ago in Anna's face had been quickly replaced by a look of angry determination.

She nodded. 'Who was trying to kill me? I want to know.'

Beckett raised his eyebrows and shrugged. 'We'll know soon. Ed should have that in hand right now.'

Ed had thought he had heard the whisper of a rifle being

fired through a silencer, but that was impossible. He must have imagined it. But he had certainly heard the crack of glass across the hall. If the lights had been on maybe he would have been able to stop the assassin.

In the dark he had lost his way. It would have been embarrassing if the situation wasn't so desperate.

The corridors from the back of the presentation hall were practically labyrinthine. Idiot. He had doubled back on himself. The killer could be well away by now, mission accomplished.

As he entered the presentation hall, the lights were still down, apart from four spotlights that barely allowed him to see around the hall. The control room's lights had flicked off as soon as he arrived.

Come on, Ros! Switch on the lights! The guy could have killed Anna. I need to see where he's gone.

Ed arrived at exit three. An emergency exit. He was halfway up one side of the hall. He hadn't passed the killer getting there. But with the lights out, the killer could have hidden himself away, or perhaps even escaped.

But Ed wasn't going to let the killer escape. Not this time. Not again.

A silhouette. A body. The killer. Facing him.

The man was short and stocky. He didn't look like he would be much of a fighter. But Ed had made that mistake before and almost lost his life because of it.

The killer's rifle was pointing directly at him.

'You again!'

Ed jumped at him before the man could fire. The assassin fell backwards onto a rack of plastic seats. Fell hard. The wind was knocked out of him. Ed struggled on top of him. He had to get the gun but Ed felt himself being pushed sideways. The rifle twisted in their arms as they fought for possession. Ed felt the killer relax his grip on the gun. An old trick. It still worked. There wasn't enough time to stop the killer pushing Ed over and down the next row of seats.

Ed grasped hold of the killer's black jacket. 'You're

coming with me, mate.'

He pulled the killer over with him. Too much momentum. Neither man could stop. They rolled over each other, the rows of seats clanged in their metal holding clamps, snapping flat, one rack after another.

Ed's world was spinning. The thuds of the slamming seats echoed in the hall. They weren't going to stop until they hit the hall's floor. Ed grabbed hold of the gun and tried to wrench it from the killer's grip.

Ed let his muscles relax and tried to let himself fall.

The killer suddenly relaxed his grip on the gun. There was a pressure on Ed's neck. Every time the killer rolled above him, the pressure increased. The man was trying to strangle him. Ed tried to twist his head from the killer's choking grasp. No good, he was too strong. Red and green spots appeared in the corner of his vision. No*NoNO*! He couldn't black out.

Ed slammed the gun into his attacker's chest but there was no reaction. Didn't this guy feel pain?

Suddenly Ed was weightless. He was falling.

They hit the floor.

The pressure on Ed's neck relaxed. The killer was on top, his knees on Ed's chest.

Ed looked up at him. Black eyes. Hatred. Anger. Madness. This guy was a complete psycho.

Ed held his arms over his head. He had the rifle and was about to swing it down when –

'Starkey! This is the SSD! Armed security!'

A megaphone. Who the hell needed a megaphone in an empty auditorium?

Ed turned to the voice. Three men walking in the beam of a spotlight. Three silhouettes. Ed could make out the shapes of pistols in their right hands. Heels clicked on the wooden floor coming towards him.

The pressure on Ed's chest abruptly lifted. The killer – Starkey? Was that his name? – reached for the rifle in Ed's outstretched arms. Ed threw it across the floor towards the three men.

A fist swiped across his head. Pain.

116

'Damn you.'

The assassin jumped up to his feet. Ed saw the killer run for the stairs. He was escaping. Ed couldn't let that happen. This 'Starkey' had almost killed him, Ros and Swift. And could have just succeeded in shooting Anna.

Ed shook his head, stood and set off at a run. He bounded up the stairs, three steps at a time. Starkey had run out of the exit.

Ed stepped out of the exit into a corridor. The lights came on. There was no one in sight. Ed paused for a second and checked behind him. This Starkey was fast. Did he have accomplices? A car to take him away from here? No time to think. Time to act.

Which way to go – left or right? Back or main entrance? Right. Back entrance.

Ed sprinted down the corridor. The back entrance was locked. Had to be, didn't it? He cursed his choice. He looked up at the door. An emergency release handle was encased in a glass box. He pulled his leather jacket sleeve over his hand and smashed the glass. An alarm immediately sounded. Cold night air rushed in as the door swung open.

No one around. Again. Like it had seemed all evening. The killer must have been inside Swift's place all the time. Arrived while the studio was still open for business and then hidden himself away somewhere. Very clever.

Something crashed to the floor. The sound came from the building site. The killer must be hiding there.

Ed ran towards the construction site. What a mess. And the only light came from the street lamps. Hardly enough to see anyone. The killer could hide anywhere.

The foundation blocks of the new building were in place. Rows of concrete columns with no roof to support. Planks of wood leaned against a makeshift wall. And there, scaffolding, tarpaulin, ladders. Bags of cement lay unopened on the floor. The odd tool left by a workman. Puddles of water from the rain.

Ed kicked a hard-hat as he ran through the site. He

had to watch his footing. One slip and he could crack his head against a concrete pillar. Maybe the killer had done the same?

Footsteps. Running. Falling piping clattered against the concrete. Planks of wood fell onto the ground in Ed's way. Ed ran through, past the pillars, leaping over the fallen planks. A street-lamp glared through the site that made huge shadows from the concrete blocks.

A shape. A man sprinting. The killer, and he didn't seem to care about the noise he was making. Feeling safe enough not to care?

A voice echoed in the night. 'Armed security. Stay still and raise your hands. Armed security!'

Oh, come on, guys! There was no point in saying who you were! They had to do something!

If this SSD lot were as bad as Beckett said then the killer would probably escape. Ed couldn't leave it up to them.

He reached the far end of the site. A car was coming towards him. Ed hid behind a pillar. Tyres screeched. An SSD car? A getaway car? Ed didn't want to be confused with the killer and end up shot in the back for trying to catch the guy. But it could be Starkey's getaway car. He noted the registration. Ros could have it checked out in moments.

Ed crouched down on all fours and stepped over to a bush that hid him from the road. He peered over through the branches. There were now three cars. Bright lights. A canal on the other side of the road. And the killer, Starkey, was trapped by the cars. He swung a pistol in all directions.

Six figures, two from each car, stepped onto the road. Each carried a pistol pointed directly at Starkey.

This must be the SSD. How had SSD known about the trap?

The killer swung his outstretched hands from left to right. His pistol could kill any of the operatives.

A figure stepped forward from the other five. A man.

He moved towards Starkey. Was the man deranged?

'I said put down your gun, Starkey. You can see my men are armed.'

My men. Was this Wence?

Starkey stopped moving. His gun was pointing directly at an agent.

Three shots rang out.

Starkey had been tricked. Fabrizi had been helped. The SSD had been close only once before but now they had him. The blond guy. Was he an agent? No. He wasn't part of Wence's squad. A freelance?

It didn't matter now. How had Fabrizi survived? It didn't make sense. He had her in his sights. She looked at him. He had shot her.

He *had* shot her.

But she didn't die. How was that possible?

Confusion. All there was. No explanations. No understanding.

Starkey had run through the building site, crashing through noisily. Easy to follow. But rational thought had gone. Only confusion. Fabrizi had cheated him, for a third time, and that was impossible.

Starkey found himself surrounded by three SSD cars and the canal behind him. Mackenzie's driver couldn't be too far away but that didn't matter any more. Cornered by six agents. Six pistols aimed at him.

He would never be captured. He would rather die fighting.

Starkey looked down at the three bullet holes. Two in his chest. One in his left arm. His pistol hung uselessly by his side. His mouth was a huge 'O' of surprise.

A burning sensation filled his body and his mind.

He had lost.

But the burning, the burning. It created a feeling stronger than the joy of destroying life.

He couldn't see. The world no longer existed, only a colour in his head. Blood red. Yet this was more than anything he had ever felt. Every time he killed he had wanted more. And the pain in his mind was so much more than all the lives he had taken.

Starkey felt his legs weaken and buckle under him. He stumbled backwards, blind with the ecstasy of the pain.

This is what he had always wanted.

All those lives. All that waste.

It had not been life he yearned for but death. The ultimate absolute.

Finally, he understood. Sweet death embrace him. If he had only known.

By the time he hit the water, Starkey knew no more.

Ed watched Starkey stagger backwards and fall into the canal. Three bullets. Close range. There was no chance that he was still alive.

In his hiding place, Ed sat on the cold pavement. Car doors slammed. He heard the cars driving off. SSD had beaten him to his prey. He tried to ignore the feelings of being cheated out of his prize. He hadn't wanted the man dead. Wanted to find out who he was, find out who he was working for.

Ed turned to walk back through the building site when he realised that Starkey might have been meeting someone. The killer had not run to the car park outside Swift's warehouse but instead run in almost the opposite direction.

He picked up his radio from his jacket pocket.

'Beckett. Ros. The killer's dead. I'm going to check out the area. See if anyone else is around.'

The radio was silent. Surely they would have answered his call immediately? He gave the radio a shake. It whistled at him and then fell silent.

He lifted the mike in his lapel to his mouth then let it fall. That was for the test-drive tomorrow. The miniaturised mike's receiver back at Gizmos.

He shook the hand radio again. 'Beckett? Ros?'

Nothing. Not even a whistle. Bloody typical.

* * *

Beckett wanted to laugh as Wence crossed the auditorium. The man was so pompous. Wence scowled. Two agents flanked him. Even over the noise from the alarm, Beckett could hear their feet clump heavily on the polished floorboards.

Beckett turned to Ros. 'Here comes trouble.'

Anna squeezed Swift's hand. 'This is the guy who organised our bodyguards,' she whispered. 'Complete imbecile if you ask me.'

Wence came up close to Beckett. Beckett resisted the urge to push him back. From the look in Wence's eyes, it was best to keep on his good side – for at least the next five minutes.

'I warned you, Beckett,' said Wence. 'We knew all about the assassination threat to Miss Fabrizi. All you've done is to put her,' he nodded to Swift, 'and her friend in grave danger.'

This was a new one on Beckett. If Wence hadn't been so damn unfriendly back at their HQ perhaps they could have worked together. That, he admitted to himself, was unlikely in the extreme. No one was allowed to play in Wence's back yard. And there was Wence's problem. Stupid, proud fool.

Wence stared at Beckett. He glared right back.

'We were both quite safe,' said Anna, putting a hand on Beckett's shoulder. 'I wanted to flush the assassin out.'

Wence sighed and faced Anna. 'Yes, well, he certainly won't give you any more trouble.'

That meant the assassin was dead. Great work, Wence. How did they find out who was behind the killer now?

Wence continued. 'There's a car outside for you, Miss Fabrizi. If you'll come this way.'

The other two agents led Anna away. She shrugged then blew a kiss at William. He looked confused by everything that had happened.

Ros said, 'It'll be OK, Mr Swift. The assassin's dead.'

Wence ignored Ros and turned on Beckett. 'As for

you, Beckett,' he spat. 'Get out of here before I close you down.'

Where did Wence get off with acting like that? Twice in one day he had been looked at like that. At least Wence wasn't as scary as Major Cardenas.

Beckett watched as Wence followed his agents out of the hall.

'Likes creating an impression, doesn't he?' said Swift.

Beckett laughed. 'He doesn't get out of the office much, so he always tries to make the most of it.'

Ros moved away from them and started glancing around the auditorium. 'Beckett, where's Ed?'

Perhaps it had been a vendetta killing. Perhaps Starkey had a grudge against Anna. No. The guy had been a professional. Perhaps he was working on his own. Ed wandered around looking for any sign of an accomplice. It was a waste of time. The gun shots would have frightened them off.

It started to rain. The film of water on the roads reflected light from the street-lamps. The street was coloured sodium orange and black. The offices were tinged a sickly yellow in the darkness. Water lapped softly at the edges of the canal. The air was crisp and cold.

Ed was getting nowhere. Time to head back to Swift's place.

White light flashed behind him.

Ed turned.

Car lights. A parked car. The only one on the road. Ed strained to see the driver.

The headlights flashed again.

A signal. It had to be.

But that meant the driver didn't know what Starkey looked like. Otherwise, why the signal? Must be a pre-arranged meeting place.

A choice. Ed knew he should leave the car and ignore its signal. Just turn away, walk down the road and head back to Swift's workshop. Check on Anna. Let Beckett and Ros know what had happened to the assassin.

But as soon as he had seen the flashing lights, Ed also knew he had to investigate.

The signal was meant for Starkey. The driver didn't know the killer was now permanently retired. Ed could find out who was behind the plot to kill Anna. Find out who was behind the guy who had tried to kill him. Risky. But life was risky. You didn't balk at risk. You shook it by the hand, patted it on the back like an old friend, learned to live with it and even welcome it.

And he knew he could blag his way out of anything.

Ed turned and walked slowly towards the car. A rear door opened. The guy who stepped out was huge. As tall as Ed, shaved head, large flat nose, looking like he'd been in a fight or ten. Black leather trench-coat. Army boots.

Here it was: the missing link.

The thug stood behind the opened door.

'Are you Starkey?' It was more of a grunt than a question.

'Who's asking?'

The thug looked Ed up and down. 'Don't try to be clever.'

Damn. He could have had a name and then just walked away. Asked Ros to check it out. Even Wence could have helped.

The thug's grey eyes stared at him. It was Ed's move.

Say nothing. Don't give yourself away. Stare back. You don't know who this guy is.

And then a very bad idea hit him.

'We heard shooting,' said the Neanderthal.

'SSD agents,' said Ed, unsmiling. 'They need the practice.'

He really shouldn't be doing this. Why wasn't he walking away? The sober part of his brain screamed at him to turn and get away as quickly as possible. It wasn't cowardice. It was called sanity. But Ed had never run from anything in his life. This might be the best chance he had to find out who Starkey was working for.

'So, who are you?' asked the grunt.

Don't do it. *Don't do it. Don't do it.*

'I'm Starkey.'

Too late.

The thug smiled. That was wrong. Guys like him only smiled when they were about to make someone's life extremely uncomfortable.

The pistol was aimed straight between Ed's eyes.

'Get in.'

There was no arguing with that sort of reasoning. Ed walked around the man and stepped into the car. It smelled new, as if it had just been driven out of the showroom. The car door slammed shut. The thug stepped into the front passenger seat. Ed heard the flick of locks shutting. There was no way out.

The driver, similar in shape, bald and thick-set, turned the ignition key. The engine purred as it rolled slowly down the street.

The car turned left onto a main road. Ed looked at his watch. 8.27. Didn't time fly when you were having fun?

The button microphone. A chance of rescue. A loose thread hung from the lapel. The over-size button only looked strange up close. Would Beckett and Ros be listening? Doubtful. Probably still at Swift's warehouse and wondering by now where he had gone.

Ed looked at the two men in the front of the car. He couldn't risk talking. Ros would be able to pick up the tracker but only back at Gizmos. He prayed they would go to the office soon.

The carphone rang.

'Spencer here. Yes, we've got him, sir.'

Pause.

Spencer listened to the man on the other end of the phone.

'The woman's still alive?'

Ed wanted to let out a sigh of relief. Then it hit him. His stomach clenched and he suddenly felt very cold.

Starkey had been employed by someone to kill Anna. Starkey had (thankfully) failed. But if he was being Starkey . . .

Ed smacked his forehead. Why was he so stupid?

'We'll take him to the office. Yes, sir. See you in the morning.'

Spencer replaced the receiver and turned to Ed. 'That's three times you've messed up, Starkey. The boss isn't pleased.'

Ed met the man's gaze. What was there to say? Spencer laughed and sat back in his seat.

Great. Just great. There he was, in the back of a car, posing as a failed assassin, about to meet his employer. The prospect of blagging this one out was becoming more and more remote.

« Eleven »
« The secret »

The morning was glorious. A bright blue sky. Thin slivers of clouds crossed the sky. Skyscrapers glistened with reflections of the early morning golden sun. From her hotel room, Anna could look over the entire city. A medley of a thousand different designs, old and new.

Her shadow was back. He stood in the corner, unsmiling as always. Did they receive training in looking so serious? He was almost enough to put her off breakfast. She had asked for room service knowing full well that she should have gone to see Corelli and told him of her plans for the day. After last night, however, she needed pampering. A rather delicious young waiter, tall, dark-haired with deep brown eyes, served breakfast at her table by the window. Not before Mr Misery had frisked him for any concealed weapons, checked the waiter's trolley for hidden explosives and radioed someone to check that the waiter did really work at the hotel. Anna thought the bodyguard was going to taste the food. He didn't go that far. Croissant, coffee and fresh orange juice. The croissant was soggy, the coffee repulsive and the orange juice was fresh from a carton. Not the greatest breakfast in the world but it definitely was not poisoned. Anna took another sip of her orange juice. It was foul but that didn't matter one jot. Nothing and no one, including Mr Misery in the corner, could

126

spoil this day. The assassin was dead and, with luck, Wence's men had scared any potential killer off.

Gina sat on a sofa, tapping away into her laptop. Did she ever stop working? Anna snapped open her newspaper and scanned the news about the Italian elections. Her lead in the polls had extended, even though she had been out of the country. Obviously, absence did make the heart grow fonder. Soon she would become one part of the one per cent of Italian politicians who were female. She would have to do something about that.

'Is everything arranged for later?' she asked Gina.

Gina didn't look up from her computer. 'Yes, Miss Fabrizi.'

'Good.'

There was a knock at the door, and William stepped into the room. He smiled.

'It's all right. He's my fiancé,' said Anna to the bodyguard.

William walked over and sat on a chair at Anna's side. He picked up a croissant and bit on it. Anna slapped the back of his hand lightly and laughed.

'Seeing the bride on the morning of the wedding is supposed to be bad luck,' she whispered. Bride. Wedding. Her heart started to pound in anticipation of the day's events.

William's smile faded. 'I know. I wanted to give you a chance to change your mind.'

What was going on inside that head? Was he starting to think that marrying her was a bad idea?

'Why?'

'Suppose Wence interferes?'

Anna glanced over at her bodyguard. He was watching them intently.

'Mr Wence won't know anything about it.'

'We could cancel,' suggested William. 'Wait until after the election. I could fly back to Italy with you and we could get married there.'

Anna shook her head. 'No. We planned to do it here

127

in Britain and that's what I want. Nobody is going to stop us.'

'But is it going to be safe?'

Anna shrugged her shoulders. Was anything really ever safe? 'Hardly anybody knows anything about it. Anyway, Wence said the man had been killed.'

'They haven't got the people who hired him, though, have they?'

That, she admitted to herself, was worrying. It wasn't much of a concern at the moment, however. She had told almost nobody of the wedding – certainly not the SSD who would have put a stop to it. And Anna Fabrizi wasn't the sort of person who let anybody stop her doing exactly what she wanted. She had been careful. Her own little security system for the wedding would be fine.

'I know they haven't caught anybody,' said Anna. 'And it could be down to a number of people. But William, I cannot spend the rest of my life in hiding.'

William sighed. He always let Anna have her way. Just as it should be. She was in control of her own life. No one else.

William changed the subject. 'Your secretary's happy to be a witness?'

Was he kidding? Gina had leaped at the chance. 'Of course.'

'And Alberto?'

Her stomach tightened. 'I haven't asked him yet. I was leaving it until this morning for maximum surprise.' A white lie. She wasn't about to admit to anyone that Anna Fabrizi found it difficult to tell her partner of their marriage.

'You do trust him?'

She didn't believe William could say that. 'He and I could be running the country together in a couple of weeks. I can't let him learn about the wedding from the papers. Now. Pass me my mobile. Alberto said he would be at the embassy this morning. I'll tell him now.'

* * *

Ed hadn't slept.

Spencer had locked him in a small office. No furniture. Grey carpet. White walls. Windows from floor to ceiling on two sides of the room.

It had been a cold night, but now the sun was beginning to rise Ed felt like he was on death row, about to face his final day.

Which, in all probability, he was.

Ed stood up and banged his fist on the door.

'Hey! You guys! Where's the condemned man's hearty breakfast?'

Spencer hadn't even given him a blanket to keep warm. As far as Starkey's employer was concerned, he was a failure. From what Spencer had implied, failures didn't live too long to regret it.

At least he might find out who was after Anna. As if the knowledge would do him any good. He'd probably be dead the minute he found out.

No. He shouldn't think like that. There was a way out of every situation. He had got himself in and out of plenty of tight corners before. He would just have to find the right moment to make his move.

As long as he got the chance.

Mackenzie sat back on his leather sofa and crossed his legs. Spencer stood by the door. Corelli sat at the desk, talking animatedly to someone on his mobile. It wasn't hard to work out who was on the other end of the line.

Fabrizi. The target. She had the luck of the devil. Or perhaps her guardian angel was looking over her shoulder, keeping an eye on her?

Hadn't he hired the best?

Hadn't he trusted Starkey to get the job done? How had the man let him down for a third time?

Mackenzie knew he would have to get rid of his employee. It would be the only way to save face with Corelli and his 'friends'. And they were better friends than enemies. But that sort of friendship could be lost so easily. They were people even Mackenzie would think twice about before crossing. Alliances based on respect and fear. No trust. You gave people an ounce of trust and they let you down. It had happened before. Mackenzie had vowed it would not happen again. People were either for you or against you. No in-between. And Starkey had crossed that fine line with his triple failure. Starkey had become a burden. Mackenzie wasn't about to change the habit of a lifetime and let him get away with it.

Perhaps his faith in Starkey's abilities was misjudged – to say the least. Mackenzie alone would have to answer for the assassin's failures. That made him uncomfortable.

Keep calm. See what you can pick up from this mess.

Corelli switched off his phone and slowly, almost theatrically, put it back in an inside jacket pocket. He turned to Mackenzie. He said nothing. The room was silent. Corelli's dark eyes stared at him.

Don't say anything. Don't risk saying a wrong word.

Eventually: 'Married!' Corelli spat the word out as if he had just been insulted. 'Not only is she still alive,' he said, 'but she's getting married this morning! What the hell went wrong last night?'

So, Swift and Fabrizi were tying the knot. If only he had known. A bomb in the pew, in the vestry, in the bloody priest's cassock, for crying out loud. So many opportunities to kill someone. Even Starkey would not have failed.

As to what went wrong, they would soon find out.

'We picked up Starkey,' said Mackenzie. 'Do you want to see him?'

Corelli's voice was low. 'Yes. I do.'

'Spencer. Bring our guest in.'

Spencer opened the door and left the room.

Mackenzie avoided Corelli's eyes. The man in his beige Italian suit was furious and he had to make sure Corelli didn't take that anger out on him. Get it transferred to Starkey.

The door opened wider and in stepped the legendary Starkey. The soon-to-be-dead Starkey. There was a look of failure in his eyes. Or that could just be Mackenzie's imagination.

The man was tall, blond and handsome. He didn't look much of a killer. Looked like he could handle himself, though. Thick-set arms and strong legs.

It was annoying they had to meet in such inauspicious circumstances. He had wanted to meet Starkey for some time.

'So, you're Starkey,' said Corelli. Quiet. That dangerous quiet. The calm before the storm.

Starkey glared back. Arrogance? A lack of fear?

'Yeah. Why am I being treated like a prisoner?'

Something was wrong. His voice. Australian. Starkey didn't talk like that. The inflections on the words were all wrong. He spoke in an almost monotone. This wasn't Starkey. An *operative*? A damn SSD agent in his office? It would just be like one of Wence's mob to stumble their way into his operation.

'Because,' said Corelli, his voice dripping with anger, 'you keep failing to do the job I'm paying you for.'

'Where did you get that accent?' said Mackenzie. 'You're not the person I spoke to on the phone.'

'Are you kidding?' said the Australian after a pause. 'I always use a voice synthesiser on phone calls.'

That sounded more like the Starkey he knew. Paranoid idiot. Probably suspicious of his own shadow.

'You mean as well as that stupid tape you always play?'

The blond man paused again. 'Haven't you heard of security?'

The phone call. Yesterday afternoon. Weren't those almost Starkey's exact words? Anal bastard. Yes. This was Starkey.

'Sure we've heard of security,' said Corelli.

The gun came out of nowhere. Spencer always frisked everyone when they came in. But you didn't

131

go round checking if clients were carrying. That sort of behaviour was bad for business.

The gun was pressed hard under Starkey's nostrils, pushing his head back.

'That's why I want you dead.' Corelli flicked the safety catch.

Starkey was scared. He stared down the barrel of a gun. Staring death in the face.

If the Italian fired now, there would be blood everywhere. His new suit would be ruined. Not to mention the mess on the carpet.

'Hey, come on guys,' said the Australian. 'I thought we had a deal.'

'The deal's off. I don't like failures.'

'Look, it wasn't my fault. Fabrizi hired some people to protect her. The whole thing was a set-up.'

So the Aussie assassin had been outwitted. It was still failure.

Corelli sounded more interested. 'Yeah?'

Starkey was talking for his life. It had better be good.

'Yeah. The security services turned up in a big way. A man was killed. A passerby, I think.'

Ha! Wence still couldn't catch a bus. 'Trust the SSD to get the wrong man.'

Corelli relaxed his hold on the gun. Starkey looked relieved.

'At least they killed someone. That's more than you've achieved.'

And Starkey had plenty of chances to finish her off. 'Not only is Fabrizi still alive, Starkey, but she's getting married this morning.'

'Married?' Starkey's voice changed. From one tinged with fear to one filled with hope. 'Where's the church? I can do it there.'

Corelli laughed. 'Kill her at the wedding? You think I should trust you again?'

'Yeah.' Cocky. Sure of himself. Starkey was very different from how Mackenzie had imagined the man to be.

'I can have her dead,' he continued, 'before the ink's dry on the wedding register.'

Good line.

Corelli let the gun fall to his side. The idea had merit. Perhaps he and Corelli would have to spoon-feed Starkey every single step of the way but the job would get done. Fabrizi would die.

'OK,' said Corelli. 'One final chance. But screw up again and it will be your last mistake.'

And Starkey couldn't really expect fairer than that, could he?

They were on full alert.

Since the killing last night, Wence had almost every available man watching over the hotel. Perhaps calling in the extra manpower was a waste of money but who knew if there would be another attempt at killing Miss Fabrizi? Would Starkey's employer be scared off? How many people exactly were after Miss Fabrizi?

Watching the hotel was starting to become tedious. Morale was getting lower. That was just too bad. Anyway, his men would be glad of the overtime.

Now, all Miss Fabrizi had to do was be where she was when she said she would be. His men were everywhere and able to watch her back at all times, so why hadn't she turned up for the conference that morning? Why wasn't he told of any changes in her plans until they had happened? Why couldn't she remember that he was protecting her life? How on earth was she able to take the threats and attacks on her life so damn coolly? She was either a foolish or a very brave woman.

He tapped lightly on her hotel door. Open, of course. Acting as if she didn't have a care in the world. That could be considered a good tactic. By pretending she was not scared of anyone, any would-be killer might think twice about attempting to end her life. No one would behave in such a manner unless they had excellent security. Or, they could think 'sod it' and kill her anyway. There really was only so much he and his men could do.

Anna sat on a sofa in a white silk dressing gown, reading a newspaper. She smiled as he entered the room.

'Your secretary – Gina, isn't it? – tells me you're not attending this morning's session of the conference.'

'No.'

What did that mean? No, Gina's wrong or no, she wasn't attending the morning session?

Be polite. Smile. You wouldn't want any complaints brought against the Division.

'What are you doing? May I ask?'

'I shall have a swim in the hotel pool. If that's all right with you?'

God spare us all from Italian women. What did Swift see in her?

No one could simply vanish.

Ros needed information like she needed air to breathe. Ignorance, in her book, was not bliss. Once Wence had left William's warehouse, she and Beckett had checked every single street within a two mile radius but found no trace of Ed.

Ros cursed herself. Why hadn't she taken equipment with them to Swift's place so she could have listened to the mike she'd sewed onto Ed's jacket? She should have been prepared for the unexpected. All her talk about back-up plans was just so much hot air. But berating oneself didn't get you anywhere. She had suggested going back to the office to see if she could pick up Ed's trace. If not, she was sure she could rig something to boost the receiver.

Ros worked through the night, spurred on by the thought of the danger Ed could be in. Also, she felt guilty by what she saw as a lack of foresight on her part.

Beckett was no help. He had whined on and on about how he should have covered the assassin. He hadn't said it outright, but he'd implied that Ed could be dead. If his experience was anything to go by, Ed could have met up with the assassin's employer and God knows what might have happened. She wouldn't let herself think that Ed had been killed, so she tried to ignore him and got to work cannibalising parts of other radio receivers. As soon as Beckett realised that he was being worse than useless, he curled up on a sofa and went to sleep.

The silence was wonderful.

Now they were sitting by the strange receiver. But there was no trace of a signal.

Ed might not be able to speak. A gun could be pointing at his head. Buildings could be blocking the transmitter. A whole range of things could have stopped Ed being traced. The mike could have been damaged. Whatever.

Ros shivered as she adjusted another control on the radio.

'Beckett? Ros? Can you hear me?'

Ed's voice. Ros wanted to scream for joy. His voice was echoing, whispering. He was too close to the mike. His 's's were like hisses. Someone was watching him?

She heard the sound of running water in the background. A bathroom? Probably. Made for a good place for privacy. Ed's voice showed more than a little stress.

'I don't know how long I can talk. I lost my radio. I'm using this button thing. I hope it's working. The people I'm with think I'm a contract killer –'

Beckett leaped up from the sofa. 'Ed! What the hell are you doing?'

'He can't hear you,' said Ros. 'The button's just a mike.'

'Anna's getting married this morning, and I'm meant to kill her. Don't ask.'

'Next time sew a couple on, Ros,' said Beckett. 'Then one can be a receiver. Ed's not trained for infiltration work. It's highly dangerous.'

'I'm playing along to find out who's behind it.'

135

Ros waved Beckett to be quiet. She needed to listen. A clue to where he was being held. Anything. She had to get Ed back. 'Sh, Beckett. He's trying to tell us something.'

'I should have covered the assassin, not Ed.'

And that solves all our problems, does it?

Ros yelled, 'Beckett!'

Banging on a door. Wooden.

'You finished in there?'

Another voice. Male. Gravelly. Aggressive. Sounded like he smokes. The flush of a toilet. A door sliding open. The bang of a door closing.

'Ros! Beckett! If you can hear me: just get to the church on time!'

« Twelve »
« Dream killer »

How was he supposed to look inconspicuous, sitting by the pool in a suit? How?

Anna's bodyguard checked over the pool area. They were in the hotel's basement. Exits to changing rooms were on the left. Entrance to the hotel gym on the right. It wasn't busy. Half a dozen people. White everywhere. White walls, white floor, white pool. Looked almost clinical.

Wence said follow Fabrizi, so that's what he had done. Of course, Miss high-and-mighty Fabrizi didn't like having him around. Her dislike was easy to cope with. Knowing she called you Mr Misery behind your back didn't faze him. And being an intrusion in her life wasn't a problem. Some people didn't realise that the SSD had their clients' interests at heart. After last night's farce, if it was up to him, he would have told Fabrizi to look after herself.

But it wasn't. He just had to get on with his job.

God, it was warm. The air was humid. It was a pity he couldn't join Fabrizi in the pool. Looked very inviting. His suit was becoming clammy. He couldn't take the jacket off. Wouldn't want the hotel's residents getting jumpy at the sight of a gun, would he?

Trying to read the newspaper was pointless. He couldn't let Fabrizi out of sight for a second. He tried to

137

look at ease as half-naked people pointed at him, laughed and seemed confused. He gave them a hard stare to make them look away. He checked them over. Concealed weapons in a pair of trunks or a bikini? That didn't seem too likely. But Starkey had been a clever son of a bitch. The things he'd done in the past. He wouldn't be doing them any more.

Wence had been after the assassin for some time. Probably feeling a little proud about downing that one. But Starkey's successors might be of the same school. And there were no two ways about it: being rid of one killer meant another would pop up almost immediately. He sighed. An operative's work was never done.

What was Miss Fabrizi doing now? Was she finally going to leave? He'd had enough of being in the stifling atmosphere of the swimming pool.

She stepped out of the pool. Her blue swimming costume was stretched over her softly curving body. Certainly not waif-like. Stunning. Long black, lightly curled hair. Beautiful. And she probably knew it.

She headed for the changing rooms. At last.

Damn. The changing rooms.

There was no way he was going in there. Probably cause a riot.

Man's Battered Body Found in Women's Changing Room.

Not the best idea in the world.

Miss Fabrizi stepped into the changing rooms, turned at the entrance and waved at the bodyguard. He had to let her in there on her own.

Not to worry.

She'd be out in a minute.

Hired by Swift. Lied to by Swift. Almost blown to pieces by assassin. Assassin cornered using revolutionary holographic techniques (OK, Ros – that's enough self-congratulation). Assassin killed. Not our fault. Anna saved. We *do* claim the credit for that one. Ed kidnapped. Idiot. Idiot. Idiot. Anna getting married.

Anna getting married *this* morning. Ed pretending to be the killer. And he has to kill Anna at aforementioned wedding. Nice one. And they still had work at Tronix to complete. Not that it mattered much if they didn't have a driver for the test car.

This was getting really good. All they had to do was stop Anna going to the wedding. And that should be easy enough.

Then they had to save Ed. Heaven knew how.

One problem at a time.

Ros and Beckett were back at the hotel. It wasn't the time for dodging Wence or any of the SSD. They could help by making sure Anna stayed in the hotel. But security seemed to be only adequate. Beckett wanted to crack their heads. Ros had to keep him in check. Finding and breaking into the HQ of the most secret security department in the country was not likely to make them your lifelong friends. So out came Diplomatic Ros who could get questions answered at any time and anywhere.

By pretending to be hotel residents, it was possible to bypass SSD. Ros was annoyed that they were never stopped and asked for any identification.

Ros was happier when she bumped into Gina. Ros asked her the way to Anna's suite. Anna's secretary was nice although she looked a little stressed. Gina had assumed that Ros was part of the SSD. God forbid that anything so terrible would happen to her.

Ros walked through a pair of double-doors. Beckett stood, waiting patiently.

'They said she's in the pool,' said Ros.

Beckett nodded. 'So that's why she didn't answer her mobile.'

Ros stopped. *Think about what you just said, Ros.* Anna couldn't have.

She could. Damn. If Anna could get by the SSD last night then she could do anything.

'Beckett. Swimming's an odd thing to do before your wedding, isn't it?'

Beckett set off, running for the lift. Ros followed. Anna was going to make a break for it. Why the hell didn't she tell them her plans right at the very beginning?

Secrets. Didn't you just love them?

Someone wearing a white dressing gown covering a blue swimsuit stepped out of the underground car park entrance to the hotel. Her breath condensed in the cold, still air.

A car rumbled along another floor, its engine roaring.

Where was Gina with that limo?

Anna started hopping from one foot to the other.

Ah, ah, ooh, ooh, ah, ah! Cold feet!

If Gina didn't have the wedding dress in the back of the limo, the whole thing was ruined. But, Anna reminded herself, Gina wouldn't fail on this one. She couldn't.

Wait till William heard about this. Anna was determined that the SSD would not stop the most important day of their lives. Hotel reception had thought it odd when a grown woman had darted through the hotel, wearing a dressing gown and sporting almost fatally bad hair. She laughed and quickly clamped a hand over her mouth. She felt guilty and excited by her daring escape from what she saw as the SSD's overprotective clutches.

The poor bodyguard. If he hadn't been such a prude and followed her into the changing rooms, the wedding would have been off.

Wence would probably fire the bodyguard for losing her. It might be politic to apologise to Mr Wence later.

Come on, Gina! Standing in the middle of a freezing car park was no one's idea of fun.

The limo pulled up and the passenger door opened. Gina was clutching a suitcase to her chest. Was it right that the bridesmaid looked more excited than the bride?

Finally, Anna was out of the freezing cold car park and into the nice warm limo. Blood started circulating through her chilled, bare feet.

'Well done, Gina. You've got everything?'

Gina opened the suitcase. A crumpled bunch of flowers lay on top of a folded dress. Anna didn't mind. Gina couldn't have walked out of the hotel holding a wedding bouquet without arousing some question or other from Mr Wence or one of his cronies, could she?

'Bouquet,' said Gina, lifting the battered flowers out. 'And here's the something borrowed.'

Anna's mother's jewellery. Hmm. Mother had not been happy that the wedding wasn't being held at home. But Anna had promised that they would celebrate even more loudly back home.

'Something blue.'

'Oh, *hello*.'

The sky-blue knickers looked exceedingly saucy. Silk. She couldn't wear anything else on her wedding day. Well, perhaps something a little more adventurous for afterwards. If William behaved himself.

'Now,' she said sternly. 'No peeking, driver!'

He didn't even look back. Anna's heart skipped a beat. The black-suited driver could be anyone.

'It's OK, Miss Fabrizi,' said Gina, reading her mind. 'He's a friend of a friend.'

Anna hugged her secretary. Gina had sorted out practically every single engagement. She was an absolute star. Minister for Home Affairs when she became the prime minister, possibly? Ha! No. She couldn't. Who knew what Gina's replacement would be like? And good secretaries were so hard to find. And Alberto wouldn't stand for it.

Stuffy old Alberto. He had been so surprised by her announcement. And amazed to hear that the wedding was this morning. Anna had half expected him to start complaining. Why hadn't he been told? What if the press found out before the election? Et cetera.

Anna rummaged through the suitcase. It was time to get changed and look completely irresistible for William.

* * *

Who the hell were they, barging into the swimming centre demanding to know Miss Fabrizi's whereabouts? They weren't SSD. But there was something in the young woman's voice. Urgent. Almost desperate. No time to argue with them. The bodyguard pointed at the changing rooms. The woman sighed, shook her head and went inside. The well-set young man stayed behind.

The man looked familiar, but he couldn't place the face. Ex-employee? An SSD target?

'What's going on?' he asked.

'SSD have done the usual,' said the dark-haired man. 'Cocked everything up. Put the woman you were supposed to be guarding and our partner in danger.'

What the heck was he going on about?

The woman reappeared from inside the changing rooms. 'Anna's not in there.'

Oh, no. Damn. Miss Fabrizi had done it again. Wence would have his guts for garters. Brilliant.

Oh, she'll just be a minute. Just wait for her outside.

He should have gone in after her. Sod the complaints from any other swimmer. Too late now.

The woman stared hard at him. 'This is what happens when you don't employ enough women.'

And what could he say to that?

Beckett and Ros had rushed out of the hotel and were now in Ros's car, moving fast away from the hotel. The car was quicker than the Jeep. Ros was ignoring a few traffic laws. The back seat was full of junk. Devices of various shapes and sizes, disks, CDs. And only one of her toys will help us find Ed. Beckett hoped it would be before Ed had to kill anyone to survive.

Things were falling apart.

Anna was off on her way to get herself killed by Ed. He might not have any choice but to kill her. His life was on the line. Uncomfortable thought.

Ed couldn't do it. There was no way he would let it happen. He would die first. He would put anybody's life before his own.

142

Beckett knew Ed shouldn't have asked to chase the assassin. And Ed shouldn't have been allowed to chase the assassin. Becket blamed himself. He should have been firmer.

He just didn't want to lose a friend.

The tracker was a simple machine. Another of Ros's upgrades. It picked up the signal and the tracker's liquid crystal display magnified as it moved closer to the bug.

Ros and he could get Ed out of this. They had managed to rescue Ros from a remote-control jumbo, hadn't they? They could do this. If time was on their side.

'What's the range of your button?' he asked.

'Eh?'

'This new mini-tracker and microphone of yours.'

'A couple of miles. Why?'

Good question. 'Well, let's hope the wedding isn't in Rome then.'

Break his face.

Smack him against the inside of the limo window. Daze him. It would give Ed maybe a minute's head start at the very most.

Mackenzie. Those staring steel-grey eyes. He was an evil-looking bugger. Even with the cuffs on, Ed could knock him out. He could make a break for it. Maybe. But then with cuffed hands how could he open the doors? And what would Mackenzie's driver, Spencer, do? Being cuffed wasn't exactly conducive to unarmed combat.

But if luck was on his side, there would be no attempt on Anna's life. That was what was most important. Ed had to risk it.

He started to lift his cuffed hands, then stopped.

It was madness.

My brain is trying to kill me.

And then there was the gun pointing straight at him. That would stop anyone in their tracks. If Ed moved a muscle Mackenzie didn't like – no more Ed. But who would do their dirty work for them, then?

Hell. No one was irreplaceable – especially a guy who wasn't even a contract-killer but – for some reason that slipped his feeble mind – was just pretending.

He had to keep cool. Act like no worries. The cuffs bit into his wrists. His moment would come. A chance to make a break for it. Or Ros and Beckett would show. They would defeat the bad guys and they would all go home happy ever after. Stranger things had happened.

Ros's button hung by a thread. If it was given even the slightest tug, it would fall.

Ed was distracted from the miniaturised mike as the car door opened.

Corelli. Nice suit. Designer. White carnation in the buttonhole. Smart tie. Not everyone's cup of tea. Showed the man's sartorial taste was better than his taste in friends.

It was hard to believe this guy was Anna's partner in politics. Liberty Party. What a joke. Corelli must be a good actor. Anna didn't seem the type to be fooled easily.

Ed moved over on the seat as Corelli sat down.

'Mr Starkey,' said Corelli, 'I trust this time you'll complete your assignment?' Corelli smiled slightly. A lizard's smile. Creep.

'Touch of disunity in the party?' asked Ed. 'Or is Miss Fabrizi just marrying the wrong guy?'

Corelli's smile vanished. 'You're not paid to ask questions. Just kill her.'

'Unlucky in love?'

'Love has nothing to do with it. This is politics.'

No it wasn't. This was murder. How did Corelli think he would get away with it? Probably by framing Ed for Anna's death. If they let him live.

'So whereabouts is this wedding?' asked Ed.

It was Mackenzie who answered. The man had hardly spoken a word since they left his office. 'You'll find out.'

What a mine of information. Ed kept fishing. 'In a church?'

'What's it to you?' snapped Mackenzie.

Beckett heard Ed's voice come clearly over Ros's radio.

'Idle curiosity . . .'

The image on Ros's tracker magnified. If they had been in his Jeep, the tracker could have been linked up to the computerised traffic map. Finding Ed would be a lot easier. That was tough. This was the best they had.

Two men were with Ed. One of them he had heard before – when they had first heard Ed was alive. The two men were not providing any information that would help save Anna's life.

Life couldn't be that easy, could it?

Ed had to be careful. He shouldn't push too hard or his kidnappers might permanently dispose of such an inquisitive employee.

Ros's car stopped at a set of traffic lights. She slapped the steering wheel with the palm of her hand.

'Corelli!' she announced.

Anna's partner? What did he have to do with this?

'Sorry?'

'That was Corelli's voice.'

'How do you know? You haven't even met the guy.'

The lights changed slowly from red to red and amber then green. Ros put her foot down and sped down the empty road.

'Remember when I couldn't quite place where I'd seen William's logo for the Liberty Party?'

Beckett nodded. It had been at Swift's warehouse.

'Well, I remembered it was from a television interview with Anna and *her partner* Alberto Corelli.'

'And?'

Ros tutted. 'Come on, Beckett. Once I've heard a voice, I never forget it.'

It certainly made sense. Another piece of the jigsaw firmly in place.

145

'Had to be, didn't it?' he said. 'I mean, whoever heard of two politicians being best mates?'

Ed was getting nothing out of them. Corelli would only have known about the wedding arrangements a short time ago. He kept muttering about the wedding being sprung upon him.

Judging by Starkey's failures, Corelli and Mackenzie were staying with this job and were going to watch Ed very closely. Mackenzie would make sure the job was done.

'Put this on,' said Mackenzie.

Ed was handed an odd-looking waistcoat. Leather. Very padded. Lots of pockets. Plenty of thick, gold-coloured zips.

Ed carefully removed his jacket, aware of the mike and its loose connection, then took the waistcoat.

'It's not quite my style,' he said, putting it on. 'I mean, I normally like Italian clothes, but –'

'Shut up, Starkey,' said Corelli. 'You won't have to wear it long.'

Mackenzie moved to Ed's right. Both Corelli and Mackenzie tugged the top of the waistcoat over Ed's shoulders.

Ed picked up his jacket by his side and put it back on. The mike dangled even more precariously from the lapel.

Mackenzie gave one last tug on the waistcoat.

Damn. Don't react. Don't draw attention to it.

The button would be fine on the floor. Ros and Beckett could track him and listen to their conversation just as well with it lying between their feet. If either Corelli or Mackenzie spotted the mike, then it was *ciao* Ed. When the button was seen up close, it was obvious it was a mike.

Ed looked out of the window. He couldn't see anything. Smoke-glass side windows. He just didn't want to look at the floor.

'I'm sorry about the weight of the waistcoat,' said

Corelli. 'It's lined with plastic explosives.'

What?! Ed the human bomb?

And on the menu tonight is flambéed wedding guests?

Forget the tracker! They couldn't ask an assassin to go right up to Anna and then detonate the explosives – could they? No way. Starkey was a top-rate killer. Mackenzie didn't look the sort of bloke to waste a valuable resource.

'A sort of insurance policy?' Ed asked, trying to stay calm.

'Exactly,' said Corelli. 'So, if for any – and I mean *any* – reason you fail again, we'll terminate your contract.'

Nice euphemism. If Anna wasn't killed, they triggered the human bomb. The waistcoat suddenly felt very heavy. Enough explosive to bring a house down. Or a church. And certainly enough to leave no trace of him.

Corelli checked his watch.

'What's the church called?' asked Ed.

There was no response.

'Look. You don't want me to walk into the wrong one, do you?'

'Don't worry, Starkey,' said Mackenzie. 'We've taken precautions against that eventuality.'

Mackenzie placed an earpiece in Ed's ear. Corelli fixed a small microphone to the waistcoat.

Mackenzie whispered, 'We'll be telling you *exactly*, where to go, Starkey.'

Corelli fetched out a portable monitor. 'We will know every move you make. We can tell if you're not following instructions. Even be able to tell you if you're aiming too high.'

So where was the camera? Corelli would be part of the wedding ceremony. As far as poor Anna was concerned, Corelli was as good as her best man. Corelli wouldn't be keeping an eye on Ed.

Corelli passed the monitor to Mackenzie. He waved it in Ed's face.

147

'And there's me thinking it was so you could follow the football on satellite.'

Corelli and Mackenzie ignored the joke. It wasn't that bad. At least he could still crack a funny. Probably the first signs of hysteria.

Corelli zipped up the waistcoat. As it reached the top teeth, Ed heard a gentle click.

What the –?

'And don't try to take the waistcoat off,' said Corelli. 'This zip completes a circuit. Try to undo it and you'll detonate the explosives.'

Thought of everything, hadn't they?

Wriggling and squirming into a wedding dress in the back of a limo might not have been the most romantic way to go to your wedding but it was certainly different. And fun.

'See!' said Gina. 'I told you it would fit.'

The dress, designer naturally, had looked very small when Gina pulled it out of the suitcase. Various shades of purple, from the lightest lilac to rich, violet braiding.

She felt like a soldier when the suit had been laced up at the back. Military-style braiding ran across her chest and the boots seemed a little excessive. Maybe just a tad too retro? She had loved it when she had been fitted for it. She remembered looking amazing and William had thought so too. So what was wrong with her now?

Maybe it was nerves. Maybe the events of the past day or so were taking their toll. Anna dismissed the feelings. Ridiculous. There was no way Anna Fabrizi got cold feet. She was going to get married to the most wonderful lover in the world and nothing as silly as butterflies in her stomach would stop her.

Ed felt as if he had been travelling for hours, but it couldn't have been more than ten minutes. The limo stopped. Corelli stepped out of the car.

The button.

Neither Mackenzie nor Corelli had noticed it.

As Ed made to follow Corelli, he kicked the tracker out of the car – too forcefully. It shot out, landed on the pavement and rolled along for a few feet. Corelli hadn't seen a thing. Mackenzie had gone to the back of the limo and opened the boot. Ed couldn't chance trying to pick the button up. Too risky to start making suspicious moves.

He could only hope he was close enough to their destination for Ros and Beckett to track him there.

The building he faced certainly didn't look like a church, more like a civic centre. It was a square white building. A number of columns supported an ornate pediment which covered steps leading up to an entrance.

Of course. A civic wedding.

Smart and brightly dressed people hovered outside. Anna's guests? Guests of other newlyweds?

Mackenzie tapped Ed's shoulder. He turned. Mackenzie thrust a decoratively wrapped, long rectangular box into his hands.

'What's this?'

'A little present for the bride,' said Corelli who walked back to the limo and knocked on its roof. The limo drove away slowly. The present had to be a rifle of some sort. They had arrived all right. And still no sign of Beckett or Ros.

Come on, guys. Get a move on.

Mackenzie gripped Ed's left arm firmly. A small black box on an elasticated band was fitted over his wrist.

Mackenzie pressed a button on the side of the box. An LED reading appeared. 15.00. 14.59. 14.58.

A timer. Great.

'An extra incentive,' said Corelli. 'If you haven't done the job in fifteen minutes, the explosives will detonate.'

Mackenzie let go of Ed's arm. 'Boom!'

It wasn't linked up to the explosives. Had to be a

radio detonator. It didn't matter if Ed took the timer off. A signal would still trigger the bombs. Unless he managed to get far enough away before the signal could be sent. But, no doubt, Mackenzie would have another detonator handy. One false move and no more Ed. Even if he had to kill Anna, he couldn't trust Mackenzie not to detonate the explosives. They had made sure that Starkey couldn't fail.

Ed had no tools with him to disarm the trigger. Not that he had any good idea on what to disarm. If he tried, he'd more than likely blow himself to kingdom come. Where the hell was Ros when he needed her?

And if they didn't reach him within fourteen minutes and thirty-two seconds, Ros and Beckett would have to start looking for a new partner.

« Thirteen »
« Time to die »

Roads. Offices. Cars. A few people. Young, old. Male, female. A man walking his dog.

No Ed.

Ros drove like a woman possessed. Her tracker bleeped constantly. They were very close. The display showed an unmoving target.

'Wherever he is, Ed's got there,' said Beckett.

Ros didn't speak, just nodded, as if talking would waste time.

By the main entrance, Ed noticed you could walk three ways. To the left and right were stairs that led up to the next level. Straight ahead was a door that he presumed led to the actual registrar's office.

Mackenzie opened the ornate wooden door and beckoned Ed to follow.

From the outside, the building looked nothing more than functional. Its interior was much more elaborate. Smooth marble walls, polished floor and high ceiling. Mosaics on the floor. Two balconies. One above Ed and Mackenzie and the second directly opposite on the far side of the building. Pillars stretched up to the vast ceiling. In the ceiling's centre was a large, slightly flat glass dome. Coloured light shone through the stained glass. The place smelled of polish. The air was still. It was so quiet. The sort of quiet that would make you tip-toe around and talk in whispers.

'Right, Starkey. Out of here and down the corridor to your left,' said Mackenzie. 'Up to the gallery.'

'Where will you be?'

He held out the portable monitor. 'Somewhere I can keep an eye on you.'

Mackenzie headed for the other corridor. His footsteps echoed in the corridor. 'Now get a move on.'

As if Ed needed reminding. The timer read 13.50.

Ed ran up the steps two at a time to the gallery. He was looking directly over the hall. Four chairs were lined in a row and a table stood before the chairs. There was a single chair beyond the table. William and Anna hadn't invited a lot of people. Hadn't invited anyone, in fact. Must have been a spur of the moment kind of arrangement. That seemed to fit with Anna's personality. Do everything at once, as quickly and with as little fuss as possible. The way in which she had been determined to catch her would-be assassin proved it.

This was where the wedding would take place. Two chairs for the bride and groom. Two chairs for the witnesses (of which, he presumed, Corelli was one) and the chair and table for the registrar.

A man's voice in his ear startled him. Mackenzie. For a second Ed thought it was Beckett. He was too used to hearing his voice or Ros's on his head-set.

'*Get the gun out, Starkey.*'

The paper ripped open easily. Ed flicked the lock on the case inside.

Hell's teeth. The box contained some type of military issue rifle. A tiny video camera was linked up to the sights and a miniaturised transmitter had been attached to the camera.

'Don't spend too long looking for a firing position,' said Mackenzie. 'Remember: your time is limited.'

12:37.

* * *

152

Beckett jumped out of the car. The tracker bleeped frantically. He swung it in a wide arc. The display didn't change. But there was no one around. Ros had parked in front of a modern building with a tacky Georgian façade. He looked around for any signs of a church. Nothing.

They were right on top of Ed.

Either Ed had turned invisible or the tracker was going haywire. Beckett wasn't about to suggest to Ros that one of her miraculous devices was faulty.

Ros scanned the area with her own tracker. Suddenly she bent down. Beckett walked around to her side of the car.

She held out something to him. Looked like a button.

The tracker.

'Electronics, grade I,' he said. 'Sewing and needle-work, failed?'

Ros ignored the jibe. 'So where's the church then?'

There was no answer to that. Italians were all Roman Catholic, weren't they? Ed was going to the wedding to kill Anna so there had to be a church around here somewhere. Beckett wouldn't let himself consider the possibility that Ed was miles away from the button mike by now. Ros stepped away from the white building. The sun glinted on a golden plaque on one of the columns.

'We're here!' cried Beckett. Ros turned around. Beckett pointed at the plaque. 'Look.'

'Register office. Excellent. Come on,' said Ros, as she ran up the stairs to the entrance. 'It might be all over by now.'

The signal to Mackenzie's portable monitor began transmitting as soon as Starkey had opened the rifle's case. Mackenzie couldn't wander too far. The signal wasn't that strong. The monitor lit up, showing a view of the office from the balcony. Good. Starkey was in position.

There would be no failure. Not now. It was rare that

he became quite so involved with a job. Mackenzie saw himself as an administrator. His clients contacted him. He hired a pro. The job was cleanly and efficiently carried out. Everybody got paid very well.

He was treating Starkey like a trainee. A killer on a job for the first time. He had rarely spoken to the man before now. Meeting him hadn't been the pleasure Mackenzie had imagined it would be. Starkey seemed soft. The constant questions in the limo on the way to the register office had been unusual. Not like Starkey at all. Previously, all Mackenzie had to do was tell him where and Starkey would work out the rest.

And this was his fourth attempt at killing Fabrizi. If Starkey failed again, he would pay for his failure. Not only that: Mackenzie could also be in the firing line.

So it was best to keep an eye on Starkey. The video link did that perfectly. And once Fabrizi was dead, maybe – just maybe – they wouldn't kill Starkey.

Mackenzie fingered the secondary trigger for the explosives in his pocket.

After all the extra work that Starkey had caused, maybe not.

Ed's hands were becoming clammy, the gun slippery with sweat. He sat back against the wall of the balcony. There had to be some way out of this. Maybe he should try to defuse the timer. No way. He had no tools. Perhaps try and rip the waistcoat apart without breaking the circuit. No can do. He didn't know how the circuits were lined into the jacket.

Call out a warning? Possibly. No. He couldn't do that. Mackenzie or Corelli were bound to have another trigger for the plastic explosives in the jacket.

There was another choice. He could shoot Anna. All he had to do was make sure he didn't actually kill her. What was he thinking of? Maybe graze her head? Knock her unconscious? Too risky. It probably wouldn't work. Either she remained conscious which would show his failure or his aim might not be quite

154

right and he would be a murderer.

The final choice was to wait until the explosives were triggered. Yeah, right. Anna would get out alive. But with this amount of explosives in the waistcoat, even that could not be guaranteed.

Ed set the rifle so it was pointing down at Anna's chair. Doing that made it look to Mackenzie as if the gun was being aimed. Then he could go and find Mackenzie and overpower him. There were two problems with that. One: there was nothing with which the rifle could be propped. Then, two: Mackenzie could wander round, find the rifle and no Ed and decide to detonate his plastic explosive-lined waistcoat.

Ed couldn't move. He couldn't do anything.

And even if he killed Anna, he was left with little doubt that Mackenzie and Corelli would kill the man they thought was Starkey. The guy had failed before. Let people down – thankfully. Mackenzie and Corelli didn't seem like people who coped with failure very well. There seemed no way to win.

Ed peered over the wall on hearing two men talking. Swift and Corelli.

'You must be William Swift. Let me offer you my congratulations.'

The two men shook hands. Corelli all warmth and smiles. Yeah, right. And he would be the first to offer his condolences when Anna was dead.

Mackenzie: 'They're coming. *Take aim, Starkey. Show me your shot.*'

Ed looked over the balustrade. The double-doors of the main entrance to the hall swung open. Anna and another young woman strode in. Swift walked over, arms outstretched. They held each other tight and kissed.

The doors opened again. A black, middle-aged woman in a tight yellow suit stepped in. The registrar. 'This is the party for the Swift wedding?'

Anna nodded.

'If everyone could take their places?'

Ed knelt down and aimed. One bullet. That was all it would take. Pull the trigger. End a life. It was time to decide once and for all.

He wasn't going to kill Anna. He could not kill her. If there was going to be a death in the register office today, he wasn't going to be responsible for one of them. He wasn't even going to try and wound her to make it look to Corelli and Mackenzie that he had attempted to carry out the job. It was too risky.

An auburn-haired woman Ed didn't recognise walked into the hall with Anna. Ed's heart leaped into his mouth. Time was running out. Anna sat in a chair. The unfamiliar woman stood behind Anna's chair, totally blocking the bride. Ed felt jubilant. Mackenzie couldn't expect him to murder anyone who was in the line of fire, could he?

'I can't get a clear shot,' Ed hissed into his microphone.

'Whoops. Sorry. Wrong room.'

Half a dozen faces turned to Ros. Smile. Look apologetic. She closed the door gently. That was the third room they had checked. The third room of admin staff pushing papers.

And still no sign of Ed.

Beckett was already halfway down the corridor. He checked over every part of the building as they ran up a flight of stairs to a balcony.

Ros looked over the balcony. There was Swift. And that was Alberto Corelli. Both chatted happily as if they were old friends.

She looked up again. And there was Ed. On the balcony on the other side of the register office.

Ros resisted the urge to shout. She had to be careful. You never knew who could be listening. The rifle in Ed's hands was pointing down at four chairs. The padded waistcoat. Probably held enough explosives to rip the balcony apart.

Anna and Swift sat in their chairs. Gina stood behind them.

'Beckett, there's Ed.' Ros pointed over to the balcony. Ed didn't see them. He was aiming the rifle. Was he going to kill Anna?

Beckett glanced over and then turned and walked down the flight of stairs. Ros followed.

It wasn't too late.

Mackenzie looked closely at the monitor in his hands.

'It's no good.'

Starkey's voice sounded desperate. As it should be. The man's life depended on killing Fabrizi.

'She's in the way.'

Starkey was right. The woman, Fabrizi's secretary, was covering her boss's back.

A decision.

'Kill the secretary as well, if you have to. Kill them both.'

God, no.

Ed looked down the rifle sights. Mackenzie might as well trigger the explosives now. There was no way he could kill one person, never mind two.

A hand fell down on his shoulder. Ed turned. He almost dropped the rifle.

Ros and Beckett. About bloody time.

He jumped up, putting his finger to his lips. He pointed to the rifle, to the wedding guests, to the camera linked up to the rifle's sights, the explosive trigger on his wrist, the explosives in the waistcoat, showed them the timer, all the time shaking his head.

Beckett nodded his understanding and tried to calm Ed without saying a word. Beckett touched the lapel of his jacket and then pointed to his ear. They had heard everything. They knew what was going on.

Ros examined the waistcoat. She ran her fingers along the zip.

'Don't undo the zip –' Ed whispered.

Ros nodded and whispered, 'It completes a circuit. We heard.'

157

'And there's a timer.'

Ros sighed. 'We know.'

The hiss of a radio in Ed's ear: 'Is there someone there with you?'

Ed gulped. He shouldn't have relaxed with the rifle. All Mackenzie would be seeing was the floor. He had to think of an excuse. And quickly.

From the hall below Ed heard, '. . . in accordance with the . . .'

There was the answer. 'No. It's the ceremony.'

That might throw him off the scent.

With his left hand, Ed pointed the rifle carefully away from Ros and Beckett and directed it towards the floor of the hall.

He looked at the timer and wished he hadn't.

3:25.

Ros fished out a large canvas wallet from her jacket pocket. Opening it, she revealed something that looked similar to a large screwdriver. Looking at the screws on the timer, she pressed a button on its handle. The screwdriver's thin metal rod shrank into the plastic handle and became thinner. She smiled at it once it reached a certain length, less than half the original size and let go of the button.

'Handy, isn't it?' she whispered and set to work undoing the cover of the timer.

Starkey was pointing the rifle at the ceiling. What was the man thinking of? Mackenzie went for his pistol.

The voices. Not having done the job. The questions in the limo. The time wasting. The excuses. The accent. Starkey's talkativeness.

Fabrizi hadn't been the clearest shot in the world but Starkey could have killed her by now. Something was going on up in the gallery. Someone was interfering.

So the blond man wasn't Starkey? That's what his gut feeling told him. But instinct could be wrong.

Was he SSD? That didn't make sense. SSD agents didn't work alone. And Spencer had said that there was no one else around when he had picked up Starkey.

Best to check it out.

The timer was a wonderful little piece of machinery. Pity she had to take it apart.

Ros let its cover hang loosely to one side. Might as well keep track of how much time remained. But the timer was trouble. There really wasn't enough time to work out what every miniature component did. Her mind raced over the myriad possibilities as to the function of each chip.

'Go on then,' urged Ed, whispering. 'Cut the wires.'

'That's the problem. There aren't any wires.'

Ed looked down and groaned.

As well he might. There, in the corner of the black box, was the timer's power source. But it looked too exposed. Too obvious. Remove that and she might set off a booby-trap and then the balcony walls would be painted in a lovely shade of Ed, Ros and Beckett. But there would be a chip that released Ed. She had to try and remember other circuitry like this.

Come on, Ros. Think!

Beckett whispered, 'I'm going to take a look around. The signal from the camera's transmitter can't be too strong.'

He didn't sound nervous. Faith in her abilities? Possibly. More like acting the ultimate professional. Anyway, it was for the best that at least one of them was out of harm's way.

They would need someone to mop up the mess if she removed the wrong chip.

Beckett moved silently down the stairs. The marble floor made him walk slowly. He didn't want to alert anyone to his presence. He turned around. Ros stared at the opened timer. Ed looked out over the balcony.

A sound. Something brushing against the wall. Soft footsteps.

Wait. Don't leap out.

The curving of the walls meant that whoever approached wouldn't see him until it was too late.

A pistol. A hand holding the gun. Finger ready on the trigger.

Hold on a second more.

Now!

Beckett leaped out and crashed into the man with the gun. Shaved head. Dark blue-grey eyes. Nasty piece of work. Must be Mackenzie.

He had to push him against the wall. Wrestle the gun off him. He smacked Mackenzie's head against the marble. It didn't seem to have any effect.

No. Mackenzie couldn't push back.

Beckett's footsteps faltered. The bald man was pushing him up the stairs. He had got the better momentum. The gun was pointed at the ceiling. Beckett couldn't let it go off. It would alert Corelli. Anna would be at risk.

Beckett grabbed hold of Mackenzie's left hand and his right wrist. But Mackenzie still pushed Beckett down to the floor. Where did the guy's strength come from? Beckett knew that if he fell on the floor then Ed, Ros and Anna were as good as dead.

He turned his head for a second. Ros ignored the fight. Ed looked over, anguish on his face, unable to do anything.

Beckett couldn't let go of Mackenzie. He had to push him back. Twist him. He forced himself to relax for a second. Make Mackenzie think he had won.

The bald man fell for the oldest trick in the book. Beckett gave one massive amount of effort and pushed.

Yes. There was a look of total surprise on Mackenzie's face as he was forced backwards. They both stumbled over to the balcony and smacked into the balustrade. Mackenzie turned and kicked Beckett's legs from under him.

The ceiling swung into view. Beckett was underneath Mackenzie and was slowly pushed closer to the edge of the balcony. Either or both of them could fall any second.

Mackenzie suddenly let go – but only for an instant. *Stranglehold. Can't breathe. Confused. Don't panic.*

Mackenzie kept pushing. Beckett felt himself slide on the smooth marble.

Mackenzie was winning.

Beckett got a grip on Mackenzie's jacket. He didn't want to do this. Mackenzie knew what was about to happen. It was in his eyes. Beckett didn't want to do this. But Mackenzie wouldn't let go.

Greyness slowly started to fill Beckett's vision.

Beckett wanted to plead with him to let go, but he couldn't speak. There was no time now. Beckett bent a leg up to Mackenzie's chest.

Don't want to do this. Mackenzie's eyes. *He knows he's lost.* Disbelief.

Pushing Mackenzie over was a risk.

Beckett pushed his knee on Mackenzie's chest. He lifted up. Beckett couldn't support the man's weight and felt his knee falling back down but also forward. Too far forward. Mackenzie couldn't not fall.

Mackenzie suddenly and inexplicably let go.

He fell silently. He twisted in mid-air, looked up, his mouth wide open in surprise.

His body hit the floor with a dull thud.

A scream filled the hall.

Now for Corelli.

'Anna!' shouted Ed. 'Corelli's the one trying to kill you!'

Everyone turned and looked up at the balcony.

What? Alberto?

Anna felt herself being pulled away from William's side. Alberto. There was a gun in his hand. They stepped away from William.

William moved forward. Alberto waved the gun at him. William stopped.

'Alberto! What are you doing?'

161

'Teaching you a lesson. Honesty never pays.'

The years they had worked together. Building the party up into the most popular Italy had seen for decades. Bringing all the different ideologies together. Asking Italy to trust them. Wanting to lead the country in one direction with everyone believing. All for nothing. Alberto was behind it all. The death threats. The assassination attempts. Alberto.

How could she have been so blind? So stupid?

Belief. Trust. Double-edged swords. So easy to betray another.

Where were they going? Why had Alberto left it until now? An assassin could have done his job any time over the last six months.

Political mileage. Obvious. The death of a popular party leader just before an election. It would win a lot of votes. Smart.

Doors were banged open. Wence strode in.

'Alberto Corelli. Let Miss Fabrizi go.'

Agents ran from all sides of the hall, rifles pointed at Corelli.

Corelli. Her friend. Her most trusted colleague. The man who shared her dreams and hopes.

'Let me get away,' he cried. 'Or Anna dies.'

All for nothing. All that work. *Bastard.*

'Open fire!' she shouted. 'Kill him!'

A stand-off.

Ed lifted his rifle and aimed.

Corelli and Anna stood still. Corelli's gun stabbed into her neck.

Operatives, both standing and kneeling, waited for the order to fire.

Wence was under the balcony. Ed could hear him but not see him.

But Corelli. A clear shot. Easy to wound. No danger to Anna at all.

'I can do this,' he said to Ros.

Ros pulled his right arm down. The timer's cover

gently tapped the leather jacket. 'But I can't do this if you move.'

'I just need a few seconds.'

'You haven't got them.'

A quick glance: 0:06.

'Give me safe passage out of here,' called Corelli. 'Don't make her into a martyr.'

One shot.

Now or never again.

The rifle recoiled. Just one shot. It had to be enough.

Ros had the screwdriver in the timer's mechanism. She prised a chip out.

0:01.

Corelli fell to the floor clutching his shoulder. The gun dropped out of his hand. Anna ran over to William and wrapped her arms around him. The SSD mob swarmed around Corelli.

0:01.

0:01.

0:01.

Thank God. Ros had done it.

Ed turned to see her smiling face. He ripped off the timer and started to undo the waistcoat. A few kilos of plastic explosive weren't his idea of a fashion accessory.

'Took you long enough to work out which chip to remove, Ros.'

'Who worked it out? I guessed.'

Bloody hell!

There was a dead man on the floor. Corelli lay wounded, moaning incoherently. Wence and his men formed a circle round him.

'Get a paramedic team here! Now!' snapped Wence.

Gina sat crying in a chair being consoled by the registrar.

And Anna. His precious Anna. William held her so tight. He didn't think he would ever let her go.

That she could have died. So close. Too close.

William Swift would become her shadow. He would

follow her everywhere. Her husband and protector. It was a surprising feeling, wanting to reach out and love someone so totally. Suddenly he appreciated how valuable life was, and he just wanted to live it.

'I love you, Anna Fabrizi.'

She didn't respond. She didn't have to. Her head lay on his chest.

'Excuse me?' The registrar. 'How are you?' she asked.

Anna looked up at her. 'We'll be fine.' She smiled. Swift's heart was fit to burst.

'I know this hardly seems fitting with all this.' The registrar, looking appalled, pointed at the dead man and Corelli. 'But I was about to give my congratulations now that you are husband and wife.' The woman shook her head, then turned and walked away.

Anna said nothing. What was there to say? After all this was over, they were a thousand miles away from all this, then there would be time to celebrate.

« Fourteen »
« The joy circuit »

Round and round and round he goes. Where he stops, nobody knows.

The engine roared. The test car's shell vibrated. Ed's hands shook on the steering wheel. The noise from the engine was incredible. At least the suspension system gave a smooth ride. But this bucket on wheels wasn't a car. Cars were something you enjoyed, felt liberated in. In a car you could taste freedom. All he needed was an open road, good music playing on a cool stereo, beautiful scenery, best friends sharing the journey. This thing was a prison. Shouldn't driving the best in automotive technology be exciting? Shouldn't they be putting the car to the test instead of driving around on the most boring roads in the country? And at a steady 85 kph?

Cray had given Ed the quietest, simplest route imaginable. There wasn't much traffic. Ed had never been so bored in his whole life.

It was wet. The clouds were grey. The world seemed as dead as he felt.

This was embarrassing. Ed had driven everything from a stock car to a helicopter and had jumped at the chance to drive the test car. But did it have to look like a hunk of junk in a style that had been abandoned a decade ago?

Shouldn't they be testing the wind resistance? Well,

not really, Ed reminded himself. Not since the Trancer shell had been stolen. That was a cheery thought. O'Neill must be browned off to have had his baby stolen. And misery always loved company. If Ed had to put up with the monotony of this drive, he was glad that someone else was feeling as bad.

Ros had asked for no radio contact unless unavoidable. Terminal boredom was kicking in. It had become unavoidable. Even over the din from the engine he had to talk to someone. Thank heaven for their head-sets.

The rear-view mirror moved slightly as he checked for Beckett. Beckett's Jeep kept a constant distance from him.

'I hope I don't see anyone I know. How did I fall for this?'

Beckett answered. Ed could hear the smile in his voice. 'You volunteered.'

That just made it worse. 'I should have gone for the shadow car. At least that sounds sexy.'

Ros joined in the conversation.

'Is this what we call minimal radio contact?'

Time to protest. 'I'm bored out of my skull here, Ros. The seventh circle of hell is a place where you drive round forever and never arrive.'

Silence. Not a jot of sympathy from either partner.

The car turned another corner into yet another stretch of empty road. If Ed didn't get out soon, he would go out of his head.

'Keep going,' said Ros. 'You'll see a roadside tea-shop in about four kilometres. Stop there and switch off the engine for fifteen minutes.'

'Can I get out?' It was more than a question. Ed was begging for merciful release.

'Sure thing.'

Ed kissed the head-set's mouthpiece. Ros laughed.

'Just don't take your eyes off the goods.'

The way he felt, Ed didn't care if he never saw the thing again.

* * *

The café was by a village green. A statue of some local dead dignitary. A few benches. Red telephone box. No traffic about. All very quaint. All very Middle England. Looked like it hadn't changed for the past few decades. A street of small shops a hundred metres away. Wooden signs above each shop. Probably selling ye olde worlde tack.

Beckett pulled up by the test car. If you didn't look too closely at it, it wasn't that bad. And with all the technology inside, surely it handled well?

Ed stepped out of the car. He looked in need of something stronger than a cup of tea.

'So what's it like?' asked Beckett.

'What's what like?'

'The car.'

Ed shrugged, then removed and pocketed his headset. 'It's OK. I guess.'

So, the result of the jury on the most technologically advanced car in the world was 'It's OK. I guess.'

The café smelled of fresh coffee, bread and polish. Wood panelling everywhere. Wooden tables and seats. Two lads tucked into a full breakfast at a table by the window. Beckett looked for the waitress.

'Plasma cages, eh?' Ed whispered. 'What else do you suppose they get up to in that place?'

Beckett pulled up a chair. 'I'm not sure I want to know. Whatever else O'Neill's working on has nothing to do with us. Sometimes, ignorance is bliss.'

'I mean, weapons are worth being secretive about. But military vehicles. Aren't they just wheelbarrows without the comfort?'

'That depends on what or who they carry.'

A blue van pulled up alongside the test car, almost obscuring it from Beckett's view.

He tapped Ed on the arm. 'Hey.'

Ed looked out of the window. 'Nah. No worries. We're OK.'

Maybe Ed was right. But some instinct was kicking

in. A gut feeling. Or maybe it was paranoia? As long as he had his eyes on the car, it should be OK.

The waitress arrived. Blonde in obligatory black and whites. 'What can I get you?' Her pen was ready at her notebook.

'Just two coffees, please.'

She smiled and snapped her notebook shut. 'Fine. Back in two ticks.'

'So what did you reckon to O'Neill's client – the man in black?' asked Ed.

Beckett didn't take his eyes off the car. 'Major Cardenas looked like a nasty bit of work and I'm going to do my best not to bump into him again.'

'And that car. What a noise.'

Ed was interrupted by the arrival of the two coffees.

'Anything else?' asked the waitress.

'Just the bill, please. We don't have very long.'

Knife. Rear windshield. Rubber seal.

Sarita smiled. Too easy.

All Davina had to do was keep the driver and his shadow occupied in the tea-shop while she broke into the car.

She slapped two large hand grips on to the windshield, leaned against the car and cut quickly around the seal. She had to hurry. The two blokes could come out of the café at any second and catch her red-handed. Or a passerby could stop her.

The windshield fell in slightly. Sarita grabbed the grips and heaved the windshield from its setting. Damn, but it was heavy.

Windshield on the ground, Sarita dived into the back of the car. They couldn't park the van right alongside the car. Couldn't obscure it totally. That would have been too suspicious. She kept low and out of the way of the car's front side windows that were visible from the café.

Sarita tapped her jacket pockets. Where was that tape machine? Got it. Camera? Good.

Right. It was time to pilfer all of the Trancer's secrets.

Davina had been surprised that Mrs Pearce had been convinced by Sarita. Apparently, her house smelled of joss-sticks and joints. Strange paintings hung from the walls and dried flowers stood in a multitude of ceramic pots. Classical music blasted out of an ancient stereo. But Sarita had said that the woman wasn't as mad as she had seemed.

Mrs Pearce had wanted to help as much as she possibly could with the *investigation*. A criminal using her tea-shop as a rendezvous? Whatever next? Sarita had obtained the keys and the code for the café's alarm. She had said she felt a little guilty about duping Mrs Pearce, but needs must when the devil drove. Davina had volunteered to pretend to be the waitress.

Mrs Pearce had taken some convincing, apparently, not to directly involve herself with their plan. And there was her 'criminal'. The blond driver of Tronix's test car, sipping coffee with another dark-haired man. It was strange and worrying that duplicity seemed to come so easily to the both of them.

Sarita pulled the coverings from the instrumentation on the dashboard. There was enough light. Her automatic camera wouldn't flash. She started taking one photo after another.

The dashboard looked ultra-modern. It would take time to work out every function embedded into it but Bob would help out there.

She held the tape machine to her mouth.

'It looks like it has a fully automatic gearbox with touch selection. The handbrake includes a transmission lock. The rearview mirrors all self-adjust to the driver's eye-line. There's nowhere for an ignition key. It could be a code system. No. It's thumbprint recognition. I'll get a close shot and then I'll fully dismantle the dash.'

* * *

169

The fifteen minute break had allowed Ros to get a cup of coffee. The computer could start analysing all the data it had received from the test car.

Cray could have monitored Ed's progress in the car. It was all on Tronix's computers after all, but Ros had wanted to try out their system. She saw it as another toy to play with.

Cray and O'Neill hovered behind her, chatting quietly to themselves. The office, like the rest of Tronix, was immaculate. Clear surfaces. Gleaming white walls.

The computer screen showed nothing moving. The temperature reading slowly reverted to its normal setting. The graphics along the top of the screen had all levelled out.

Except one.

Using the mouse, Ros clicked on the image. The screen filled with a three-dimensional drawing of the suspension system.

The computer was registering movement. The rear suspension was rising gently up and down.

'Beckett,' she asked into her head-piece, 'what's happening with the car?'

'*Nothing.*'

'So what's making the suspension bounce?'

Beckett froze. His coffee cup was at his lips.

The gut feeling had been right. Someone was messing about with the car. Could be kids. But he would have heard them.

There was no one in the car. Not as far as he could see.

A flash.

A camera flash. Someone taking pictures inside the car.

Time to leave.

Ed looked up at him. His look of confusion was replaced immediately by one of determination when he caught Beckett's sour expression.

'Trouble?' Ed asked.

170

Beckett didn't answer. Get out the door. Sneak up on the photographer. Not professional using a flash. Catch them. Find out who the amateur was working for.

The waitress walked from the café door and headed for the kitchen. Good. Stay out of the way.

The door was locked. Beckett shook it violently.

What?

Beckett turned to the waitress. 'Hey, miss –'

She turned to look at him. Gone was the smiling waitress, replaced by a hard-looking woman. She flashed a sardonic smile.

A trap. They had fallen into a trap. But how could the waitress have known about the car?

The woman turned away and then stopped by a red box suspended halfway up the wall. The fire alarm. The waitress smashed the glass cover. A siren blared. A good signal for her partner from the blue van. He really should trust his instincts more.

The waitress ran into the kitchen. Beckett wasn't about to let her escape. He and Ed had to get out and stop whoever was in the car.

The café's kitchen was narrow and long. No sign of the dummy waitress.

The back door was unlocked. It led into the street. Beckett looked left then right. She'd disappeared. How?

He had to check on the car. They dashed around to the front of the building. Still there, but the rear windshield was on the pavement. A dark-haired woman jumped into the van through its side door and slammed it shut.

She had trapped herself. They ran to the side of the car and Ed quickly let the air out of the van's rear tyres.

Ed straightened up and banged on the side of the van. 'Come on. You're going nowhere. Come out and let's get a look at you.'

'Back doors, Ed.'

Ed nodded but stayed where he was. Two of them. Two exits.

171

A sound came from inside the van. Something shuffling. What was she up to?

The rear van doors burst open. Beckett leaped backwards. A motorbike flew into the air. Ed would have a better idea of what make. Some sort of scrambler? It looked pretty lightweight.

The rider skidded the bike in a circle and stopped by the café's kitchen entrance. Her helmet concealed her face. Another helmet rested on the handlebars. For her waitress friend?

And there she was, leaping on to the back of the bike, and grabbing the helmet. Where had she hidden? Didn't matter. The women sped off.

Beckett picked himself up and dusted himself down. He ran round to the side of the van.

Where had Ed gone?

The test car. Its ignition fired. The engine roared. Beckett turned to see the car race after the motorbike.

'Ed!'

It was pointless shouting. Old gung-ho Ed was at it again. Beckett could imagine Ros's face back at Tronix. And O'Neill's.

Well, there was no choice. He just had to go after the lot of them.

The computer read-outs were going wild.

Ros stared at the screen. O'Neill and Cray stood behind her, looking over her shoulder.

The car was seriously in motion. This wasn't the same terrain as before. This wasn't even part of the test route. The car was being driven over rough terrain, and at vastly varying speeds. The car twisted, rose and fell. Was it going over a field? Had to be. Had Ed gone mad? OK, so the job wasn't the most exciting ever but from the data displayed on the screen, it looked as if Ed was going AWOL with the car.

Unless, of course, it wasn't Ed. That was even more worrying. Someone had taken control of the car. That wasn't right. The test car could only be driven by three people: O'Neill, Cray and Ed. Their thumbprints were the only prints that the car recognised. You couldn't start the car without a recognised thumbprint.

What happened if you chopped someone's thumb off? Would the car recognise a thumbprint then? Maybe it was best not to think like that.

This was more like it! This was what he called driving.

Ed was off the beaten track – literally. The motorbike had driven through an open gate and he swerved the car in pursuit. He could feel the car's power. Yes, the frame was shaking, rattling, doing everything a car shouldn't do and the noise was terrible but with his hands firmly on the steering wheel, he suddenly felt the tremendous power contained within the test car.

If he didn't know better, he would say the car was being run into the ground. But not the Trancer.

The test route wasn't a test. It wasn't even an hors d'oeuvre. This was how the boys at Tronix R&D should have tested the car. Pushing it to its limits. Seeing what it could really do.

Oh, the power. Ed knew he had barely begun to scratch the surface in discovering what this car could do.

Nothing could get away from him. Certainly not the two amateurs on their flimsy scrambler.

'Ed? What are you doing?'

Ros. She didn't have to worry. He could more than handle the test car. This was wonderful. The sort of experience he lived for. What made life worth living. Racing across green and pleasant land. OK, so he was tearing up the countryside a little. Hell. Nature would look after itself.

'It's lightning time!' he shouted into the head-piece. 'Clear those decks and call me Captain Speedy!'

He was getting closer to the bike. A couple of minutes more and he would have them. Break into this little darling of a machine, would they? Those who crossed the path of Captain Speedy lived to regret it.

The bike sped down a path. The women were trying to make for another open gate. He would intercept them at the gate. Maybe.

'Yes! Yes!' he shouted. 'You cannot run! You will be mine!'

Ed put his foot down. The car was swinging a little erratically over the damp earth. Nothing he couldn't handle.

He flicked a switch on the dashboard and the side windows slowly retracted. The wind ran through his hair. That and chasing two women in the greatest car the country had ever seen. What more could a man want?

Maybe a little less sexism, said a little voice in his head.

'There's no point in trying to run!' he yelled, ignoring his little voice. 'You're being chased by the Prince of Pursuit! The King of the Car!'

The scrambler made it through the gate before he could reach them. They turned a corner. A mud track. Great for scrambling. And no problem at all for the Trancer.

'And I love a bit of mud!'

Music. That was what he needed. Something classical blasting out. He looked down at the dashboard and wondered which of the peculiar devices was the stereo.

It was all right for Ed. Going bananas in the test car, miles away from Tronix HQ. Yeah, fine. Ros had the Tronix MD and his technical director breathing down her neck.

Cray stood by her side, silently watching the rapid changes in the information relayed by the test car. O'Neill was standing too close to her for comfort. He leaned by her computer. It wasn't good to be so near to him. He put you on edge. And he was wearing nasty deodorant.

'Your boy's an idiot,' he said.

174

'I know.'

Ros spoke into the head-set. 'Ed, for God's sake, don't wreck the prototype.'

He was driving like a lunatic. All over the place. Skidding everywhere. Taking corners at speeds that made her shiver. Make a mental note: never, ever let Ed drive you anywhere. If you are incapacitated in any way at all, do not accept a lift from him.

'Don't worry,' said Cray quietly. 'He *can't* wreck it.'

Now what was that supposed to mean?

Sarita hadn't got enough information from the Trancer. A few pictures and a few hurriedly spoken words into her tape machine weren't going to be enough for Bob.

And the test car was catching up with them.

On her own, she could have weaved the bike through the trees. It was light and easily manoeuvrable but with a passenger weighing it down she had to stick to the dirt track. And speed was becoming a problem. The scrambler wasn't designed for two riders.

Sarita looked at the mud-splattered rear-view mirror on the handlebar. The car was right behind them. Damn it to hell! And she couldn't increase her speed.

They had planned for every eventuality. She knew they were definitely getting better at the espionage business. Except now they were being chased by a rather formidable vehicle. Hadn't foreseen that, had she?

She was not about to give in. The test car might be nudging the rear wheel but she wasn't finished yet.

The bike turned another corner. Keeping control of the bike at that speed was becoming more and more of a fight. The test car was moving in even closer.

They had been quite daring so far. Stealing the car from under O'Neill's nose was audacious to say the least. And they were becoming more ruthless, much more determined. Nothing would stand in their way.

That wasn't a good sign. No compassion. No consideration for other people. Just like Uncle Dave.

The next mile was straight dirt track. Trees along both sides. An opening on to a tarmacked road ran from the track on the right. On a straight track, the car would soon reach them. No problem. It could outstrip the scrambler in almost every department. She had to accelerate. No good. On a bigger machine maybe they would have outrun the car. Even that was unlikely.

Sarita checked how far behind the car was.

Suddenly, it wasn't there. That couldn't be right. The car had vanished.

She slowed the bike to a stop. It couldn't have disappeared.

A trap? Had to be. Maybe the car had joined the main road. But what good was that? The road led away from the field.

Sarita revved the bike. What was the use of worrying about it? They'd escaped, hadn't they?

Ed had almost had them. A minute more and they would have been his. That was all he had needed.

Then all hell had broken loose.

No. That was not the way it felt. The complete opposite, in fact. He had been driving like a bat out of hell. Ed had the skill to handle any motor. That wasn't arrogance.

But, somehow, he had lost control of the car.

The car slowed down to an infuriating forty kph, and refused to respond when he put his foot down on the accelerator. He tried the brake. Nothing. The steering wheel spun uselessly in his hands. All illumination on the dashboard blinked off. But the car was still moving. It turned a corner on the dirt track, then took a right onto a tarmacked road. Like the thing was driving itself.

The car took another right. Unbelievably, it was doubling back towards the tea-shop.

'Ros. Something's wrong.'

176

'What are you doing now, Ed?'

'I'm not doing anything. That's the problem. The car's driving itself.'

Cray picked up a head-set and slipped it on. It was time for some explanations.

He looked over at O'Neill. The man was impassive, though it wasn't hard to guess what he was feeling or thinking. Ed's impromptu drive was excellent for obtaining good solid data.

But things were travelling too fast and too far. The car was the only prototype they had, after all. Heaven knew in what sort of state Ed would bring back the car.

'Excuse me, Ros. I need to show you something.' Cray gestured at the computer. 'If I may?'

Ros pushed her seat away from the computer terminal. Cray flexed his fingers and then tapped one instruction in after another, accessing parts of the operating system that only he and O'Neill were authorised to use.

The image on the screen of the Trancer and the read-outs of the data from the car disappeared. For a second, the screen went blank.

Four images suddenly appeared, one in each corner of the screen. They changed constantly but not randomly. That was good. The system was functioning perfectly.

Ros stared hard at the new pictures. 'That's the view from each side of the car, isn't it?'

Cray was impressed. She was very quick. The garish multi-coloured images took some getting used to. 'Well, to be accurate, that's a representation of what the car sees. It only looks that way to our eyes.'

He hoped Ros would be surprised by the system. It was an odd thought but, from their meeting yesterday and that afternoon, he had learned that Ros knew a damn sight more about computers than he. The old adage 'forgotten more than you've learned' came to mind.

Trancer. From the word 'trance' meaning a condition

of intense euphoria and triumph. And they had triumphed. The system had taken years to perfect. Once, it was only something to dream about. Tronix had made it a reality.

The Trancer was a car that could see. A car that could sense where it was. He could see in Ros's face that her mind was working overtime on the concept.

'And Ed doesn't have to do anything but sit back and let the car do the work.' Cray knew the headstrong Australian would be listening.

'He's triggered the passive safety system,' Cray continued. 'The Trancer is a car that you can't drive recklessly. If you do, it takes over.'

Ros stared at the computer screen. O'Neill looked on disapprovingly. Well, if they had told Beckett's team about the passive safety system then none of this would have happened.

Cray was proud that he had worked on such a project. And it was good to be able to tell someone what they had been doing for the last few years. He knew for a fact that their rivals were working on nothing like this. Tronix had their spies in other camps. But maybe it was best not to let Ros in on the fact that Tronix were at least as bad as their competitors.

'The car can sense its surroundings and read the road ahead,' said Ros. Not a question but a statement.

'Correct,' said Cray. 'That's what makes it so special. Link that to a routemaster program, feed it with updated traffic information, and we're talking about one hundred per cent accident-free motoring within the next ten years.'

Ed felt sick. He was totally useless sitting behind the driving wheel. The car was doing what it wanted to do. Nothing he attempted would rectify that situation. Unless, of course, he turned off the passive safety system.

The woman who had broken into the car had removed all the covers on the dashboard. He was wary of taking his eyes away from the road. Hell.

He wasn't driving. Fighting his instinct, Ed took a closer look at the dash.

All the screens were dead. Presumably, as the driver had suddenly been transferred to passenger status, he or she didn't need to be told what was happening to the car.

'How do I turn the safety system off?' he asked.

'You can't,' Ros answered.

Cray joined in. 'It has a default setting which automatically guides it back to a preset point. In the case of the test car, that means right back to the lab. Just sit back and enjoy the ride. We'll meet you down there.'

Sit back and enjoy the ride? What was that guy on? He should read a book, maybe? A bit of bird watching, perhaps? Catch up with some paperwork? Ed hated being a passenger when someone else was driving. How could he relax when the car was doing the driving?

'Is this what the girls are trying to get hold of?'

'It's what everyone's trying to get hold of,' answered Cray.

The mud-spattered Trancer drove slowly into the bay and stopped. O'Neill could have cried.

His little baby. His dream come true. Treated as if it were nothing more than a cross-country rally motor.

Technicians in white coveralls moved up and down the car. They scanned every inch of the vehicle. Perhaps he should know what they did exactly. The equipment they used was becoming more bizarre every day. Nah. That was Cray's department.

The car was a mess. Mud everywhere. And if the engine wasn't in exactly the same condition as when it left the building, that Aussie idiot was looking at a couple of broken ribs and a pretty huge repair bill.

Beckett's team had to go. They made O'Neill nervous. He needed people who would check over the place and keep an eye on the car. If they saw anything they shouldn't, they would leave well alone, keep their mouths shut and not poke around. This lot wouldn't do that. Too inquisitive.

Beckett, he could relate to. A professional. Hard working. But still a bit of a wild card. Neither was he back at the bay.

Ros looked the car up and down. Now, she knew her stuff. Computers, security, the works. She had a look in her eyes, as if she would never let something go if she got her teeth into it. Like yesterday afternoon. What did she think of that? The plasma cage was pretty heavy security. She had not said anything to either him or Cray about it. O'Neill wasn't the best person to judge – he knew he had all the sensitivity of a brick – but there was a definite feeling of distrust. He didn't need someone with a conscience.

The blond Australian, Ed, stepped out of the car. He seemed a little shaky from the drive back to the bay. What a grade-A prat. Could've done himself a lot of damage driving like that. More importantly, something might have happened to the car. With people like that around, who needed industrial spies to ruin Tronix?

Ed pointed at the car. 'That's going to take a lot of getting used to.'

'Don't worry about having to,' snapped O'Neill. 'You're all fired.'

Ros and Ed spun round to face him. Even Cray was surprised by the announcement. Tut-tut. Cray should know the way it worked there. He had been with Tronix long enough. You botched things up and you were out on your backside.

'Wait a minute –' said Ros.

'No. You wait a minute, darling. After last night's escapade and now this? I thought I was hiring people I could rely on.'

'Trust is a two-way business, Mr O'Neill,' Ros replied. The way she spoke was good, too. She wasn't afraid of him. So many people were.

'You sent us out there with less than half the story but we still did the job that you hired us to do, Mr O'Neill. If things change and we have to improvise, we improvise. Look. We kept your investment intact and the egg off your face.'

Improvise?! They almost lost the car and they call it *improvising*? 'Only by luck did your boy manage to keep hold of the car!'

'Luck? Mr O'Neill, if Ed hadn't –'

Beckett arrived. 'Hang on a minute! Hang on!'

Ros and O'Neill shut up.

'You didn't give us the schedule for the drive until this afternoon,' he said. 'Yet you must have planned this days ago, right? Those women knew exactly where we'd be. Every piece of electrical equipment in this building needs to be checked, Mr O'Neill. You've got a leak. And you need us to find it.'

What? A leak in this place? It couldn't be true, but it did make sense. This time, heads were going to roll in Security.

But if his own staff were about as much use as a dog in a desert then there was no choice. He had to use the three youngsters staring right at him. And they knew it.

He hated being put in this position.

OK. They could carry on.

But if they fouled up again, heaven help them.

« Fifteen »

« Tricks »

The hired help had split up.

Cray smiled. It wasn't fair to call them that.

Cray's office was one of the few in the building that wasn't open plan. No glaring white walls with light that flooded the rest of the building for him. Subdued, restful half-light. A retreat from everyday tribulations. Another day, another problem. The blinds were shut and the walls sound-proofed. Peace at last. Or at least the pretence of it.

The team certainly didn't believe in wasting time. Ed and Beckett had gone over to check out the car labs. He and Ros were checking the offices. He didn't really need to be there but it was good to watch Ros work. And he was trying to pluck up the courage to ask her out. There had been no indication that she was even remotely interested. Still, he had the rest of the day.

There was no doubt in Cray's mind that Beckett and Ros were the technical experts in the team. Ed was the vehicle expert and quite the fish out of water with the security stuff. The way Ed handled the test car was nothing short of masterly. Plenty of hard data for the lads in Development to play with. But Ed was not in the same league as the other two when it came to checking security.

There had been no luck in tracing the owner of the

van. The car's licence number wasn't registered. Judging by their actions so far, the two women could hack into the vehicle registration computer and remove any incriminating evidence.

O'Neill was with Major Cardenas. The boss wasn't happy being caught out by Beckett. O'Neill wasn't the sort of man who would back down even when wrong. The team had crossed him and made an enemy. But they would not – luckily for them – be around for much longer. They should check the security system and then get out of the place without looking back as quickly as possible. O'Neill was getting himself into deep water.

And, like an idiot, Paul Cray, you're still around.

Some people, including him, knew too much about certain generations at Tronix and would find it difficult to leave on good terms. The thought of being stuck there indefinitely was not a cheery one. The money was good. Really good. But how long was that money going to last?

The Major's men were out testing one of their machines. The trucks were truly terrifying. In the wrong hands, they would be lethal. And the Major irrefutably felt like the wrong hands. One scary man. And his cronies were almost as bad. Cardenas termed them technicians. A nice, harmless title. They were as much technicians as he was a humpback whale. Those black uniforms. Whatever military they came from . . .

No. Don't think about it. The stress level in this place went through the roof months ago. There was no need to add more.

O'Neill said it was best to keep an eye on Ros. He didn't need asking twice. As well as having the pleasure of her company, it also meant not hanging around with Cardenas. And that was just fine. Two thousand miles away from that man was not far enough.

Ros worked at his computer terminal. She had

laughed when he gave her the passwords necessary to access certain parts of the security program.

She was checking the security layout of Tronix. She examined the connections of the security cameras, the infra-red beams located at strategic points inside and outside the building. She could be there a long time. Tronix was not a small place.

'What's he like to work for?' Ros asked.

There was only one answer. 'Very tough. He came up the hard way.'

From nothing to self-made millionaire. A regular working-class hero. The media had loved him. Articles in every Sunday newspaper, regular interviews in the car mags, all that sort of thing. But that didn't happen any more. O'Neill was heading on a downward spiral. Very few people knew that fact. Not even the investors.

'So he's made a lot of enemies?'

It was true that O'Neill had stepped over a few people. Crushed a few more. There were even rumours of how he had removed a couple of people permanently. But they were just rumours, ones that O'Neill did nothing to disprove. It built him a reputation of being a hard nut, which he was. No doubt about that. And, anyway, you didn't succeed without treading on a few toes in life.

'His enemies aren't half as scary as some of his friends.'

Ros didn't take her eyes away from the computer screen. 'I can take from that you mean Major Cardenas?'

Cray checked the door to make sure no one could hear. He shouldn't be talking about this. O'Neill would have a fit if he found out. 'Look Ros, we developed the passive safety system for military use and we fit them for all kinds of clients.'

'But why take these jobs on at all? I mean, if dealing with these people makes everyone so nervous?'

It was a good question. Ros had probably worked out why already, just wanted him to confirm it. 'Money. We're desperate for cashflow.'

And, boy, was Major Cardenas paying for those trucks.

Tiny blue lights from the computer screen danced in Ros's jet black eyes. 'But the Trancer must be worth an absolute fortune.'

'In the long run, yes. But we're taking huge losses on development. The boss is making deals with the devil just to keep us going.'

The military division. The annexe to the main building. No one had told Beckett that the place was out of bounds. O'Neill might have been reluctant but he had finally agreed to a full security sweep. He and Ed had found nothing in the car labs. Ed decided to look for Ros.

When O'Neill had permitted a full sweep of Tronix Ltd, Beckett decided that meant checking the military division.

The spotlights in the annexe were moving with their peculiar motion. Five of the eight bays were occupied by covered machines. There had been six vehicles. One of them was being used. But for what? Didn't matter. It was nothing to do with him. He really, really didn't care. He had to keep reminding himself that. He didn't care. If you found yourself on the wrong side of a dodgy military outfit, heaven knew how long you would live. Probably not for long. So why was he checking over the annexe?

Just check the phones and the cameras. Get out of there as quickly as possible. He didn't want to run into the Major.

The vehicles were covered but he still felt their presence. Military vehicles. Heavy duty. Massive and very, very threatening. Being in the same room as them was disquieting. Beckett found it difficult to keep his attention on the job.

Right. Skirting board. Junction box. Grey. He opened it. Nothing unexpected there. Basic electrical cabling. Nothing being interfered with. The two women hadn't broken into that. But they had broken in somehow.

Beckett checked the phone and took its back off. Nothing unusual in there, either. Nothing that didn't fit in with the rest of the circuitry.

He hoped that was the only phone. The other, Ros had fried. There were an awful lot of security cameras. Did the building need that level of security? There were, admittedly, plenty of reasons to be paranoid in this world. Someone, somewhere was probably watching you. Keeping tabs. Maybe just as a name on a computer, or only a bank account number. Possibly more. A high street camera watching you walk down the street or a government operative keeping track of your movements. Not the healthiest way to live but, Mr O'Neill, ten cameras in one room? That was excessive.

Beckett had the feeling that whatever O'Neill was up to with the Major and those machines, it had to be very illegal. He caught himself. He was doing it again. Worrying about something that was most certainly not his concern.

From across the large room came a hiss of hydraulics starting up. The door to the annexe slowly rose. It had to be the missing vehicle.

'Take it carefully, now.' O'Neill's voice.

It was best to hide. A pillar. From behind there Beckett would be out of O'Neill's direct line of sight.

There was a strange humming noise and the sound of five – maybe six – sets of footsteps.

There was O'Neill. And there was Cardenas. He and his little band of helpers were dressed from top to toe in black. Cardenas wore a black baseball cap. It was one of the few ways to distinguish him from the rest. All his men were tall and well built.

And there was the machine that O'Neill was so protective about. Not quite as big as a normal truck but ten times more threatening.

The shell of the vehicle was strange, as if it had been made from a mould. Thick, unreflective steel.

186

Bullet-proof. Bomb-proof. Missile-proof? It would take a serious amount of power to even scratch its surface. Its dozen huge black wheels partially covered by its massive frame. No windows. That was scariest of all. A blind machine. Where the windscreen should have been was a solid sheet of steel. Probably reinforced steel at that. The driver would navigate by using monitors inside the machine. So there had to be at least one camera on its body. Now there was a weakness. If somebody shot the camera out it made the vehicle worse than useless.

Wonder what it carried?

The vehicle reversed into a bay. O'Neill lifted his hand onto a pillar. Cardenas stood, watching him closely. As before, Beckett saw a panel in the pillar light up. And, again as before, thick green beams of light suddenly surrounded the vehicle. The plasma cage. Impenetrable. The pulsating thrum of the beam's power source filled the dark chamber.

One of Cardenas's underlings handed O'Neill something to sign. He scribbled on it for a second and handed it back.

'Your unit will be completely safe with us,' said O'Neill. 'I'd stake my life on it.'

It was difficult to hear what O'Neill was saying but he could just be heard.

'You already have,' the Major replied.

O'Neill looked up at Cardenas. There was at least one foot in height difference between them. O'Neill's face was made uglier by the reflection of the green light on his pale skin. His eyes were wide open. Now there was a frightened man who suddenly looked very human and vulnerable. The arrogant son of a bitch was eating a lot of humble pie around these people.

O'Neill wasn't calling the shots. He didn't know how to deal with suspect military outfits. It was like playing Russian roulette. You were never quite sure if a bullet was aimed at your head.

And maybe it was the same for Ros, Ed and him.

Maybe, for the first time, they – like O'Neill – were completely out of their depth.

It had taken a while sitting at Cray's computer, digging around the security system, but Ros finally found the source of the leak. She couldn't believe it. The two women had the cheek of the devil. Not only had they broken into one of the most secure premises Ros had come across but the women had tapped the phone line directly from Cray's office.

The skirting board had come away all too easily. They had not fitted it back properly after pulling it away from the wall. And there was the bug. It fitted snugly in a cluster of cables. Just an ordinary mobile phone but in a very unusual place.

The phone's motherboard was exposed. It had been connected to a specific phone line and could intercept any calls that came through the line. The work was primitive but more than adequate.

'There's your spy.'

Cray crouched down. 'What's it doing?'

Now she had to be careful with the phone. The connection was functional but looked delicate. Judging by the cabling, the phone line being tapped was a recent addition. Now, Tronix was at least a decade old and here was a new phone line. There were no outward signs of expansion at Tronix. From what Cray had said, there would soon be cutbacks.

'How do your departments communicate with each other?' she asked.

'E-mail. The network system's only been installed for a few months.'

Thought so. 'Somebody got in here one night and put this cellphone link on your wire. Now they can call it up and read all your e-mail from any phone, anywhere.'

It was quite brilliant stuff. Not the most neatly executed job Ros had ever witnessed but it was proficient. And breaking into Tronix and not being spotted.

The team were dealing with people who were up to their own standards. Well, almost.

Unless, of course, it was an inside job.

Oh, there were at least a dozen possibilities. It could be someone on the inside working for a rival company *and* helping the two women. Things could become more complicated than they already were. It was better if she worked on the premise that the potential thieves were operating by themselves and for themselves.

Still, there was that doubt. It could even be Cray. His own office. Technical director. He had the know-how. He could make it appear as if someone else was tapping into Tronix's computer network when all the time he passed information to a rival company. Somehow, Cray didn't seem the type to betray his boss. He looked too clean cut. But mud stuck and how much got thrown over you when you worked for a man like O'Neill?

Hell. Anybody in the building could be working for a competitor. The solution was to simply keep an open mind and look out for any trouble.

'Get that thing disconnected,' snapped Cray. 'Then we can worry about how they put it there.'

And what would that achieve? It was much better to turn a weapon against aggressors.

'I've another suggestion. These two are obviously going to keep coming at you. Why don't we set them up?'

The malicious smile from Cray told her everything. He badly wanted those girls caught. He wasn't involved with them at all.

Ed paced up and down in the car park. Beckett leaned against his Jeep patiently. God, it was getting him mad.

Why weren't the girls taking the bait?

The car park was empty at this level. A cloudless sky. Wintry chill. A car horn beeped a few floors down. There was a rumble of traffic in the distance. People living their lives while they were stuck up there on the seventh floor, keeping watch on the test car that stood alone on the top floor.

Ros was waiting at Tronix just in case anything did happen with the car. Ed hoped it would. They hadn't set up the e-mail message for nothing, had they?

Ros and Beckett might be used to hanging around but he wasn't. Where were those girls? They were late. It would be good to see them. The way they rode that scrambler, the audacity of trying to steal the test car. Man, they were something. No plan seemed too big for them. Thinking big. Someone after their own hearts. It would be good to find out who they were. Find out what else they did, how they got into the business, what they knew, compare notes, all that sort of thing. Even Ros sounded quite impressed by the tap on Tronix's e-mail.

The test car sat alone on the roof. All that lovely engineering in the ugliest car in the world. Criminal. And he had only seen models and pictures of its real shell. It looked superb. Macho, aggressive, sleek and fast. Just the way he liked his cars to look. What had to be done to get a chance of driving the real thing? Put a stop to the two girls. Return the shell to Tronix. Find out who they worked for. All that jazz.

But the girls weren't going to show. He and Beckett had been waiting too long. The women would know where the car was supposed to be and at what time. It had been all set up on Tronix's e-mail. Perhaps they had given up? That would be a real shame. The blonde one was very nice. Especially in that waitress outfit.

'It's been standing there an hour. Nobody's even been near it,' said Beckett.

Beckett wanted to leave. Ed could hear the impatience in his voice. Couldn't they give the girls a little longer to turn up?

'Maybe yesterday scared them off.'

'You're disappointed,' said Beckett.

Too right. 'I had them down as the type who'd go for a challenge.'

So, they had dropped out of the fight. That was probably for the best. They were up against tough opponents, even if he did say so himself.

A small white van entered the empty car park and sped up to the roof. It stopped immediately by the car.

Ed's muscles tensed. This could be it.

Weapons. What if they used guns? All he and Beckett had were their bare fists. How desperate were these people to get hold of the car?

'Ros?' said Beckett into his head-set.

The van carried on. It had been a false alarm.

'Yes?'

'Oh, nothing.'

The test car looked unusual. No two ways about it. That was probably what caused the van driver to stop for a minute. Matt black painted shell, decade-old design. It looked like an old banger that had been deserted by its owner.

Beckett relaxed and turned to open the Jeep. 'Nothing's moving.'

'Come on. Let's get back.'

'Ros? They didn't take the bait. We're heading back.'

Beckett opened the Jeep doors as Ed walked up the ramp that led to the car park roof. The white van was parked in a far corner. A man stepped out of the van and walked through a set of double-doors towards the car park's lift. Ed checked him out. Tall, beige trenchcoat, dark suit. Wispy, thinning hair. Didn't look like either of the girls. Unless it was a damn good disguise.

The car door was opened by a press of the driver's thumb. Another Tronix speciality. Wonder what that would add to the price of the car?

Cold metal jabbed into the side of his neck.

'Don't move.' A woman's voice. It was the waitress. The blonde woman.

They hadn't given up.

Ed wasn't moving. Not for anything in the world. A gun pressing against his jugular was an excellent reason for doing exactly what you were told. Where was Beckett? Ed heard the Jeep start up. Beckett was driving away. They were supposed to meet on the ground floor.

'Don't speak', she said. 'Just get in and drive.'

The door opened with the pressing of his thumb.

He should have realised the girls would wait until they had the driver and the test car together. They wouldn't be able to steal it any other way. Why hadn't he realised earlier? But how had they managed to pass unnoticed? No one had passed them.

The lift. Of course. You didn't need a car to get in a car park.

His lack of foresight was just about to cause O'Neill to lose his most prized possession.

Well, he might have been stupid but at least there was one good thing to come out of it. The girls hadn't disappointed him. Ed had given up on them, but they were as determined as ever to have the car.

The two women were putting up a fight.

« Sixteen »
« Face to face »

Two exits led from the car park. The front exit led to a road heading to the city centre. The rear exit ran directly to the town by-pass. From there, Tronix was less than five minutes drive away.

Beckett tapped the steering wheel. Ed should have reached him by now. Cars left in dribs and drabs, but the test car wasn't among them. Beckett checked his watch again. He had waited in the Jeep long enough. What was Ed hanging around for? There was the uncomfortable thought that Ed had picked up someone on his way down. An unwanted guest.

There he was. Even from the other side of the car park, the shape of the test car was unmistakable. But Ed was leaving by the front exit. That was not what they had planned. And was there someone in the back seat?

Beckett wanted to turn the Jeep around but stopped himself. He couldn't go through the car park.

Sod it. He'd risk it.

Oncoming cars beeped their horns as he cut in front of them. An estate car screeched on its brakes, narrowly missing the Jeep.

Beckett waved apologetically and smiled to show he was sorry. He turned on the tracker. A road map came up on the computer screen.

Frequency. What was the damned frequency of the bug on the test car?

Come on. Think!

16.2 megahertz.

Beckett fished out his tracker and input the frequency into it. He linked it to the road map. Nothing happened. Beckett adjusted the tracker. No pulsing red dot.

Beckett knew the bug worked fine. He checked every piece of equipment before it was used. That meant only one thing: the signal from the test car was being blocked.

'Ros? I think we have a problem.'

'I'm ahead of you, Beckett. Ed just dropped out of radio contact. And there's someone in the car with him. I'm going to the trackers.'

Waiting around for something to happen had been tedious. But it was better than the feeling of panic that had gripped Ros's stomach. She had seen everything on the computer screen. The test car had been opened by Ed. There was no one else who could have done it. But the suspension system had registered movement that was greater than if Ed had been in the car on his own.

They had set up a trap but fallen into another.

Suddenly, the information being relayed by the test car cut out. The computer screen showed only a blank screen. That could be a fault with the equipment but it wasn't likely. Not with Ed's passenger on board.

She was grateful neither O'Neill nor Cray were around to see this. O'Neill would have flipped his lid. Cray would have squirmed while his boss ranted and raved. Neither of them would be clear headed. And that was what she needed.

Another plan had bitten the dust. Some days, no matter how hard you tried, everything went wrong.

There was nothing she could do about the blocked transmission from the car. There was always a back-up. With the trackers on board, the route map should show the movement of the car, but there was no signal coming from the tracker, either.

Ros slammed her fist on the workstation in frustration. Every signal from the car was being jammed. This theft had been meticulously planned.

She should have anticipated this.

'They've blocked the trackers, Beckett. We have a problem!'

Too confident. That was their trouble.

The woman in the back of the car snapped his head-set in two. Vandal. Did she have no respect for other people's property?

The rear-view mirror adjusted itself to his eye-line. The waitress stared back at his reflection in the mirror. Those were stunning bright green eyes.

'Drive.'

The streets were busy with late afternoon traffic. School kids played in the backs of cars, annoying their parents. And Ed had a gun pointed in the back of his neck.

He had fought his way out of pretty formidable situations before. It was becoming second nature. But having a gun stabbing into you while you were driving wasn't comfortable. And being kidnapped twice within twenty-four hours was almost embarrassing.

Was he getting soft? Defeated one villain too many and thought he was invincible?

'So where are we going?'

The gun jabbed harder into his ribs.

'Just keep heading on this road,' said the blonde woman. 'I'll give the instructions as and when you need them. Now shut up and drive.'

Wonderful manners. Having a gun in your hand allowed you to dispense with pleasantries. Some gratitude seemed in order, seeing how he had basically handed over the greatest vehicle of the century.

Ed started to think about escape. He had started the

car. After that, he was a mere chauffeur. The blonde woman didn't need him now, but it seemed she had no intention of killing him. That meant that she wasn't as hard as she sounded.

With the trackers planted on the car, Ros and Beckett would be able to follow the car to their destination. There was nothing to worry about. Maybe it wouldn't be wise to push her. Keep on her best side. After all, she had the gun.

The blonde woman held up a black box so Ed could see it in the mirror.

'And don't think your friends will be able to follow us. This handy little device blocks all transmissions.'

She smiled triumphantly.

What was she, psychic?

There went that plan, then.

The traffic on the road began to thin out. The three-lane road became two lanes. Green fields replaced industrial sites. Woods appeared in the far distance.

Ed stopped the car at a crossroads as the traffic lights switched to red. Two men in day-glo orange overalls walked across the road and looked the car up and down. A queue of vehicles formed behind. Beckett's Jeep was one of them. He was only two cars back. How on earth had he found them? Luck. Nothing short of luck.

Beckett waved slightly.

Ed sat up straight in the car. If Beckett was planning anything he would have to be ready for anything.

The blonde woman turned her head. 'That's your friend, isn't it? The guy in the Jeep.'

Hell, she *was* psychic!

'Go through the lights,' she ordered.

'In case you hadn't noticed –'

The gun was pushed hard against his neck. 'Do it. Now.'

Was she mad? A steady stream of traffic passed in front of them. Did she reckon they could get past that lot?

Then again, they were in the fastest car in the country.

'I said –'

'And I heard you.'

There was an opening in the traffic. A huge truck was heading towards the traffic lights. A couple of cars were coming up behind it.

In this car, they could make it across. But that would mean losing any chance of rescue. But there was no choice.

Ed put his foot to the floor. The tyres roared on the tarmac.

The crossing was 50 metres at its widest point. In less than two seconds Ed had accelerated up to 70 kph.

Don't look left. Don't see how fast the truck is bearing down on the car.

The truck's horn blasted out.

The woman began to panic in the back. 'Oh, shit.'

She stared at the truck. Stared death in the face.

Then Ed couldn't see the truck. They had passed it. He'd made it.

Ed had to check what happened to the truck he had cut up. Tyres screamed on the tarmac behind the car. The truck jack-knifed, its cab swung around in almost a full circle, its load turning in a wide arc. It stopped in the middle of the junction, cutting across all the lanes. Luckily, nothing had crashed into it. It would take a while before that jam was sorted out.

There was no way Beckett could follow now.

Ed hadn't realised how desperate the women were for the car. If they were prepared to risk their lives to steal it, there was nothing they wouldn't do.

Beckett turned the steering wheel, drove the Jeep along the pavement, turned left and joined the road again. There was no traffic. It was being held up by the truck.

Ed was mad but he wasn't that mad. Even he wouldn't voluntarily risk his life like that. He had been forced to run the lights.

There wasn't a chance in hell of following the test car. Not with the lorry blocking everything in its path. That would take at least an hour to sort out.

'Ros? It's Beckett. Caught up with Ed but lost him again. And how.'

'And we're receiving no signals from the car.'

'What about the transponder? Surely that can pick them up?'

'It might work. We've no idea how strong the jamming signal is.'

'Look. I'll get myself in position and wait for the word from you. OK?'

'Sounds like a good idea. I'll call you later.'

Ed had to sit on a crate while the two women tied him to a metal post with a band of cloth. The band was strange stuff. The more he resisted, the tighter the material became. He had to relax but that was difficult. Thinking about his dance with death still made his stomach clench.

The garage was a mess. The shell of the Tronix sat in one corner, gathering dust. Bits of long-dead cars were all over the place. But it smelled good. Engine oil. A friendly, reassuring smell. A reminder of simpler times.

Neither of the women had spoken since they entered the garage. The dark-haired woman who had driven the scrambler was there. She wore a pair of dark-blue dungarees and a black T-shirt.

There was a family resemblance between the two. Probably sisters. The dark-haired sister had taken a hoist and lifted the engine out of the test car as easy as if it was something she did every day – though who was he to say she didn't? She started to take photos of the engine from every possible angle. She went through a roll of film in under a minute. Ed wondered why she wasn't using a video recorder. It would have been easier.

And they should have known that. It was common

sense. She was using the wrong tools for the job.

Their way of working confused him. In some things they excelled, such as kidnapping, but in others, amateurish was the only word that described them. Why hadn't they known that the car they stole from the studio was only a presentation model, for example?

'I don't know your names,' said Ed.

'Sarita,' said the brunette. She carried on taking pictures.

'Davina.' The voice was muffled. Davina sat in the shell of the car. Very professionally and very quickly she had taken it apart as soon as they had arrived at the garage.

They certainly had very original names. At least Ed had been given them. The women could easily have ignored him and carried on working. Perhaps they weren't so callous.

'One of your trackers?' asked Davina as she poked her head out of the car and held out a tracker in a set of long-handled grips.

It was his favourite. The one he had stuck under William Swift's desk.

'Kind of a family pet.'

And then she would find Beckett's bug in a minute. Perhaps he could distract them?

'You're quite a pair of operators.'

Sarita looked over. She was checking whether he was being sarcastic. But he meant it. In some aspects, they were almost worthy of his own team. And it was also worth trying to start up a conversation. Make friends. It was harder to kill a friend. But he wasn't distracting Davina from the car.

Sarita walked over. Her forehead was lined with engine grease. 'We were going to be a rally team,' she said, 'but this looked like a better career move. Stand up, please.'

Ed stood.

'I'm sorry we had to drag you along,' said Davina, dangling Beckett's bug in front of his face.

Not half as sorry as he was. 'Don't think of it as a problem. I agree to most things when there's a gun at my neck.'

A tube of metal a centimetre thick was thrust in front of his face. He could have kicked himself.

'It was only a grease gun,' said Davina.

'Now you tell me.'

'Couldn't do it without your thumbprint, could we?'

'You take a hell of a risk,' said Ed. 'How much do you make out of this?'

'So far, we're making a loss,' said Sarita. She began rooting in the crate Ed had been sitting on. Tied up, he couldn't turn around to see what she was doing.

'Mind you, this is one job we'd do for free.'

That sounded personal. 'Why?'

'O'Neill put our dad out of business ten years ago. Losing it all as good as killed him. So when we decided to move into the commercial espionage business,' she paused, 'O'Neill was a natural first choice.'

It wasn't a surprise they kept making mistakes. Personal motives and emotions got in the way of doing a good job. Angry people tended to make mistakes. Not as bad as the ones he, Beckett and Ros had made, though. None of them had anticipated the trap.

A personal motive suddenly made things clearer for him. It was no wonder they were so determined to have the car, even if it meant risking their lives. Ed could believe O'Neill was an easy man to hate. If the women were right about their father, O'Neill had made two very bad enemies.

Davina waved something under his nose. It smelled like wet paper bags. She let him have a better look.

'Dynamite?' Ed tried to sound cool.

Sarita smiled sweetly. 'Another little set-back for Mr O'Neill.'

From now on, O'Neill would trust his instincts. And his instincts were telling him to batter someone around the head for this failure. He was sick of people letting

200

him down. Cray was keeping out of his way. Very wise.

He should have fired them after Cray had found them with the military equipment. He should have brought another security team in. Surely they were two-a-penny? This lot were worse than useless. Not only had the bimbos not been caught but now they'd managed to make off with the test car.

Whoever had it in for David O'Neill was going to pay.

Ros sat in front of the computer, staring at the route map. Why wasn't she doing anything to get the car back? They had the transponder. Its signal might be jammed but an attempt had to be made to get his car back.

'Why are you wasting time?'

'They've jammed the trackers,' said Ros.

O'Neill sighed angrily. As if they both didn't already know that.

Ros continued. 'But they won't know about the transponder until I activate it from here. We'll get one chance to trigger it. If they're as equipped as I think they could be, they'll notice the signal straight away. And if the car's still on the move when we do it, then we'll have lost the chance to find the car, Ed and the thief, Mr O'Neill. If the car is stationary when I transmit a signal to the transponder, Beckett and I can fix its position.'

She moved over to another part of the workstation. The transmitter for the transponder was linked up to a computer. As soon as a signal was received, the computer would work out the direction of the signal. Beckett would be able to calculate the direction from wherever he was and together they would be able to determine the location of the signal.

But O'Neill's limited patience was exhausted. Anyway, patience was for the virtuous and he had never scored highly in that department. Those bitches needed to be caught and soon. God alone knew what sort of damage they could be inflicting not only on the car but its engine. And also to his company. His life's work. Details of the make-up of the car could be transmitted to anywhere in the world in a matter of minutes. All those years of work lost in minutes.

Beckett's voice came through on Ros's head-set.

'Ready when you are, Ros.'

Soon, they would have the location of the car. With a little luck, O'Neill would catch both of the women. And then, as God was his witness, they would damn well pay.

Ed had managed to turn around so he had a better view of what the women were doing. It did not look good.

The engine had been crudely dropped back into its compartment. The car wasn't a pretty sight at the best of times but Davina had attacked it with gusto. Doors and panels littered the floor.

But that was the least of his problems. They had not stopped at tearing it apart, stealing all its secrets and photographing every single section of the engine in minute detail.

They were about to utterly destroy it.

There was an awful lot of dynamite in the garage. Sarita and Davina were planning a display of pyrotechnics that no Bonfire Night could ever match.

There was dynamite taped to the walls, inside the car, on the engine, scattered around the floor. At least a hundred packs of the stuff. Where on earth had they got it all? Who did they know?

Davina carefully pushed one detonator lead after another into the packs of dynamite.

'Er, ladies!' Ed shouted.

No reply.

'Hello! What's going on? Get me out of here.'

They ignored him and continued to carefully place the dynamite in every available space. The band around his wrists constricted as Ed involuntarily pulled against the metal supporting beam. He wasn't about to be left here, was he?

It wasn't easy ignoring O'Neill's wittering. Neither was his ranting unjustified. The team had messed up badly. They had to get the car back and stop the two women before they did any further damage. They could be looking at a very big bill if they didn't.

Cray entered the room and O'Neill started to shout at him. Ros was grateful for the diversion. She could concentrate on the task at hand.

The transponder's activator was one of her own designs. A powerful signal would be transmitted to the transponder and, with luck, it would respond with another signal. She and Beckett would be able to pick up the signal and triangulate the location of the test car.

It would only work if the jammer wasn't stronger than her transmitter.

'Here goes.'

The women were still ignoring Ed. No matter what he said, they refused to listen to him. Ed became certain that when the dynamite went off, he would be there with it.

They wouldn't do that. They couldn't do that. They would be no better than O'Neill.

'Can I be somewhere else when –'

A high pitched beep filled the air. An oscilloscope on a workbench registered a signal.

The transponder! Yes!

Davina came up to his side. 'Transponder. Where is it?'

They could have it. A lot of good it would do them.

'Inside the spare tyre,' Ed replied, happily.

'One-oh-four degrees.'

O'Neill had made sure he was wearing a head-set. He wasn't about to miss a thing this time. The transponder had worked perfectly. The power of the bimbos' jamming signal had been no match at all. Just as the bimbos were no match for him.

He would have them now.

Ros typed the triangulations into the computer. Two thin lines, one red and the other blue, crossed on the map on the screen.

A circle appeared where the lines crossed.

'They're close. Very close,' said O'Neill.

'I can be there in ten minutes,' said Beckett.

O'Neill could be there in less. Ros would want to be in on this. Tough. Her team had screwed up once too often.

He threw the head-set on to a bench.

Time to leave.

Finally, cornered like the rats they were.

O'Neill had never let anyone in his life give him a hard time. You didn't mess with David O'Neill. Not healthy. He wasn't known in the trade as a complete bastard for nothing.

These women were ruining his life. And they were going to regret the fact that they had ever even heard of the Trancer.

the Australian go.

« Seventeen »
« Glitter and ash »

The Australian was brave, but foolhardy. What else
was to be expected from one of O'Neill's employees?
Failing to tell them about the transponder had put all
their lives in danger. He knew they weren't about to let
any trace of the car be found. It was almost tempting to
leave him with the dynamite. No. He wasn't as bad as
Uncle Dave. He had done nothing wrong. He was
looking quite anxious about his situation, tied up by
the pillar. He looked kind of cute.

Davina set the timer for the dynamite. That left them
three minutes to pack up and get out of the lock-up.

'Sarita. Are you ready?'

'Give me a moment, sister.'

This was almost a job well done. From the dismal
failure of not stealing the right car to compiling a
complete photo-library of the test car and its engine,
they had every right to be feeling proud of themselves.
It was a shame that the transponder had ruined the
party.

Now if she and her sister didn't get a move on, the
Australian's friends would arrive before they had a
chance to get away. All their hard work would be for
nothing.

The briefcase snapped shut. Twenty rolls of film.
Audio cassettes. A mass of information that Bob would

205

pay for through his nose. And, if they could also wangle an arm and a leg, they should do it. Maybe even bypass Bob? Try to find the highest bidder?

No. The sooner they were off the job, the better. Davina was right. This job was too dirty. Anything involving Uncle Dave was bound to be.

And they should have used a video camera. More info would have meant more money. The dummy e-mail message had given them no time to organise one. And had the Aussie's friends thought their charade would trap them? What sort of set-up was O'Neill running?

Sarita picked up her Stanley knife. It was time to let the Australian go.

'Don't get any ideas about interfering with the dynamite. They're war surplus detonators. Very tamper-resistant.'

'As if I would.'

His look of innocence might fool some people but not her.

The band was undone. The Aussie rubbed his wrists and stepped over to the briefcase that held the cassettes and film.

Oh, he wasn't going to be boring was he?

'What's to stop me just grabbing that case and making a run for it?'

Yes, he was.

'Try it.'

Before he had even touched the case, Davina was on him, pulling his left arm up high behind his back and holding him in a neck lock. To his credit, he did try to throw her over his shoulder, but he really shouldn't mess with the best. She kicked his feet from under him and he fell down hard, flat on his face. Davina pulled his arm higher up his back.

'Well, I'm certainly glad I tried that,' he said, the breath well and truly knocked out of him.

Davina released him.

A sound. Someone behind them. Something snapping shut. A shotgun breech being closed. O'Neill.

Even before Sarita turned, she had no doubt.

'Well, well, well. If it isn't the bimbos from hell. Why are you so persistent?'

His voice. That snaky rasp to every syllable. It made Sarita want to retch.

'Don't know, Uncle Dave. Better just get used to it.'

The pictures in the magazines did his face a favour. It had been a long time since the sisters had been that close. His hair had thinned away and what was left was grey. His face was so pale, as if he were ill.

Life was never that kind.

The shotgun was pointed straight at them all. It meant nothing. Sarita had no fear of the pathetic little man. He was a huge part of her life, even part of what was essentially her. The hatred that his name brought had once almost consumed her. He was an obsession. Neither she nor Davina could let go until he was financially ruined.

But they weren't meant to meet like this, with O'Neill playing the part of the victorious champion.

O'Neill didn't know about the timer. Davina looked at her sister. The same thought: they wouldn't tell him. They wouldn't save his miserable life even at the expense of their own.

'I'm not your uncle,' said O'Neill, looking confused.

'But you were Dad's best friend till you ruined him,' said Davina.

It had been more than a decade ago but Uncle Dave would remember. You didn't forget ripping somebody's life to shreds.

The realisation suddenly showed on his face. The shotgun slipped slightly in his hands.

'You? You're Jack's daughters? Sarita and Davina?'

'Excuse me –' said the Australian.

Immediately, O'Neill re-aimed the shotgun. They could have warned the blond Aussie that this was how you were rewarded when you worked for a slimeball like Uncle Dave.

'Shut up, Ed,' growled O'Neill.

So his name was Ed. They really should have asked earlier. Not Eddie or Edward but Ed. Sounded like he was a bit of a lad. Looked the part, too. Not that they were ever going to find out. The timer read one minute and twenty seconds. Hardly even enough time for goodbye, never mind proper introductions.

They had been discovered because of the transponder signal. O'Neill had found the Trancer shell and the car. Everything looked as if he had won. He looked so bloody smug. The man who always got everything was about to get more than he had ever bargained for.

He couldn't be allowed to win. This was for Dad. And, amazingly, Sarita felt no fear at all, only a feeling of numbness in her chest.

'You.' Who was he ordering about? 'Come here.'

Ed leaned forward. 'Listen –'

'I said shut up!'

'But –'

O'Neill raised the shotgun and fired. Ed flinched instinctively. Davina didn't move. That was impressive. They wouldn't give him an ounce of satisfaction from his macho posturing.

Dust from the garage ceiling fell slowly over the dynamite. The noise was startling. Stupid fool had probably deafened them all.

'Why don't you do the job properly, Uncle Dave?' taunted Davina. Sarita realised she was trying to keep O'Neill's eyes away from the dynamite. 'It's the only way you're going to stop us.'

He pointed the shotgun straight at her. The man was utterly furious. His eyes were wide and bulging. 'Don't imagine it isn't in my mind.'

The shotgun was an inch away from Davina's face. The timer read forty seconds. Davina didn't move a muscle, but stared defiantly at him.

He cocked the hammer on the gun.

Thirty seconds. She just had to hold his attention for a little longer.

A man stepped in from the doorway. Shorter than

Ed but stockier. He had probably heard the gunshot and come to investigate. Why did this little do-gooder have to walk in? He was about to die for his concern. Or he could ruin the whole thing.

'Beckett!' shouted Ed.

What? Ed knew this guy?

The man looked around the garage. Damn! He couldn't not see the dynamite. He was about to ruin everything.

Davina and O'Neill continued to stare at each other.

Twenty seconds.

'Hey!' shouted the man called Beckett.

Nobody moved.

'Is that a bomb?'

O'Neill turned. He saw the timer. Twelve seconds. He dropped the gun. He smashed past Beckett and headed out of the door.

Damn O'Neill to hell!

Ed pushed past. 'That's what I've been trying to tell everyone!'

Davina looked over. There was no choice. They had to leave. If O'Neill made it out of the garage in time, they'd have to live to fight another day.

Seconds later, they were outside the garage, running hard. O'Neill's little legs carried him as fast as possible away from the garage.

But the test car had been left behind. Though O'Neill was going to survive, his dream machine was about to be obliterated. His dreams were about to be shattered into thousands of tiny pieces.

Oh, no. The briefcase. All the photos, the audio cassettes. All the information was about to go up in flames. Wasted. How could they have left it behind?

It wasn't important. Not right then. They just needed to get away.

Ed stopped, looked behind and shouted, 'Come on!'

What did he think they were doing?

A huge blast. A deafening roar as the packs of dynamite exploded. Again and again and again. Nothing else.

No other sound. The shock wave knocked everyone off their feet. Sarita didn't hear herself fall. The intense heat from the explosion made it hard to breathe.

But she had to see the end of O'Neill's dream. She forced herself to turn round. Ignoring the noise, she faced the blasts of hot, dry air.

There was a wall of flame where the garage had been. Explosion followed explosion. The garage walls were knocked out. A giant hand seemed to pulverise the walls from the inside.

The wolf huffed and he puffed.

O'Neill should have been in there.

Another detonation. Louder than any of the others. Windows shattered. Sarita tried to cover her eyes and ears but she needed to see O'Neill's life ruined. She wanted to rejoice in the flames rising high above the garage. Massive balls of flame devoured the flimsy building.

Another explosion. Would it never end?

Oh, my God.

The burning car shot out above where the roof had been. A shell. Its wheels were gone. A metal husk was all that remained.

And it was flying straight towards them.

The shell climbed higher into the air then slowly arched downwards.

It crashed into the concrete. The frame cracked, buckled and broke. No clue as to what it once was. It was just a huge chunk of twisted metal.

The fire raged in the garage but there were no more explosions.

Davina stood. Sarita shook her head, feeling dazed. She had to keep a clear head. She felt dizzy as she stood.

Beckett and Ed stirred. O'Neill gaped at the shattered building.

Maybe now he knew what Dad had felt. It had been worth losing the photos if O'Neill learned his lesson.

Davina darted to the driver's side of a burgundy car.

Where had that come from? Something good. Classy. She couldn't remember the make. Her head felt as if it would fall off any second.

The car was O'Neill's. Brilliant. Perfect.

Davina laughed and climbed inside. In seconds she had hot-wired the car. Sarita jumped in beside her. She hoped Ed and Beckett hadn't been hurt. It was tough if they were. Shouldn't be involved with a man like O'Neill.

The car accelerated.

Sarita held Davina's hand. They were still together. That was all that mattered. The rest of the world could go hang.

She took one last look at the total devastation they had caused. The fire continued to rage. O'Neill knelt and watched his dreams burn down.

All in all, it hadn't been that bad a day.

Ros turned the car around a corner when she heard another huge explosion and was so startled, she almost skidded off the road.

You could probably hear the explosion right across the city. Black smoke billowed into the sky.

Ros wondered if the explosions were O'Neill's fault (likely), the work of the two women (possibly less likely) or that Ed had triggered something that should have been left alone (not very likely, but you never knew with Ed).

Concrete concourse. A saloon car raced by. Ros saw the two women. Looking determined but annoyed. Somebody had spoiled their party. There was Beckett's Jeep and unrecognisable pieces of junk lay burning on the ground. Flames were dying in something that looked like it might once have been a car.

A building was on fire. The flames reached high into the sky. That must have been the girls' base.

Beckett and Ed were stretched out on the ground. Moving. Good. They were OK. O'Neill was on his knees.

Ros stopped the car. The outside air was warm with the heat from the burning building.

'Beckett, Ed!'

Dirty faces. Spoiled clothes. Dust and ash covered them both as they sat up in puddles of oily water.

'We're all right,' said Ed. 'Just about.'

Ros checked over O'Neill. He didn't move, just stared at the fire.

'Mr O'Neill?'

'Gone. It's all gone.'

Was that shock? She had to get him out of there. Take him to a hospital, or something.

The test car. He must mean the test car. So it was gone. But that didn't mean it was gone forever.

'Mr O'Neill? You've lost nothing. The designs for the Trancer are still held in your computers back at Tronix. All the data from the road tests, too.'

O'Neill turned then slowly looked up at her. Not a pretty sight. Blank. Emotionless. A look of defeat.

'You.' He pointed at Ros. 'You. This is all your fault.' He stood up and snarled, 'You did this to me.'

He was shaky on his feet. If he tried anything, one good shove would have him back down on the ground.

He wasn't going to see that the destruction of the test car was only a minor set-back.

'Mr O'Neill –' she began.

'Shut up.' He was coming round. The dazed expression replaced with a more familiar one of contempt and anger. 'Because of you, they've destroyed my car and are on their way to sell all the information to the highest bidder.' He looked around the concourse, confused. 'And where's my car?'

Ed stepped in. 'They left all the photos and information they'd put together in their garage.'

They left it behind? Ros couldn't believe it. What sort of amateurs were these people?

O'Neill started to laugh hysterically. 'Just like their father. Couldn't do anything properly. Complete idiots.'

'They've taken your car,' said Beckett.

'I can see that,' he snapped, his mood changing instantly. He pointed at Beckett. 'Give me a lift back to the office. Mr Cray and I have work to do. After that, I don't want to see your ugly faces again.'

They were all sitting in the lounge at Gizmos. A retreat. A shelter from O'Neill's dangerous world. Now they had time to plan their next move. Peace at the end of a very long day. He was tired and uneasy. Feelings he wasn't used to having. Ed would have been much happier never to darken O'Neill's door again.

They should back out of any further deal with O'Neill. Walk away. Forget about him. O'Neill had acted like a lunatic. The way he had pointed the shotgun at Sarita and Davina. The way he had stared at them all. One hundred per cent certifiable.

Ed forced himself to try and see the situation from O'Neill's point of view. Tronix was his life. The Trancer was everything to him. Having it stolen must have felt like a child being kidnapped and O'Neill had been prepared to do anything to get it back. But even putting himself in O'Neill's shoes didn't make Ed feel any more sympathetic to the man.

Cray had told his boss that they still needed a full security check and, as far as he was concerned, Ed and the team were the best people for the job. O'Neill had very reluctantly agreed. Reluctantly! They had tried to help the man, for crying out loud. And Ed had tried three times to tell him that the garage was rigged with dynamite. What thanks had he been given? A double-barrelled shotgun being let off over his head.

Ed concentrated on sewing the button back on his leather jacket.

Ros was sitting on the floor, cradling a cup of coffee in her hands. She slipped off a shoe and began massaging her foot. 'Are you any good at ironing as well?' she asked.

'Do me a favour. I'm just repairing your faulty

213

workmanship.' He was done. He snapped the loose thread off the button and held it up to Ros. 'There! Good as new.'

Beckett walked in carrying a teddy bear. He threw it at Ros who caught it above her head.

'I've got some socks that need darning,' said Beckett.

'He'll make someone a wonderful wife one of these days,' said Ros.

'You left your teddy at William's workshop.'

'Yes, I know. How are things there?'

Beckett shrugged. 'Anna's party seem to be suffering in the polls. The Italians don't like to think they've been supporting an anti-corruption party with one of its heads as one of the country's biggest criminals.'

'And so she's out of the running?'

'Looks that way. She didn't seem to be particularly bothered. Quite philosophical about it, really. Said there was always next time.'

Ros sat down on the sofa with the bear on her lap. 'Ed!'

'Yeah?'

'Not you, him.' She nodded towards the teddy. 'His name's Ed too.'

Beckett took off his jacket. 'Maybe we should take him on. He can take your place next time you go missing. That's twice now in a matter of days.'

Ed ignored the jibe. He was just a very popular guy. He picked up the stuffed toy. 'Yeah. We should have him on the team. Why not? And anyway, you know what they say, don't you?'

'What?' asked Ros.

'Two "Eds" are better than one.'

Beckett groaned. 'You get worse.'

'Anyway. O'Neill. What are we going to do?'

Ed knew Beckett wouldn't want to jack the job. Sort of professional pride. Hell, none of them would normally back down from a fight. But O'Neill was different. Ed's gut feeling was screaming at him to turn and walk out of the situation as fast as possible. If Ros backed him, then today would be the last they would see of O'Neill.

'The man's a psychopath,' Ed continued. 'If it was down to me, we'd walk.'

Ros put her teddy bear on the table. 'I've never walked out on a job yet. His problems are personal. Ours are professional.'

There was no hope of back-up there, then.

'You can say that, Ros. You didn't get a twelve-bore parting in your hair.'

O'Neill's eyes glinting. His threat to kill them all.

O'Neill wasn't a case of lights being on and no one home. Inside the girls' lock-up O'Neill had the biggest rave of the decade in his head. There was nothing O'Neill wouldn't do to protect his investment.

'Here's the new deal,' said Beckett. 'This time we don't just sweep the place. We give the entire Tronix operation a complete security overhaul. We make it airtight and then we stay on it all the way down the line.'

Shouldn't they just give it a miss? They weren't O'Neill's favourite people in the world.

'What about Cardenas and his Boys' Brigade?' asked Ros.

Good point. A quasi-military group didn't inspire any feelings of joy. If he had to make a guess, to Ed they looked like mercenaries. No flags on their arms. No sign of rank on any of them. And the vehicles they were buying from O'Neill were almost as bad.

'We work around them,' said Beckett. 'They're not going to like it, and we'll probably like it less. But that's how it's got to be.'

So it was decided. A majority vote for further involvement with Tronix. Fair enough. After this evening, Ed would never mention it again.

'I don't know,' said Ed. Ros and Beckett looked at him. 'I just don't know. Look guys, I'll go along with anything. You know me, right? But I think we're getting deeper and deeper into something that we may seriously have cause to regret.'

« Eighteen »

« Out of sight »

Bob had been waiting for them long enough.

The café was all chrome and uncomfortable stools. Music, if it could be called that, blared out.

People everywhere. Superficial kisses. Forced smiles. Hollow laughter. Tables and chairs were arranged on two levels. Huge windows looked out onto a busy street. A coffee machine spurted and hissed. Glasses and cups chinked. Cigarette smoke and the smell of fresh coffee drifted in the air.

All the customers were young. Too young. Anyone looking over at Bob as he supped his second cappuccino could have mistaken him for someone's dad. His beige mac wasn't exactly the height of fashion.

The music. The fashion. God, he was feeling so out of it. He was so old.

Once upon a time, all this would have been fun. Computer terminals sat on each table. Groups of people chatted to a friend on a computer screen.

Conversations became louder as the music was turned up a notch. He really did want to leave now. He would give them a few more minutes to find out what they had salvaged.

The sisters hadn't sounded too optimistic on the phone. The test car had been scrapped in a permanent way. God alone knew how they managed to obtain the dynamite. That wasn't his concern. Information was all he needed. He had been authorised to pay up to a couple of hundred thousand for the info on the Trancer engine. Potentially, it was worth much more to his employers. Tight buggers. But wasn't everybody trying to screw everybody else for every penny they had?

Bob stopped himself. He didn't want to be going soft. If he wasn't careful, he would be giving up his houses, the lovely salary, adoring wife and mistress. He would be working the land if he kept thinking that way.

Sarita and Davina walked in. Both wore long black woollen coats, black jeans and colourful T-shirts. Sarita looked around the café and smiled when she saw him.

They were carrying nothing. Not even a handbag.

They sat.

'Hello, Bob.'

'Good morning ladies. I trust you're well after yesterday's little incident?'

Davina barked a laugh. 'Oh yes. We got on very well with O'Neill. Like a house on fire.'

There was no point in asking why they had blown up the car. Bob knew only a little of their grievance against O'Neill and, quite simply, he didn't care what their personal motives were. Just as long as they had the information.

A notebook was slammed down onto the table.

'What's this?'

'Read it,' said Davina.

The notebook was mostly empty. On only a few pages was there any writing. And all in red biro.

Info on the engine's design. Brief notes on the dashboard lay-out.

This was not what he wanted. Not by a very long way. Bob wanted disks full of hard data. Engine schematics, the works. Photos of the engine.

He didn't want their scribblings.

'This is all of it?' he asked, trying to remain calm. He

217

hadn't waited for almost an hour to be brought this rubbish.

'All we could put together from memory.'

The stupid idiots had blown up the car without compiling any information on it.

'You seem to have got things the wrong way around,' he said. 'You destroy the evidence *after* you know everything about it.'

'That's what we had done,' said Sarita.

'So where's the information?'

Sarita picked up the notebook and tapped it on the table. 'We got a little distracted.'

'How?'

'One of O'Neill's cronies alerted his boss to our outfit.'

'Tell it to someone who cares, Sarita.'

Davina sighed, becoming impatient. Tough. He was the one who had to go back to his bosses and explain he had nothing on Tronix's new car. He was the only one justified in feeling impatient.

'Look,' said Davina. 'We almost went up with the car. There was literally no time to grab the briefcase and make it out of the garage alive.'

How his heart bled for them. 'What sort of operation are you running?'

No answer.

'I know you've not been in this line of work for very long but it's one thing after another. I'm sorry but the only word I can think of to describe how you work is amateurish.'

Again, no answer.

He finished the dregs of his cappuccino. 'You know as well as I do that this is nothing like the level of hard data we need.'

The two sisters looked at each other and shrugged.

'We'll get more,' said Sarita.

'What's to get? They found your wiretap on their e-mail and you blew up the technology.'

'Come on, Bob,' said Davina. 'We're broke.'

218

And what did they expect him to do about that? Did they see him as some sort of charity?

'I'm sorry. What can I say?'

There was a great deal Bob could say, but a blazing row in the middle of the café would have been embarrassing. And he shouldn't even be seen with them. If O'Neill was as bad as all the reports said, there would be a hunt for the two girls.

'Maybe you should think about another line of business,' he suggested and stood up.

Time to leave. The women were a waste of time and effort. They had been lucky not to get caught so the less involvement he had with them from now on, the better.

'Wait.'

Davina took out a photograph from her coat pocket. It was bent at the edges. A crease ran through its middle.

A blurred picture of a truck. Taken at a distance and then enlarged. Where were the truck's windows? Steel grey. Massive wheels. Bob felt an impression of formidable power. The picture quality was poor but good enough for him to tell that what they had found was good. A military vehicle. He had only heard rumours of machines like this. You didn't see pictures like this in the latest issue of *Autofuture*, that much was certain.

'Is this at Tronix?'

'Could be,' said Davina.

So that's what the sly bugger had been working on. It suddenly made a lot of sense. O'Neill hadn't produced anything for years and he still managed to fund R&D. The truck was serious diversification. From on-the-road sports models to the latest military hardware.

'This is what I most definitely call a red-hot item.'

'You want it?' asked Davina.

'So you two think you can get it?'

Davina shrugged.

If nothing else, Bob knew that information on O'Neill's involvement with the military would be appreciated by members of the board.

'At the moment, all I want is information. All you can get.' He stood. 'One last chance. We'll pay well for data on this. Just don't mess it up.'

Cray's office was in almost total darkness. In the half-light from the outside corridor, it looked meticulously neat. Not a speck of dust to be found. On the desk was a PC, a pen lying next to a notebook and a lamp stood by the computer.

Let there be light.

Beckett and Ros were in Tronix's security suite, checking all the cameras. Ed had left them to it. Dismantling monitors and looking over every single circuit board looked boring. Besides, O'Neill kept popping his head round to see what they were doing. The further away Ed could be from that man, the better he would feel.

Ed was keeping out of everybody's way by walking around the building checking for bugs. There was a nasty chance of bumping into Major Cardenas, so he felt it wise to keep away from the military division.

It was surprising to feel like that. Not wanting to be somewhere. The jobs the team had done together had been dangerous and this wasn't turning out to be an exception. Ed thrived on challenge but he was ready to hang up his hat. Only Ros and Beckett had made him change his mind. If one of them was involved, they all were.

He picked up the notebook on the desk. Empty.

His scanner detected nothing as he swept it around the room. He checked the desk drawers. Locked. A light on the bug detector changed colour from green to amber.

There was something in the bottom drawer.

The light flicked from amber to red. The detector let out a string of beeps.

Where was his electronic lock-pick? Ah. Jacket pocket.

The lock-pick fitted snugly into the lock of the bottom drawer. Ed activated it and – Bingo! The lock-pick beeped and the drawer slid open.

Ed saw some large sheets of computer print-out and a mobile phone. There was the bug. The phone hadn't been switched off. Mr Cray should be more careful. Ed turned it off and replaced it in the drawer.

Was it worth having a look at the papers? Why not? He had nothing better to do.

Blueprints. It took a moment for Ed to realise what exactly they were for. They were extremely detailed, computer-designed technical drawings.

'MPV?' he muttered. 'What's that mean?'

There were four rolls in all and Ed decided he might as well take a look at them all. Might get an idea what the plans were for. There was plenty of room on Cray's desk. He spread them out.

They were plans for a vehicle. A very, very large vehicle. The designs for the trucks in the military division annexe. What Cardenas wanted to buy. The MPVs.

The engine schematics were bizarre. Nothing quite like anything Ed had ever seen. The motor functions were all rearranged. To Ed, it looked as though the vehicle's engine had been engineered on an entirely new set of principles.

And then he saw the reason why.

A shiver ran down his spine.

'Wow.'

That couldn't be right. No one in their right minds would get themselves involved with building such machines.

Cardenas. O'Neill. They were not the most stable of people. Hell. O'Neill was desperate if he was messing with this type of technology. It was well removed from the Trancer. As far removed as possible.

In fact, the six vehicles made the Trancer seem like a kid's go-kart.

The trucks in the annexe were nuclear.

A glum security guard sat eating a sandwich. The guy did not want to be there. Neither did Ros. Of all the enjoyable things she could have been doing, going through the circuitry of Tronix's security system did not rate at all.

She was staring at the motherboards in the security console with all of its thousands of minute connections. And she and Beckett had to check them all. Beckett seemed quite happy with the monotony of the job. After the explosion in the garage, he might see it as light relief.

A monitor showed one of Major Cardenas's grunts. Outside. Dark. And was that one of those monster trucks? The man stood by the truck, walking up and down. A guard. What was the point of having a security team *and* a guard? The soldier was holding something. Ros had difficulty making it out. A thick black rod. A truncheon of some sort? The guard swung the rod closer to the vehicle. There was a flash of light. A vicious electrical charge sparked between the rod and the truck.

Ouch.

'Look at this, Beckett. That guard's armed.'

Beckett trundled his chair over to the monitors. Light continued to play between the rod and the truck.

He didn't seem too bothered. 'Those are tasers.'

'What? They're using stun-guns?'

Beckett nodded. 'Yep. A high voltage shock disables the target, but you can take them alive. This has got to be the most hush-hush armoured car in the world.'

So why was O'Neill bothering with a security check? Why were people wasting her time?

A voice behind them: 'Don't speculate. Just get it protected.'

O'Neill. Creeping about. They hadn't heard him enter.

'Those patrols are a complete waste of time, Mr O'Neill,' said Ros. 'Between us up here and the Gates of Hell down there, it's all well covered.'

Davina breathed a sigh of relief as she climbed on to the roof. She saw her sister open up a sky-light.

It had been a close thing, climbing the wall. Almost spotted by those scary-looking guards. Almost caught before they had even started.

Armed guards. Something neither of them had anticipated. That didn't matter. The guards were on the ground and they were up on the roof. As long as they were quiet, no one would see them.

The armoured truck was almost theirs.

The rope dangled down from the roof through the opened skylight. If they had planned this correctly, they would climb down into Tronix's annexe and into the only position in the military division that was camera-blind. If they hadn't, they would be saying hello to dear Uncle Dave far sooner than they would have liked. Thank heavens they had printed out the Tronix floorplan while they still had the e-mail link.

'You've got your glasses?' asked Sarita. She sat on the opened skylight's edge, tugging at the rope.

'Of course. And why are we whispering?'

'Because that's what you do,' hissed Sarita in mock-seriousness. 'Don't you watch television?'

With that, she grabbed hold of the rope, slid off the skylight and climbed down. There was a gentle tap of booted feet as Sarita touched ground. Davina grabbed the rope and followed.

This was completely mad. The plan didn't allow for any mistakes nor any unplanned entrances and a lot could go wrong. The security cameras could have been moved. The guards could be a problem, but not if they got inside an MPV before being spotted. After that, nothing could stop them.

Davina touched the ground. No alarms sounded. No sudden bright lights glaring in her eyes.

Five operating plasma cages. Nothing that worried her. An MPV in each cage.

Eeny-meeny, miney-moe, which one is about to go?

Sarita took out a black ball from her pocket. 'Put your glasses on.'

Davina did as she was told. Suddenly, she couldn't

see anything at all. The glasses were designed to let no light through at all.

'Turn around, close and cover your eyes.'

Sarita pressed a tiny button and then threw the small black ball into the air.

The sisters shielded their eyes and squeezed them shut. There was a sharp crack. Had the light-bomb worked? There was no way of telling.

Davina realised she had to assume the bomb had blinded the cameras and just get on with the job of stealing the most powerful land vehicle in the world.

O'Neill stepped closer to the open door of Cray's office.

Blueprints. The Australian was hunched over a set of blueprints.

The desk's bottom drawer was wide open.

Those blueprints.

Bad boy. A very bad boy.

Hadn't O'Neill warned them about interfering with things that were no concern of theirs?

Maybe it would be a good idea to fetch the Major. He would want to see who was gathering information on the MPVs.

And maybe the Major could bring a few of his men. Put the frighteners on the guy. Ed had to learn that it wasn't healthy to ignore a warning from David O'Neill.

The security suite was filled with white light as half a dozen monitors whited out. Beckett covered his eyes. It was so bright the security guard woke up.

What had gone wrong? What had he done?

Three of the monitors were showing blank white screens. What piece of circuity would have shorted to do that?

The one he was checking over.

'Beckett,' said Ros, turning to him. 'What did you do?'

Blame him for anything that went wrong, why didn't she?

'I don't know.' Shrug. Look innocent. He had been checking a circuit board. 'I didn't do anything.'

No alarm had been set off. So far, so good. The light-bomb must have done its work or security had fallen asleep on the job.

Davina smiled. 'Nice throw, Sarita.'

'I could play for my country, couldn't I?'

Davina produced an atomiser spray and handed it over. Now was the tricky bit. Turning off a plasma cage.

God, she was nervous. And excited. If this worked it would be another kick where it hurt for O'Neill. Oh, she could carry on like this forever. Revenge was such a powerful motivator. Perhaps they should blow up the building after they had finished. They did pretty well with the garage, after all. And it would finally and completely ruin Uncle Dave. Nah. Where was the profit in that? This way was much better. Stealing an MPV from under his nose and making a wad of cash in the process. Sweet as a nut.

Sarita and Davina stood by a pillar. The MPV in this cage was as good as any other.

The touch-panel, if she remembered correctly, was in the left pillar and just above chest height. Sarita pulled out an atomiser containing a clear liquid and lightly sprayed the contents over the panel. After a moment, Davina placed a piece of plain white paper on the panel. With the iodide picking up grease marks, they would see a palm-print in a moment. There was a chance they would see a mess of prints and that would be useless. They would have to move on to another panel and try again.

But no. The palm-print that soaked through the paper was perfectly clear. Wonderful.

Davina pressed her palm against the paper. A light tracked from left to right on the touch-panel, reading the palm-print produced on the piece of paper. The plasma cage lights shut off.

One MPV to take away!

Ed started to roll the plans up. Ros and Beckett would have to be told. Maybe now they'd quit this scene.

Radio-Isotope Thermoelectric Generator. Try saying that when you were half-cut.

What a power source. It would take decades before one of the trucks would even get near to having a flat battery.

His gut feeling had been spot on. It didn't make him feel any better. Nuclear power did that. Made you edgy. Made you damned scared when it was in the hands of private individuals, and terrified when in the hands of mad bugger private individuals.

The office door banged open.

O'Neill strode in. He was flanked by Cardenas and two of his heavies.

Talk of the devils.

'What did I tell you?' snarled O'Neill.

Cardenas stepped forward. He held out a black baton.

'That's not for outsiders,' he said.

The baton crackled. Light shot out from its end. The air was filled with the smell of ozone.

Ed clutched his chest as pain shot through his body.

He couldn't breathe. He couldn't stand up. He couldn't think.

O'Neill's face blurred and then faded to black.

Oh, God.

« Nineteen »
« Cold warning »

Every once in a while the roving lights in the annexe would catch Sarita's line of vision, momentarily blinding her. The lights, moving in their strange pattern, were a nuisance she could live with.

She and Davina pulled at the large silver-coloured plastic sheet that covered one of the massive trucks. Sarita pressed herself against the machine. It was freezing cold and the smell of oil and metal was almost palpable.

Davina walked to a side door and slid it open. Sarita was surprised that the MPV wasn't locked. But with all the security O'Neill had installed, why would it be?

Sarita smiled to herself. They would get into the truck and quickly get out. She clambered after her sister and slid the truck's door shut. Wouldn't want any unwanted intruders, would they?

There was still no sign of any security. No sign was a good sign.

Maybe this time they would get it right. Ruin O'Neill and become fabulously rich in one easy move.

Davina flicked on a light switch. Sarita saw that the rear section of the MPV was taken up by a huge piece of machinery. It sat in the centre of the truck. It was under a heavy covering but Sarita wanted a better look at it.

There was a small circular sticker on its side. Black symbols on a yellow background. A radiation warning.

'Whoa.'

Sarita stepped back. Was this a weapon?

Cables ran from the base of the machine to other sections of the vehicle. No. This thing was the MPV's power source. A nuclear-powered truck. That was too much. Maybe too much for Bob. Would he want to get involved with this?

There was only one way to find out: show him. They'd come this far. There was no profit in backing out now.

There was a switch on the power-source casing. She flicked it. The machine hummed and the truck's engine started up. Controls throughout the vehicle came to life. Computer screen flickered on. Electronic displays in a multitude of colours appeared. The lights reminded her of an arcade game.

Nuclear ignition. She laughed again. There was something that would never turn up in an on-the-road car.

She wanted to have a look at the controls of the vehicle. For a start, she had to find out how the driver could see outside when the truck had no windows.

A large flat screen hung in front of the driver's seat. There were the other plasma cages with their green shimmering bars of light. The roving spotlights swung in all directions.

It was not the widest view of the outside world but it would do. The rest of the controls looked pretty much standard. Sarita had driven everything from a tricycle to a tank and this machine was simply more powerful than anything she had driven before.

Driving this baby out of O'Neill's toyshop wasn't going to be any trouble. In fact, she was damn well enjoying it.

Beckett knew he should have found the problem with the cameras by now.

Whatever he had done to the circuit board, he couldn't see it. He and Ros had even swapped security consoles hoping that a fresh pair of eyes would find the problem.

The security guard had left, probably to inform O'Neill of yet another mishap. If O'Neill stormed in, Beckett would deal with the miserable old goat.

It was one thing after another with this case. This new puzzle wouldn't be beyond them for long. They would sort this out. They could deal with anything.

Ros crouched over a circuit board. Beckett looked over the blank monitors. Power was still reaching the screens, so that was OK. Some piece of circuitry had switched over to read a default setting? That's what it looked like.

But Beckett knew he hadn't done anything. He hadn't poked anything, flicked any switch, or knocked any circuit out of its setting.

The screen seemed to indicate otherwise.

Unless there was outside interference.

'Ros?'

She didn't look up. 'Hmm?'

'The three screens that have blanked out . . .'

'Yes.'

'They were showing the military division annexe, weren't they?'

Now she looked up. She laid a large circuit board flat on the console. 'You're saying . . .'

Time to get down to the military division. 'It's not the monitors at all, Ros. It's the cameras.'

Damn. Damn. Damn.

They had a security breach on their hands. Beckett knew assumption was the mother of all cock-ups, but it didn't take a genius to guess that the sisters from hell had broken in again.

Ros ran out of the room. Beckett raced after her.

The girls were probably still after info on the car. Atomising their own material hadn't been the smartest move ever made. But that didn't seem right. They could hack into Tronix's computers and download the data. Far less risky than trying to steal a car from under O'Neill's nose.

But they could hack from the outside. They had hacked into a phone line before. They could do it again.

So why break into the military division? The most closely guarded section of O'Neill's empire?

No. He couldn't believe they would be so stupid.

It was the only thing that made sense. They had to be after one of the machines. Didn't they know about Cardenas and his tinpot army?

O'Neill was just going to love this!

But how did the girls know about those vehicles in the first place? Beckett kept running. He would worry about that later. Right now, they had to stop the girls before they got themselves killed.

The vehicle was making the strangest of noises. More akin to a spaceship than a truck. What were they stealing? It hummed with power when Davina had expected the familiar growling of a normal engine.

She jumped out of the MPV as the truck's headlights flicked on. The machine rolled forward slowly out of its bay, then it turned left towards the exit.

They had the machine now. If there were any guards about, both she and Sarita would be protected by the vehicle's armour plating.

Davina pulled out a small black box from her jacket pocket. An ultrasonic transmitter. The locking mechanism on the exit would recognise a signal and only then open up. That was the theory. There were so many frequencies that could trigger the doors. They could be there with the transmitter all night.

So the sooner she started, the better.

She extended an aerial and pointed it at the door.

A small red light blinked on in response as she activated the device and waited. She had to give it time. The waiting seemed to last forever. The longer they were inside Tronix, the greater the chances were of being caught.

Don't panic. If push came to shove, Sarita could ram the doors with the MPV.

The door refused to open.

Come on!

She jabbed the transmitter's activation switch again and again. Suddenly, it clicked open. The huge door's hydraulics galvanised into action. The door rose quickly into the ceiling.

Cold night air. The smell of winter.

All clear. No guards.

Davina was sure that wouldn't last long.

The blue-painted walls showed that she and Beckett were in the military division. Ros kept running down the narrow corridor. Tronix hadn't seemed this big a few hours before. They had to stop whoever was in the basement. If any of the military vehicles were destroyed or stolen, there was no telling what O'Neill would do.

'How could they do that to the camera?' asked Beckett, catching up with her.

'Isotropic light-bomb,' she answered, still running. They couldn't stop. Time had run out ten minutes ago. Time was having a nasty habit of doing that lately.

'They're bright enough to blind anything,' she added, 'even security cameras.'

But how had they managed to bypass O'Neill's security yet again and get past the guards?

Two of Cardenas's men suddenly appeared in front of them. Machine-guns were pointed directly at her and Beckett. The guards barred their way.

There wasn't much difference between the two. Pale faced, thick set, dark-haired and dressed identically in their black uniforms. Gorillas with guns. Or maybe guerillas with guns? Whatever. They looked deadly.

'Security's been breached,' said Beckett.

The guns were jabbed towards them.

One of them barked: 'Hands against the wall!'

Beckett made to protest. They were both shoved against the wall and quickly and roughly frisked.

'Hey! Wait a minute!' said Ros.

'We're the surveillance team,' said Beckett. 'We're all on the same side!'

No answer.

After they were frisked, they were pulled from the wall and, at gun-point, forced to run down the corridor towards the annexe.

'Move!'

She and Beckett were too late. Cardenas had found out about the intrusion. So why were they being treated as if they had broken into the place?

One answer came to mind, clear, bright and so obvious . . .

Ed.

What was Davina doing?

Sarita drove the truck out of the building and then stopped. She ran back to the side doors at the back of the MPV. She slid them wide open and peered out.

Davina was trying to close the doors with the transmitter. What on earth for? They had appropriated the merchandise, now it was time to make a sharp exit. This was not the time to be polite and close the doors behind you.

'Davina!'

Her sister turned.

'Forget the doors, you little idiot! Get a bloody move on!'

The guards came from nowhere. Black uniforms and balaclavas.

Machine-guns were pointed straight at the MPV. Straight at her.

'Step down,' one of them barked. It was impossible to tell which one had spoken.

No. She would not step down. Not after all this. No more failure. This was to be perfect.

Sarita took hold of the side door. She heard the safety catches of the machine-guns flick off one after another.

She went to take a step out of the MPV. Her foot paused in mid-air.

Don't think about it. Just do it.

She fell to her side, grabbed the door handle and pushed the sliding door shut. The lock *clunked* reassuringly.

Machine-gun bullets ricocheted off the vehicle's side. The sound hammered into her head. Bullets didn't matter. She was safe inside the truck. Nothing could touch her.

But she was leaving her sister behind. What would O'Neill do to her?

It was better this way. If one of them escaped, there was still a chance of rescue.

And, suddenly, she had the perfect plan.

Sarita jumped into the driver's seat and drove off.

Bullets chased after her but fewer and fewer hit their mark.

Oh, there was no doubt about it. Now she had this thing, she would get her sister back.

And destroy O'Neill in the process.

O'Neill walked into the annexe as the bullets started firing. Who or what was being shot at? He looked at the cages. There were only four activated. Two of the MPVs were missing. What the hell was happening?

One of Cardenas's underlings ran up to O'Neill. 'A unit has been stolen. It was decided not to give chase. It did not seem prudent given your location.'

Too right, it wasn't prudent. O'Neill didn't want people like the SSD finding out what he was up to. His involvement with Cardenas could be seen as a threat to national security. O'Neill could do without a chase between a mercenary unit and a thief in two nuclear-powered trucks across open ground.

But the situation was retrievable. Cardenas would

233

just have to trust him. O'Neill's mind was working overtime. His life was on the line here. He was sick of feeling that things were slipping away from him. No one did this to David O'Neill.

Two people sat in an empty cage. The Australian and the blonde bimbo Davina. He could use them. They would prove a good incentive to Beckett and that woman to retrieve the stolen MPV.

The dark-haired woman had left her sister behind. She must have wanted the MPV very badly. Idiot. She wouldn't have a clue what she had driven away. No idea how dangerous the truck could be.

But she must have known how valuable it was. That was why she'd stolen it. And leaving her sister behind. That was callous. The exact move he would have made if he had been in her position.

But O'Neill wasn't in that position. He was smarter than they would ever be. He had built everything around him out of nothing and done it on his own terms with no help from anyone else.

And little people like these two youngsters sitting on the floor were trying to destroy him. It took more, much more than they had. O'Neill always had the best cards. He won every game and he would win this one. He had to. If he didn't, Cardenas would have him killed.

He looked down at the two idiots in the recently emptied bay. The Aussie was recovering from his introduction to the effects of the taser. He was lucky that was all Cardenas had done.

Quite handy little weapons, those tasers. He could do with one of them in board meetings. Anyone disagreed with him and zap!

'You stupid, stupid pair. You haven't the faintest idea what's at stake here.'

They both looked up. Ed was groggy and mumbled something incoherently. O'Neill simply didn't care. He didn't want to listen to their pathetic mewling.

The Major lifted a crate out of his way and walked

234

towards a pillar. He flipped up the piece of paper taped to it. A palm-print was clearly visible.

'Very clever,' said Cardenas.

Jack's girls had turned off the plasma cage with that. Ingenious. No matter how much O'Neill spent on security, it could always be circumvented. It was a waste of time and money having Beckett's people checking over the place. No security system would ever be perfect – especially with people like the Australian spy he had caught red-handed.

Talk was that these guys were good. Trustworthy. On the ball. That was balderdash. The more they got involved, the more things went wrong. Could it be put down to bad luck? No. They were worse than useless.

It didn't matter who really employed Ed or the other two to bring down the Tronix empire. O'Neill would make them work for him.

Cardenas placed his own palm over the piece of paper on the panel. The plasma cage started up, trapping Ed and Davina. Bars of green light appeared round the bay.

The Major made a fist and smashed the panel. There was no way to switch off the cage now. Drastic, unnecessary even, but impressive. The blonde girl stared out from the cage, like a dumb animal. Totally impotent.

Two of Cardenas's underlings walked up to the empty bay.

They pushed forward Beckett and Ros.

Beckett was angry. No, furious. His friend was locked up and there was nothing he could do.

What a shame, thought O'Neill. What a crying shame.

'What do you think you're playing at here?' Beckett demanded.

Was Beckett really in the best position to talk to him like that? No, no. O'Neill was taking control. The only way to get things done. Rely on other people and they, without fail, let you down.

'Don't waste your breath, Beckett,' said Ros. 'Can't

you see he's having his strings pulled?'

Now that was nasty. Partially true, but uncalled for.

'Understand this.' O'Neill pointed at Davina. 'Her sister has stolen an MPV. It has to be brought back here. I don't care how or even who gets hurt to make that happen.'

They kept silent. Good. He had their attention.

'I'm fighting for my life so don't imagine that I'm going to be too concerned about theirs. Call them hostages if you like, because that's what they are.'

Beckett had driven back to Gizmos in silence. He had slouched on a sofa, face as dark as night, then fallen asleep. Ros had curled up in a seat, pulled her jacket up about her shoulders and did likewise. When she woke, the sun was beginning to rise. Pale orange light filtered through the blinds.

Beckett woke up, looking startled that he wasn't in his bed.

'Morning.'

'Morning.'

'Any word from O'Neill?' asked Beckett.

'No.'

Beckett sat up and cursed. 'Damn. Right. I'm getting a shower. Be back in a few minutes.'

Ros watched as Beckett stomped out of the room.

So he was still in a bad mood from last night. It was all very well for Beckett to play the angry young man, but the only way she knew of getting out of a bad situation was to fix what was wrong.

She wasn't happy about leaving Ed and Davina inside the plasma cage either. Come to think of it, there were lots of things she hadn't been happy with on this job. Least of all was O'Neill holding all the aces.

Using hostages. No way was that normal business practice in the automotive industry. O'Neill's actions were those of a desperate man, someone who was grasping at straws. 'Fighting for his life' hadn't sounded like a joke.

Why was he resorting to holding hostages for a lump of metal? Why had Ed been locked up with Davina? He was part of their team. He hadn't stolen anything. Unless he had found out something. Something that made him a liability.

The image of a crate suddenly popped into her head. A crate that was sitting on the floor by the pillar with the palm-print reader that Cardenas had smashed.

The yellow and black sign. A radiation warning.

It had to be the reason why O'Neill was so desperate for the return of the truck. What made the truck so special.

She walked over to a computer and switched it on.

Beckett walked back in. 'Where can I find a towel?'

Ros ignored his question. 'Did you see the radio-active warning signs on the crates in there?'

'Where?' asked Beckett, thrown by her reply.

'By Cardenas. In the annexe. I think they're the only explanation.'

'Only explanation for what?' Beckett snapped.

She ignored his foul mood. 'Why this military vehicle is so special. I think its power unit is an RTG.'

'A what?'

Ed and Davina sat in the middle of the empty bay. Neither of them wanted to be near the deadly light-beams that ran around the cage. A guard patrolled the area and passed by them every few minutes. They kept their voices low. Ed was a good talker. Davina was a good listener. The more he talked about the stolen vehicle, the less she thought about her sister leaving her behind with O'Neill. She resented it, even though it had been the only choice.

'The vehicle's powered by a radio-isotope thermo-electric generator,' said Ed.

'What's that when it's at home?'

'A very, very big battery.' Ed laughed. 'They put them in satellites. They use plutonium for a power source and they run for years and years and years.'

Suddenly she was glad she wasn't in the vehicle with her sister.

'Plutonium?'

Ros's fingers tapped away at the keyboard. Beckett watched as she accessed a traffic monitoring system, but could not work out why. Then, after a few more instructions to the computer, a map of the local area appeared with a number of red 'X' marks that ran along one particular road.

'So where did O'Neill find his plutonium?' he asked.

'Plutonium dioxide to be exact,' Ros replied. 'And it's not important where he found it. What's important is to get the truck back.'

'How dangerous is it?'

Ros considered for a moment before answering. 'It's reasonably stable, but highly radioactive and incredibly toxic. O'Neill's flouting all safety laws to produce a new long-range battlefield vehicle.'

'What's the risk of the radiation getting out?'

'The people who make them say the safeguards are adequate. But environmental groups say these things are a disaster waiting to happen.'

That meant that if Sarita decided to take the machine apart all hell and then some would break loose.

The guard passed by. He didn't look down at the prisoners.

'Excuse me, mate,' Ed called. 'Any chance of a drink of something? We've been here for hours now.'

The guard ignored him. Ed sat on the cold concrete floor and crossed his legs.

'Is my sister in danger?' whispered Davina.

'It's real scary stuff, but the truck won't blow up on its own. As long as nothing breaches the plutonium container, she ought to be safe.'

And what did Sarita intend to do with it, anyway? Any plans for selling it to a rival firm had gone out of the window with Davina's capture. She had no choice but to exchange it for her sister.

Ed hoped the exchange would be soon. Neither Cardenas nor O'Neill seemed the patient type.

'What about, erm, dynamite?'

Dynamite?

'Tell me you're joking.'

Davina shook her head. 'If Sarita follows the usual way we work, she'll strip the vehicle, glean as much info about it as she can and then it's goodbye incriminating evidence.'

'You can't say goodbye to plutonium. It hangs around, you know? For decades!'

'Shh! You're shouting.'

'I don't care! If she destroys the MPV, the least it will do is spread fatal doses of radiation across the city. That's thousands of deaths within a few weeks. Then there will be the cancer cases. The full effects of which won't be seen for maybe another twenty years. I can't begin to guess at how many. And let's not forget the pollution to the water supply.'

Davina shrank back, suddenly afraid of him. Ed didn't care. She had to see how stupid she had been.

'Look,' she said. 'Your friends will find Sarita before that happens. And she'll probably trade me for the machine with O'Neill anyway. Don't worry. Nothing terrible's going to happen.'

'I hope you're right. For everyone's sake.'

« Twenty »
« Machine heart »

Beckett brought Ros a mug of tea and placed it by the computer.

'So what's so special about this RTG?' he asked.

'An RTG puts out intense electromagnetic interference,' she explained.

'Electrical equipment stops working properly when one of these things passes by?'

Ros nodded.

'So that means the effects of the interference are visible and it's possible to trace the vehicle. Isn't that one hell of a giveaway for what's supposed to be a covert vehicle?'

Ros took a sip of her tea. 'That's why the power unit is shielded. But if anyone messes with that shielding you get a lot of local interference.'

The red 'X' marks at irregular intervals on the map. Beckett suddenly realised what they were.

'And this interference includes traffic lights?'

'Fourteen sets of traffic lights went haywire last night.'

Ros pointed at the map on the screen. The line of red crosses ended at an industrial estate.

'She's got to be somewhere around here.'

'It could take days to find her in there.'

'So we'd better start at once, hadn't we?'

* * *

Sarita had broken into the lock-up. White wall. Concrete floor. No windows. No one outside would see what she was doing. And she wouldn't be there for much longer. Lots of space to take the truck apart piece by piece. She flicked a light-switch and was surprised that the electricity supply wasn't cut off.

She took more photos and talked into more tapes as she methodically went through everything she could find out about the nuclear powered MPV. Tools were scattered over the floor as she delved further into the vehicle's make-up.

The technology inside the vehicle was beyond her. She thought she knew her way around every land vehicle. Not this one. It was too much. And too much for Bob. There was no way he would be interested in this machine. It was too damned dangerous.

If she couldn't sell the truck, she would exchange it for her sister.

But wouldn't O'Neill have a surprise when he retrieved his precious machine?

She rang Tronix on her mobile. A woman answered. Receptionist.

'Put me through to Paul Cray.'

The line went dead for a moment as she was put through.

Then: 'Yes?'

'Give your boss this message. He'll know who it's from. We've got something the other wants. If he lets my sister go without harming her, I'll tell him where to find his truck. He's got forty-five minutes. The clock is ticking.' She told him her phone number, then switched off the mobile without waiting for a reply.

Sarita walked to the truck and stepped inside.

The concrete in the base of the truck had set hard. The dynamite was immovable. O'Neill wouldn't be able to escape that little lot.

The timer had been a problem. For some reason, the electronic timer wouldn't work so she'd had to rig a manual one. She turned it on and jumped out of the truck.

'And much good may finding it do you.'

All she had to do now was to clear away her tools and wait for O'Neill's call.

Ed was chatting to himself. He didn't seem to mind that in a few hours, if Sarita wasn't stopped, they could both be dead and half the city razed to the ground.

So many deaths. That's what Ed had meant.

Pain and misery for countless thousands. All because of their hatred for O'Neill.

No. Not true. Because they were stupid in the risks they took. Because they didn't think about the consequences of their actions.

Oh, Dad would be so very proud of them.

Maybe Ed was simply more optimistic. He was certainly enthusiastic about the machine. At any other time she would have talked the legs off him about cars. Now it didn't seem right, somehow. Not when her actions could be the death of them all.

'The RTG powers sodium sulphur batteries,' said Ed, 'which are what actually drive the vehicle.'

Electric batteries? Davina felt drawn into his conversation despite herself. 'So how come it doesn't crawl along like a milk float?'

'The batteries don't drive the car. They drive a flywheel.' He paused for a moment then turned to look straight at her. 'You're working on me.'

That wasn't entirely true. But, if he could be distracted enough by their situation, she might as well have a go. 'You did see the plans,' she said. 'Seems a shame to waste the opportunity.' And if they ever got out of this, would she sell the information? Not likely. She didn't care if she never saw the likes of Bob again.

'You're fairly incredible,' said Ed, half-smiling.

Davina raised an eyebrow. 'Only fairly?'

'It wasn't meant as a compliment.' Ed's face was serious again. He knew the trouble they were in. His

242

amiable chatter covered his true feelings.

Davina looked at him. His normally bright blue eyes seemed suddenly so cold. She wanted to say sorry but couldn't. The word didn't seem big enough any more.

Ros tapped her fingers on the Jeep's dashboard.

The buildings on the industrial estate were almost identical to one another. Long rows of three-storey units. All made of some light grey material. Bright red plumbing. Bright red window frames in the few buildings that had windows.

Ros and Beckett drove round and round. There was no sign of Sarita. Even if Ros had been able to stick a bug on the machine, the interference from the RTG would probably have disabled the transmitter. There was no choice but to keep searching.

The clock on the dashboard had gone mad. The liquid crystal display flashed on and off. Strange alien numbers appeared. Totally incomprehensible.

'She's somewhere close.'

'How do you know?'

'Look at the clock. That's the same interference that messed up the traffic lights.'

As a tracker it left a lot to be desired, but it was all they had.

Beckett turned the car towards another grey building. The clock's display went haywire. They were so close.

'She's in there,' said Ros, pointing at the building directly in front of them. 'She has to be.'

Beckett parked the car. They jumped out and ran over to the building.

The entrance was half open. Ros crouched down and lifted the huge door to peer inside. The MPV sat silently in the middle of an empty floor. No one about. Good.

They walked in, their footsteps disturbing the silence.

They walked around the colossal vehicle keeping a respectful distance from it. They had to take this mobile nuclear power plant back to O'Neill to exchange for Ed.

People shouldn't play with plutonium. In Ros's book, using plutonium for battle vehicles was the work of the criminally insane. O'Neill certainly fitted that bill.

A voice behind them. 'Where's Davina?'

Sarita. She was holding a massive wrench as if it were a club. She did not look happy. As far as Sarita was concerned, they worked for O'Neill and that made them no better.

It was time for explanations. Maybe they could work together on this.

Beckett held up his hands. Ros did the same.

'We're not your enemies,' said Ros. 'They've got our partner as well as your sister.'

Sarita dropped the wrench. 'Is she all right?'

'O'Neill's making threats,' said Beckett. 'No one's been hurt. Yet.'

'Have you tried to strip down the truck?' asked Ros. 'You've removed some shielding, haven't you?'

Sarita relaxed. 'I poked around a bit. But it's technology I've never seen before.'

'That's a plutonium-powered RTG,' snapped Beckett, as if every sane person knew what it was. Sarita looked blank.

'It's also been fitted with one of the passive safety systems,' he added. 'I hope you didn't poke around too hard.'

'Ah.'

'And what does "Ah" mean?' asked Ros.

'I, er, took off a few panels,' explained Sarita. 'Got a few photographs. And I concreted thirty pounds of explosive into the floor-pan.'

Just wonderful. Dynamite and plutonium. Such a healthy combination. Well, they would just have to rip the concrete out.

Suddenly the machine powered up. The passive safety system had activated itself. Interference from the RTG, Ros guessed. Had to be.

The wheels turned slowly and the huge machine headed for the exit. It was driving itself out of the lock-up.

How could they stop it?

Beckett ran after the MPV but it suddenly accelerated and was moving faster than he could run. It drove out of the entrance.

Beckett looked exasperatedly at Sarita. 'What exactly were you planning?'

'I set up a timer. O'Neill would have to let Davina go. I'd tell him where to find his precious van – just in time for him to see it go up.'

Ros stared at her. Stark, staring mad. Even O'Neill would draw the line at blowing up plutonium-powered trucks.

Beckett ran out of the building. Ros ran after him. Sarita ran after them both. There was no time to tell her they didn't need her sort of help.

Beckett was in the driving seat of the off-roader. Sarita climbed in the back. Beckett scowled at her in the rear-view mirror then started up and raced after the MPV.

Tronix needed to be told that the truck was heading their way. Get evacuation procedures in motion. The whole works. Not that it would do much good. If the dynamite exploded, no one would be safe.

Ros picked up the car-phone and dialled Cray's direct line.

Come on. Pick up the phone.

'Yes?'

'Paul Cray?'

'Yes?'

'It's Ros. Listen carefully. Tell O'Neill that we've found the MPV. Some of the internal shielding has been removed. Interference from the RTG has triggered the passive safety system. It's now heading back to you with a load of dynamite linked to a timer on board. If that goes off it'll spread plutonium everywhere. Half the country could end up radioactive –'

There was a crack on the other end of the line, as if Cray had dropped the phone.

What was he up to?

'Hello? Paul? Hello?'

No answer.

The Major saw Cray run out of his office looking as if he had seen a ghost.

Cray rushed past. 'Excuse me, Major.'

What was he up to?

The receiver dangled over his desk.

'Hello? Hello?' A woman's voice. One of the security team that O'Neill had hired.

What was the lad up to? Darting off like that. He had almost knocked him over.

Cardenas picked up the phone. 'Hello?'

'Major Cardenas?'

'Correct. What's going on?'

Paul, you can get out of this.

But he was shaking. He couldn't stop shaking. The feeling of panic threatened to overwhelm him. He had to keep calm.

God knew when the MPV would arrive. He had to get away. As far as possible.

He ran into reception. He was almost out of there. Ruth sat behind the desk talking on the phone. She had always reminded him of his mother.

Expensive perfume. The same perfume every day for the last four years.

Oh, God. Ruth.

'Mr Cray?' Ruth looked up at him, surprised.

'Sorry, Ruth. Don't ask. Don't have any time. Is a limo available?'

'Yes. Right outside. But that's supposed to be for –'

'I don't care, Ruth. I'm taking it.'

He hated being rude to Ruth but his instinct for self-preservation had well and truly kicked in.

The door slammed behind him. The limo. Perfect.

He might have time to get out. He jumped in.

'City airport. And damn well step on it. Sod the speed limit. Now!'

The driver nodded, started the car and drove off.

Oh, God. Oh, God no. This can't be happening.

A radiation leak of that size didn't bear thinking about. All those people. And you couldn't stop anything that had a passive safety system. No matter what you did to halt its progress, the MPV would work its way out of it. They had made it so well that it would never fail.

And, anyway, the dynamite was on a timer.

The truck would arrive back at Tronix and then it would explode. Thousands would die. Probably millions would be poisoned by the radiation. It didn't bear thinking about. The numbers were just too big.

They had been so careful with safety protocols. Nothing approaching illegal. Everything had been done by the book. All for nothing.

Cray didn't care who was to blame for this mess. He didn't care that O'Neill had involved himself with military hardware. None of that mattered any more. Blame wasn't important. Only escape. And Paul Cray was not going to die. No way. He had worked too hard. He had a life to live. He was a young man. The future was his. He wasn't about to let anyone stop him.

Family. Lovers. Friends. Children. Something he had found little time for. Now he was so grateful. So many people were going to die that day.

There was nothing else he could do except leave the country. He was one man. He couldn't stop the MPV. No one could.

He picked up his mobile. His secretary could sort out flight details in time for his arrival at the airport. 'Jason? I'll be at the City airport in about ten minutes. Get me on any flight to anywhere. Yes! And now! Anywhere! That's right!'

He was becoming hysterical. 'Just get me in the air!'

* * *

247

The double-doors of the parking bay slammed open.

Ed stood. What was happening? Had Ros and Beckett found the MPV? It would be good to get out of this cage. Davina's company wasn't the greatest in the world. He could have throttled her and her sister for being so stupid as to mess with military technology.

Davina jumped up and looked across the room. O'Neill was being dragged across the floor by two of Cardenas's men.

'For God's sake! Put me down! I can explain!'

'I'm tired of excuses, David,' said the Major as if O'Neill was a close friend. 'It's time to end this.'

The soldiers brought O'Neill closer to the plasma cage.

'I'm not responsible. Blame her, if you have to blame anyone! Do it to her!'

The soldiers pushed O'Neill forward. He grabbed hold of a pillar, narrowly missing the killer barrier. He turned to face the Major.

Cardenas grabbed both tasers from his underlings and pointed them at O'Neill. 'You know I can't abide failure, David.'

Both tasers discharged into O'Neill's chest.

His mouth opened in a wide 'O'. O'Neill fell to his knees. Cardenas kept the weapons trained on his chest. The air was filled with the smell of ozone.

O'Neill collapsed on the floor. His face smacked the concrete.

Ed couldn't believe his eyes. Could a person survive a double-dose of those things?

Cardenas looked up and smiled a smile that was cold enough to freeze hell.

The Major handed the tasers back to his soldiers. 'We're past the point of viable recovery here. Time to go!'

Cardenas turned from the cage and sprinted out of the room. The soldiers fell in behind.

Ed kneeled to check if O'Neill was still alive. If he was, they had a chance of getting out of the cage. But

O'Neill lay completely still. His eyes were closed and his face was very pale.

'Have they killed him?' asked Davina.

O'Neill's chest rose slightly. 'No. He's still breathing.'

But O'Neill was useless to them comatose. They had to get out of the cage. The Major's last words as he left didn't bode well for them at all.

'I'm starting to get an idea of why they've cleared out and left him here,' said Ed.

Somehow, the MPV had become a threat. Something had happened to it.

And it didn't take too many guesses to work out where it was heading.

The truck was doing a steady 50 kph.

Beckett had no trouble following the MPV's progress as it kept to the main roads.

The MPV turned off down a side road. Now would be Beckett's only chance.

'One of us is going to have to get on board,' he announced.

'I can't see any way,' said Ros.

'I think I can get it to stop.'

The MPV slowed down to 35 kph down the narrow road. Beckett put his foot down and the Jeep overtook the truck, turned in front and then Beckett braked.

Ros yelled out, 'Beckett!'

There was no time for him to explain.

He jumped out of the Jeep and ran towards the MPV.

Sarita and Ros stepped out of the Jeep.

'Beckett! Get out of the way!'

The MPV suddenly braked hard.

Beckett closed his eyes and held his breath. And waited.

Come on, slow down you monster.

Nothing. He hadn't been hit.

He opened his eyes and immediately took a step back. The MPV was less than an inch away from where he stood. It had almost run him over.

'The truck has to stop,' he explained. 'It has no choice. It's the passive safety system. It won't crash into anything or anyone.'

The MPV suddenly went into reverse.

Now. The only chance he'd have of getting on board.

The MPV started forward again, steering to its left to avoid the Jeep.

Beckett ran to the vehicle's side and grabbed hold of the door. He ran along with the vehicle.

That was it. Slide it open. Got it. Don't let go of the door.

The MPV passed the Jeep and started to speed up.

Beckett heard Sarita say 'I'll drive!' as he passed his car.

He couldn't keep hanging on to the door. He had to be in there. He tried to swing. *Come on.*

A little more momentum. A little more. Almost made it inside. One more swing.

Yes! He was inside!

Beckett peered out of the side door. Ros and Sarita followed the accelerating MPV.

The empty driver's seat was spooky. He suddenly understood how Ed had felt in the test car.

Above and forward of the seat a computer sat underneath a screen that displayed what was outside. Would the computer operate the passive safety system? If so, could it be over-ridden? Not if it was like the test car. Ed hadn't been able to turn off the car's system.

Beckett turned to look in the back of the truck and kicked a bag of cement.

What was that doing there? He had to get that out of the way. And then he saw it.

Concrete. Dynamite. Blocks of it. An old-fashioned timer. It had to be. Anything electronic would have gone haywire. Sarita had done this job too well.

And according to the timer there were only nineteen minutes left before the bomb exploded.

It wouldn't be enough.

« Twenty-one »
« Berserker »

The light beams around the cage kept up their constant flickering. Judging by Cardenas's hurried exit, the vehicle was on its way back to the parking bay. And if her sister had followed her usual way of working, it was packed with dynamite.

No wonder Cardenas had left so quickly.

The passive safety system must have kicked in. That's why it was returning to its 'home'.

A truck packed with dynamite and plutonium. At least it would be quick. She wouldn't suffer any radiation poisoning as would thousands of others.

Davina, you are not going to die.

She wouldn't give in that easily. With her every last breath she would fight on, no matter how hopeless she felt.

Davina and Ed had checked every inch of the bay, going over the pillars for some way of turning off the plasma cage. In the mood she was in she would have ripped any panelling off with her bare hands. It didn't matter if anything was bolted down. Just as long as underneath any panelling was circuitry they could use to terminate the plasma cage.

But the pillars were totally smooth. No joins. No cracks. Nothing to rip off.

They were trapped.

'There's no way out, is there?' she asked.

Ed sighed. 'I can't see one.'

Suddenly, O'Neill groaned. He started to come round. Davina hoped they would be able to persuade him to free them.

O'Neill's eyes opened slightly as he raised his head. 'Uurgh.'

Then his head slapped down on the concrete. His eyes closed.

Damn him!

O'Neill had fallen unconscious, again.

Beckett smashed his fist on the MPV's controls.

Nothing responded to his commands. He had tried to override the passive safety system. The driver's display screen stubbornly read PASSIVE SAFETY SYSTEM OPERATING. MANUAL OVERRIDE LOCKED OUT.

So that was that. He couldn't make the truck stop.

Beckett walked to the back of the truck and leaned out. He recognised the locale. They weren't many minutes away from Tronix.

He shouted across to the Jeep following the truck. 'Ros!'

The Jeep accelerated and came alongside the truck. He peered up the road. For a second, he was worried about oncoming traffic. Stupid. In less than ten minutes he wouldn't be worrying about anything ever again.

Ros sat in the back of the Jeep. She rolled the window down. She would have difficulty hearing him.

He shouted out, 'I can't make the controls work! I'll have to disarm the bomb instead.'

Sarita shouted back, 'You can't! It's tamper-proof!'

Oh great. One thing she did well and they couldn't dismantle any of it.

'Can you throw the dynamite out?' asked Ros.

'The concrete's solid.'

'Then I'm coming over,' said Ros. 'Where do you keep the toolkit?'

OK. Ros was coming over. Fine. He could cope with

that. OK. She was going to leap across to the truck while it and the Jeep were travelling at 40 kph. He had discovered Sarita and Davina were a few screws loose, but Ros?

He checked the timer. There was little choice. Ros had to come over with his set of tools.

The wind was making his eyes water and he rubbed them dry.

'Come on, then!' he shouted. 'The tools are underneath the passenger seat.'

Ed was in a cage with the woman who was half to blame for his predicament. His anger was beginning to get the better of him. Ed knew he had to control it. But the thought kept slipping back into his head. He was going to die because of Davina and her stupid sister.

No. She hadn't locked him in the plasma cage. She was going to die, too.

Why hadn't help arrived? Where was Paul Cray during all this? If he worked closely with O'Neill, didn't he know what was going on? Maybe Cardenas had already dealt with him. Maybe it was his day off or something.

Davina sat as close to O'Neill as she could without touching the deadly barrier. She gently called 'Uncle Dave' every few seconds. As an attempt to escape the cage, it was the best they had. But O'Neill didn't stir.

Why did Cardenas have to trap them in the plasma cage in the first place? He knew what was going on. Why couldn't he release them? Well, Davina had helped with the theft of the MPV while he had been caught red-handed with the MPV's blueprints.

It had been the same when he had pretended to be Starkey. He never learned his lesson, did he? He should leave well alone the things that were no concern of his.

But did being found with the blueprints warrant a death sentence? No. It was no good thinking about what motivated Cardenas. The Major had left them and they had to live with it – for whatever length of time they had left.

Davina turned and asked, 'What would happen if we just jumped through the barrier?'

It had been on his mind but the sight of the melted phone receiver Ros had thrown at the beams dispelled such thoughts.

'No way, José. We'd fry.'

There was a moan from O'Neill. His hand went to his head. His eyes slowly opened.

'Oh, God,' he murmured.

'Hey, O'Neill!'

O'Neill raised himself to sit up. His whole body trembled as he sat in front of the cage. The man did not look well. The results of the double taser shock were clearly visible. His already thin face seemed drawn and he was ghostly pale. His skin seemed almost translucent. Blue veins stood out on his forehead. His greying cropped hair stuck out in all directions. His eyes suddenly widened as if he had just worked out where he was.

'We think your truck's on its way back and it doesn't look good,' said Ed. 'Can you get us out of here?'

O'Neill rubbed his chest and winced. He looked down at himself. There were too large scorch marks on his clothes over his chest.

Then he stared out and looked at the smashed control panel on the pillar.

He leered at them.

'Burn in hell.'

Keeping the Jeep door open while they were travelling so fast was a problem in itself. Never mind Ros trying to get across to the MPV.

Sarita had driven the Jeep as close to the MPV as possible. Ros's heart leaped into her mouth when the Jeep had almost banged into the truck. The truck's passive safety system had registered the Jeep's presence and swerved to avoid it.

But she had matched the truck's speed perfectly and kept at a steady distance alongside it. That took some skill. Up to Ed's level, maybe?

Ed. Trapped in the plasma cage. With no idea what's happening outside.

Ros threw the toolkit to Beckett who caught it easily. She lifted herself up so that she leaned out of the car, and held on to the top of the open door. Her feet were on the very edge of the Jeep's back seat.

Now, the tricky bit.

She hooked her arms over the top of the Jeep's door. Her feet were dangling above the road. She was suddenly very aware of how fast the Jeep was travelling. The wind started to make her eyes water.

'Ros, give me your arm.'

'Beckett! Be quiet!'

Ros inched her way across.

Beckett suddenly had hold of her right arm.

'I've got you!' he shouted. 'Now Sarita will have to increase her speed. As soon as you feel the acceleration, let go of the door. For a second you'll feel like you're falling. Don't worry. I've got you. Just swing round and grab hold of me.'

Beckett made it sound so easy. 'Let's get on with it then.'

'Sarita!' Beckett shouted. 'Put your foot down.'

The Jeep speeded up. Ros resisted the urge to hold on for dear life. There was too much at stake.

All of a sudden she had let go of the door. Ros swung round and grabbed hold of Beckett. Her hand slipped, banging into the open doorway. She gripped a handrail immediately inside the truck for all she was worth. Her shoes were scraping the road.

A hand took hold of her shoulder and Ros let herself be dragged on board.

'I don't ever want to do that again.'

Standing up, she noticed the dynamite in a large and very solid block of concrete. There was no way they could move that.

'I tried everything with the controls,' said Beckett. 'Nothing responded.'

That wasn't a surprise. Not if the controls were anything like those in the car. There was only one thing for it.

Ros stared at the gold covering over the MPV's power unit. The source of the problem. Well done, Sarita. Let's all remove shielding from a plutonium power unit.

'If we can't get the bomb away from the plutonium,' she said, 'we'll have to get the plutonium away from the bomb. How far away are we?'

'Less than two miles to Tronix at a guess.'

The timer read just under four minutes.

'Maybe the parking bay doors will stop it.'

'But it'll still explode.'

Ros knew that. 'Yes, but if we get this out, it'll just be a conventional explosion in the yard. Ed and Davina might have a chance.'

'Yeah,' said Beckett. 'But what about us?'

Ed and Davina's one chance of freedom was walking away.

O'Neill was leaving them to die.

Ed couldn't believe he could just abandon them. The guy wasn't human.

O'Neill staggered over to the large annexe doors, laughing quietly to himself all the while. He fell over and laughed. He picked himself up and fell down again. He threw back his head and laughed out loud. Then he started to sob, cradling his head in his hands.

The taser blast had rendered O'Neill an imbecile. It wasn't that he didn't care about them. His brain had been frazzled.

Davina stared over at O'Neill. 'We've got to bring him to his senses. Even he can't abandon us.'

'For God's sake, man!' Ed called out. 'Do one decent thing in your life and get us out of here!'

O'Neill turned and looked surprised that there was

anyone in the same building. He walked over, swaying slightly all the time.

He stared at them. Something in his eyes changed. A flicker of recognition. His inane grin left him and was replaced by a sneer. The old David O'Neill was back.

'I don't care,' he spat. 'This is nothing. I'll rebuild it all.' He swung his arms out wide, narrowly missing the beams of the plasma cage. 'And this time nobody, absolutely nobody, is going to get the opportunity to let me down.'

And again, he walked away. This time more resolutely than before, and more steadily.

'Hey, you stupid –' Ed stopped himself. It was not the best idea in the world to curse the man who was your only chance of survival. 'Come back here!'

O'Neill stuck two fingers up behind his back and continued towards the bay doors.

The plutonium would be encased somewhere in the centre of the power unit. It would be relatively secure and stable, as far as plutonium could be.

That's what Ros had said. He trusted her implicitly but was still nervous about unbolting the unit.

The truck continued to rumble along the road. Beckett looked out of the side door. Sarita was in the Jeep, driving right alongside. Perhaps she should get out of there? The dynamite would explode in less than three minutes.

The bolts in the unit were damned tight. He and Ros had removed eight of the things but there were still two to go and they weren't budging.

'How long now?' he asked, struggling with the monkey wrench.

'Two minutes.'

Ros loosened another bolt. Only one to go. Where was Ed when you needed him?

'What happens if this thing hits the ground at speed?'

Ros stood up and walked towards the driver's cabin.

'We hope it's tough enough to take it.'

Beckett struggled with the final bolt.

'We're almost there,' said Ros. 'The door's closed.' At least Ed and Davina would be safe. 'The truck will stop and we can get the plutonium out.'

But there was no time. The dynamite was going to explode at any second. Why wouldn't the damned final bolt come loose? The RTG canister was rattling loose inside its container. He was almost there. *Come on!* They'd moved the other nine. Why not this one?

'Urff!' He had to keep going. 'Ros! Get out of here. I can't get this thing off.'

'There'd be no point – oh, no.'

Something else had gone wrong? What could go wrong now?

'What's up?'

'The annexe doors. They've just opened.'

Ros. Ed. Davina. Sarita.

Half of the damn country.

All because of one final bolt.

'Give me a hand here!'

Hydraulics geared up. O'Neill watched the bay door rise quickly and noisily.

He was getting away. Feeling good. Head fuzzy. He couldn't concentrate properly. He was certain he didn't feel like that a moment ago.

The Major. He'd done something. Burnt his shirt. Burnt inside his head.

His hands tingled and his eyes hurt. Even his hair hurt. But he was getting away from the losers.

People who let David O'Neill down. Those girls. Sweet little things. Sat on his lap. And their father. Good friend. Gone now. Dead.

That was sad, wasn't it? What was his name? O'Neill couldn't remember.

Hands. White and trembling.

Who was he? Name. Name. Gone. It'd come back. Give it time.

And he had time now. Time to escape. He had won. He knew that much.

But what was he running from? A car? Not a car. A truck. A big truck.

He turned back to the plasma cage. The trucks were in two rows. It was all going to go bang in a minute. He had worked hard. He could do it again. Tomorrow. He would start tomorrow.

And the girl and the boy. They had tried to cheat him. Bad. Naughty boy and girl.

'I'm a survivor,' O'Neill shouted. It was true. He could live forever. 'You? You're just –' What was the word he was looking for? 'Trash. That's it. You're just trash.'

The truck slowed once as it entered the Tronix site.

Trees. The ugly Tronix building. Cars parked in three rows outside. It was a weekday. People would be working in there.

It didn't matter. Beckett couldn't budge the last bolt.

And the bay doors were wide open. There was no way to stop the MPV. Ed and Davina were going to die. They were all going to die.

'Oh, no. Come on, Beckett!'

He felt his rage burn inside him. No one was going to die. No one. Not if he had anything to do with it. He wouldn't let his failure be the cause of so many deaths. So many people depended on him.

With a massive effort he twisted the bolt loose. The bolt spun crazily out of the casing. He pulled open the power unit's cover and the canister inside fell out into his hands. The RTG.

Ros had already opened the back doors wide. Beckett saw Sarita following in the Jeep.

Beckett rolled the RTG along the truck's floor. He prayed that the RTG would survive the impact on the road.

It smashed down, clanging on the tarmac.

And again and again.

Sarita swerved out of its way.

The canister didn't explode.

Ros and Beckett sighed heavily. Ros leaped out of the moving truck, landed and expertly rolled to one side.

Outside went dark suddenly. The timer read twenty seconds. The truck had entered the vehicle's parking bay.

Ed.

He couldn't be saved.

Beckett jumped out after Ros.

There was no way Ed or Davina could get out of the bay.

Ed stared after O'Neill. He had seemed reasonably lucid only a few moments before but now he was seriously gone. No lights on and no one at home.

'Uncle David,' said Davina. 'We have to go now.'

Ed didn't think you could reason with a man whose entire nervous system had just been exposed to a double taser shock. But if Davina wanted to think it could help, he wasn't about to tell her differently. They could not do anything else.

O'Neill stepped back away from the plasma cage. He looked puzzled. 'I'm not your uncle.'

A familiar sound. An MPV. Powered up.

Oh, God. The truck was inside with them.

'I'm not your uncle!' shouted O'Neill.

There. The huge, monstrous machine rolled towards them.

'I'm not your uncle!' O'Neill stamped his foot and then turned, straight into the MPV.

It carried him forward.

'Stay right back!' Ed shouted to Davina.

The MPV ploughed into the plasma cage. Sparks flew from the machine, from O'Neill's body as they passed through the green light beams. Flashes of light danced everywhere.

O'Neill's body shook violently but he still held on to the truck. Burns appeared all over his body.

The MPV was coming forward. Them next. They would be pushed into the rear barrier. Then: game over.

But the MPV suddenly stopped in front of them and powered down.

Ed looked down one side of the truck. The side door was open.

'Come on.'

'Come on *where*?'

'Out of here. The side entrance is open. And so's the back.'

'So? We can't get out.'

'The back of the truck is outside the barrier,' he explained. 'We go through. Now, *move*!'

There was no time to waste. Ed pushed Davina forward.

When they clambered inside the truck, Ed saw that the controls in the MPV were dead. A large, gold cylinder stood next to some familiar-looking packs of dynamite set in a block of concrete.

A timer.

Eight seconds.

Seven seconds.

Ed ran like he had never run before. He passed Davina on the way out of the annexe and half-dragged her out of the open doorway.

Six seconds.

Davina was not going to die. Not if he could help it.

Five seconds.

Ed let go of Davina when they left the bay into the cold morning but she ran straight ahead. Not good. She would be killed by the blast.

Four seconds.

'No!' he shouted. 'Here!' He pulled her back by the jacket.

Three seconds.

A barrel stood by the annexe wall a few metres away from the doorway. It was hardly any shelter at all.

Two seconds.

Ed crouched and held Davina in his arms. An extra bit of shelter for her.

One second.

They waited.

The ground shook with the explosion. Ed had never heard anything like it. He put his hands to his ears.

A wave of heat passed over them. He dared to turn around.

Flames filled the open bay doorway, surging outwards and upwards. The heat was incredible. Ed pressed Davina down as flames shot over their heads.

Too close. Way too close.

But he was alive and that felt *good*.

He heard a shout over the dying roar of the explosion. 'Ed?!'

Beckett and Ros ran towards him. Davina picked herself up and ran to her sister.

'The plutonium?' asked Ed.

'Nothing to worry about. We got it out,' said Beckett, smiling. He handed Ed a long, thick metallic cylinder.

He could have that back. Beckett's smile vanished. 'What happened to O'Neill?'

'What's left of him is still inside there.'

'And Cardenas?'

'Oh, long, long gone.'

'Typical.'

'Come on, guys,' said Ros. 'Question and answer session later. Let's get out of here.'

Beckett scanned the newspaper. He hardly ever read them, relying instead on his computer to retrieve news from various press agencies' computers for him. But sometimes a newspaper was more pleasant to read even though none of the articles had been chosen to suit his particular tastes.

He found a small mention of the incident at Tronix. Plutonium wasn't mentioned, neither was Major Cardenas and his gang. That came as no surprise.

The explosion had rocked the entire building. Walls had collapsed, small electrical fires had started and huge cracks in floors and walls had suddenly appeared.

There had been few injuries. Five people were taken to hospital, mostly to be treated for shock. Fortunately, no one had been killed.

Too many difficult questions would have been asked of them had the team hung around. In his official capacity as a government employee he would have answered for his actions, but Beckett worked for himself now, so he and the rest of them had simply walked away.

Maybe Sarita and Davina should have been made to pay for what they had done. But Beckett wasn't about to ask for an eye for an eye or insist that justice be done. And O'Neill had paid a high price for his military dealings. That was the way it went sometimes. Not everything worked out smoothly or the way you planned.

Beckett rolled the newspaper under his arm. Ros and Ed were supposed to be ready by now. He ran up to the lounge and opened the door.

Ros and Ed were still playing with that silly car racetrack. It covered a huge table in the centre of the lounge. It had taken hours to set it up and they had played it non-stop ever since.

'Do you know what time it is? We were supposed to be meeting a client twenty minutes ago.'

'Don't distract me,' said Ros. 'I'm hammering him.'

'It's luck,' said Ed.

'Oh, sure. If it's me it's luck, if it's you then it's skill.' Ros did her best attempt at an Australian accent. 'Clear those decks and call me Captain Speedy!'

'Ha, ha. Very funny.'

Beckett wasn't endowed with much patience but stayed calm.

'How much longer?' he asked pleasantly.

'What do you reckon?' Ed asked Ros.

'Oh, I don't know.'

Ros and Ed ducked under the table simultaneously. What were they playing at?

Beckett crouched to see what they were doing.

Oh. Shouldn't they have handed that in somewhere? Plutonium made him feel very nervous.

The RTG sat innocuously under the table. Ros, in her infinite wisdom, had deemed it fit to attach wires from the metal canister to the racetrack.

'I think we could be playing for quite some time, Beckett.' Ros stood up and asked Ed, 'How long do you think? Twenty? Twenty-five years?'

BUGS – The TV Series

This book is based on two episodes of the TV series BUGS: 'Shotgun Wedding' first broadcast on BBC1 on 29 April 1995, and 'Stealth' written by Stephen Gallagher and first broadcast on 6 May 1995. They were directed by Ken Grieve.

Producer – Brian Eastman
Co-Producer – Stuart Doughty
Production Designers – Rob Harris
Series Consultant – Brian Clemens
Script Consultant – Colin Brake
Executive Producer for the BBC – Caroline Oulton

BUGS is a Carnival Films production.

Read the full story in Virgin's non-stop action novels